Caleb's Curse

A NOVEL BY SALLY GLASS

CHAPEL HILL
PRESS, INC.

Cover photo by Suzanne Sasser Clark, Conway, S.C.

Oil paintings by Mack Spivey on display at
Kim Clayton's Blackwater Gallery, Conway, S.C.

Drawing of cabin by the late Tony Spivey

This is a work of fiction. The characters, incidents and dialogues are products of the author's imagination and are not to be constructed as real. Any resemblance to actual events or persons, living or dead, is entirely coincidental.

All trademarks (™) and registered marks (®) used in this work remain the property of their respective owners.

Copyright © 2005 Sally Glass

All rights reserved. No part of this book may be used, reproduced or transmitted in any form or by any means, electronic or mechanical, including photograph, recording, or any information storage or retrieval system, without the express written permission of the copyright holder, except where permitted by law.

ISBN 1-59715-001-0
Library of Congress Catalog Number 2004117092

Printed in the United States of America
First Printing

This book is dedicated to my mother, Hazel Spivey.

A special thank you goes out to my wonderful husband George for his constructive advice and continued loving support.

———

I would like to thank: Jennie Bickerton, Gary and Judy Glass, Bobby Stilley, Faye Thurston, and Eric and Lidia Taylor for their honest opinions.

When I look at my brother, I see a great future wasted. I can't help but wonder why he and so many of my ancestors have met with tragedy and heartbreak. It was as if demons were at work, demons that at some point in my ancestors' lives took over all conscious will and drove each to self-destruction. My brother used to say that "No one can outrun the past; it'll catch up with you in time, raise its ugly head and devour you." I guess in Tom's case that's exactly what happened. He tried for years to outrun his demons but failed. Could they be the same demons that haunt me now? Is it possible that the chains that held him prisoner in his tragic world are as much a part of my heritage as they were of his?

I sought the answers to find out why my family had been so cursed. What I eventually found in this search would explain many things. The internal powers given to me through my lineage were revealed, and through those powers I uncovered the cause of the tragedies my ancestors had suffered. I would also learn what had to be done to end this curse.

Clearly, somehow, things had to be set right for our descendants; the sins of our ancestors required atonement. Terrified, I soon realized I was the one chosen to undertake this task. —RAINEY ALEXANDER

The telling of Caleb Bland

GREETINGS: MY NAME IS CAPTAIN CALEB BLAND; I WAS A MURDERER AND THIEF, SPAWNED OF THE DEVIL. I DIED IN 1720, HANGED FROM A LIVE OAK TREE AND LEFT TO ROT IN MY OWN HELL. I AM A VERY EVIL SPIRIT WITH QUITE A STORY TO TELL.

I was born in London, England in the year 1687, in an upstairs room of the Sailors Roost Pub, along Wapping High Street. My mother, a prostitute, died from a wretched disease when I was five years old. An old sea captain who came around on occasion took pity on me and took me in. For all I know, he could have been my father. He was as mean as they come—cut your throat if you looked at him cross. Still, he was all I had, and so I clung to his side and listened to his every word. He taught me what I needed to know to survive on the sea. Pillaging was the trade he taught me. I was an excellent student in the art of killing, stealing and all the other things we notorious, bloodthirsty pirates are remembered for. I especially enjoyed the detachment of ears, noses and other important parts of the human body. Torturing a wealthy gentleman was an extremely exciting endeavor. First we would pass his wife around allowing him to observe our pleasure, and then we would begin… Oh well, I could go on all day about our sadistic entertainment. Ah! Yes, that was the good life… Now, where were we?

This New World was the place to be. Ships abounded and were filled with wealthy travelers en route to newly established ports. Lurking along the coast of Carolina were privateers, men like me, waiting to pilfer and murder. You see, these rogues, I myself, would go to any lengths to capture someone else's wealth. I was one among an impassioned lot; what belonged to me, belonged only to me. I would send you straight to hell for stealing my plunder. Though I myself, no doubt, was destined for that eternal furnace.

After many years under the old captain's tutelage, I got restless. The urge was strong to leave the old bastard and go my own way. In the spring of 1717, we dropped anchor in Barbados to take on supplies and repair our sloop. While there, I befriended a gentleman by the name of Stede Bonnet. Bonnet was the owner of a profitable sugar cane plantation, but he was far more interested in the more exciting life of a pirate. We would spend hours in the Yellow Parrot, a local tavern, drinking rum and I would tell him stories of my life on the high seas. I found him to be a most interesting gentleman and a willing risk taker, much like myself.

He became more and more intrigued with my kind of life. Finally, he sold his plantation and purchased his own ship. I will never forget his excitement the first day he stepped on her deck. He was so proud of her, naming her "Revenge"—a splendid name, indeed. Armed to the teeth with cannons, his ship was ready to set out on the high seas. He begged me to accompany him on his maiden voyage. I agreed as I was ready for a change. My old Captain was sickly and just did not have the will to control his men. They were like a pack of wolves waiting for the first sign of weakness. I was not up to defending him from the barbaric bunch (the old captain had taught me well). I would be better off with Bonnet.

We set out to rob and plunder, but, unfortunately, we met up with one Edward Teach, better known as "Blackbeard." He demanded our sloop and convinced us that we would fare better if we cooperated. We were to remain his guests for a while.

Teach and I, both thirsty for blood, got along splendidly. Killing was an art we both zealously mastered in order to reach our goals. After a few months, I convinced him to let Bonnet and me go. I begged him to give us Bonnet's sloop so we would have a means of plying our trade. Surprisingly, he granted my wish but warned me to steer clear of him.

Stede and I set out for the Virgin Islands. After terrorizing the Spanish ships in the area for awhile, we headed toward the Carolina Coast. Stede intended to go on north to Cape Fear to lie up for a few weeks and repair the sloop. Quite frankly, I was tired of sharing with Bonnet, and so I took my cut of the plunder and went ashore to find what Charles Town might have to offer.

Bonnet, earlier, had made the mistake of attacking a ship which belonged to a local ship owner. The businessman had posted a substantial reward for his capture. To be honest, I had no allegiance to our Mr. Bonnet, so I sold him out for the reward. As I counted my gold, I watched them hang poor Mr. Bonnet and his crew. The sight was disgusting, even to me. After they hanged him, they chained his body to a post between the high and low water mark while the tide ebbed and flowed three times over it, as was the custom at the time. This should have served as a warning to me, but I was convinced I was too clever. They would never catch Caleb Bland.

I had my eye on a lovely little sloop in the harbor. The owner had no interest in selling but his lack of interest was of little importance to me. I changed his mind by beating him to within a breath of his life. Before setting sail, his presence became such a distraction I slit his throat, placed him into a skiff, and then rowed out and dumped his body deep within the marsh grasses. The marshes seldom give up the dead.

I armed my new ship with cannons and stocked the armory with as many hand weapons as I could steal. I searched the roughest places in town looking for a crew. For the most part, they all had dark pasts, just the kind of men my work required. I even found a young cabin boy to take care of my personal needs. At last, I had my own sloop and was ready to rule the Carolina coast as my personal dominion.

During the time I spent there, I was drawn to a green-eyed beauty. As greedy and evil as I was, I never thought that I could have such a weakness, but this woman proved me wrong. Her name was Annabelle.

She stole my heart when our eyes first met. My black heart was melted with the love I felt for her. My usual nightmares turned to delightful fantasies of her long dark hair, flashing green eyes, and voluptuous body. I loved her more than my own soul.

We would steal away to a remote inn on the outskirts of town. Little did we know that the greedy innkeeper would later offer up information on us to her husband for a mere piece of gold. Oh, did I mention that she was married, worst of all, to an Officer in the Royal Navy?

I had given her a beautiful emerald broach that had been my most prized possession. I had taken it from a traveler while plundering in the Virgin Islands. Annabelle loved it so much she began wearing it everywhere, but only while her husband was away. Her fascination with the broach proved to be our undoing. After hearing rumors of her being seen with the broach, he questioned her acquisition of such a lovely piece and demanded that she tell him where it had come from. Other rumors included whispers regarding the possibility of a tryst with another man while her Officer was at sea.

His lack of trust led him secretly to offer a reward for information concerning his wife's clandestine activities. Finally, after having been contacted by the innkeeper, his suspicions had come true. Sneaking up the back stairs of the inn, he watched and listened in secret waiting for the right moment.

Throwing the door open with a vengeance, he found us together in each other's embrace. He cursed her to hell and dragged her by the throat from the bed. I stumbled to reach my belt and sword, but before I could draw it, he had ripped the emerald broach from her neck and shot her near the heart. My soul roared in agony; my beautiful Annabelle lay on the floor, life pouring from her body.

I stood there, half-naked, but every muscle in my body tensed ready to kill. I turned to him with my blade in hand. His sword left its scabbard with a swish. He boasted of his skill with the weapon and how he was going to cut me to pieces. We circled, sizing each other up. Anger burned deep in my soul; I glared at him with hatred like none I had ever experienced. I had murdered many a man before but never with the overwhelming hatred I now felt. As my eyes flooded with tears, I asked if he was ready to meet his maker. He let out a pompous laugh—it was his last. My blade sliced through his neck so fast it surprised even me. His bloody head rolled onto the floor; his limp body fell as his heart pumped and spurted blood everywhere.

I ran to my Annabelle and looked into her fading green eyes. Holding her in my arms, I knew she was dying. Begging her to hold on, I caressed her forehead with my trembling hand. I told her I loved her dearly and could not live without her. She had enough strength to reach for the broach. I could see the desperation in her eyes when she found it gone. I promised I would keep the broach safe forever and return it to her when we met in the afterlife. She smiled and whispered softly, "I love you."

Those were her last words to me; she died with her dark hair next to my heart. In a rage, I screamed curses to God for taking her away.

My anger burned at my soul as if the devil himself had seized my black heart. I was filled with hatred, hatred for every living soul. Never again would I experience love such as I had felt for Annabelle. I would not allow it. I would forever be a disciple of evil.

Using the bed linen, I managed to clean the blood from my hands and then finished dressing. I retrieved the broach from the dead man's hand and glanced back at Annabelle one last time. I found the back stairs; taking the officer's horse, I rode like a man possessed back to the dock where I found my sloop. The safety of the sea would be my sanctuary. I quickly set sail with no destination in mind as I turned my bow northward up the cold Carolina coast.

After finding the bodies, the bailiff questioned the innkeeper. He told him about the pirate that Annabelle had been meeting. He naturally assumed that I had killed them both; so the Royal Navy was sent to capture me. Up the coast I sailed with the British Navy in hot pursuit. I slipped into a small inlet where I hoped to hide. In my haste, however, I failed to consider the tides as the keel of my ship dug into a sand bar. We were aground—giving the British a clear view of our masts. How could I have made such a mistake?

I ordered all but two of the men to escape. The rest scattered into the savage forest that surrounded the inlet. I placed my jewel chest into the skiff. Then, taking the cabin boy with me, I ordered the men to row to a nearby small island. I had a plan, if we could only move fast enough. As the skiff beached itself in the shallow water, the two crewmen grabbed the chest as I followed, carrying the weapons. The frightened cabin boy trailed behind us with the digging spades. Reaching the interior of the island, I found a gangly old live oak tree covered in moss and lichen. Its lengthy limbs reached almost to the ground. Looking up through its thick growth, I could hardly see the blue sky. The tangled under-growth a short distance from the tree, and the sandy clearing under it would be ideal for burying the chest. This place I could find again.

I ordered the men to dig a deep hole. After the hole was dug and the treasure safely at the bottom, I executed the two sailors, but not the cabin boy. Pushing the two bodies in on top of the chest, I worked quickly to cover the hole. I then used a leafy tree branch to smooth the sand carefully. I even scattered leaves and a few palm branches in the area of the freshly disturbed ground to make it look more natural. When I had finished, even I could hardly tell where the hole had been.

I just could not bring myself to kill the young cabin boy, a mistake I would later regret. Instead, I chased him off into the woods. I assumed the wild savages or animals would dine on him long before he could be rescued. I should have killed him along with the other two, but I had no way of knowing then the trouble this young lad would create for me. My great plan was to later return and recover the treasure.

Next, I needed to hide the skiff on the island where I would wait until the British gave up their search. I would return to my sloop, and hopefully some of my men would also find their way back. We would wait for the tide, and just maybe we could escape the sand bar. I would return for my plunder at a later date. It seemed like a good plan. However, luck was not on my side. As I started for the brush, I came face to face with the muskets of several British soldiers.

There I hid my treasure with the emerald broach, and there is where they captured me. I never imagined that I would be caught so easily.

I am not sure of the exact day they hanged me from that mighty old oak. I believe it may have been in October of 1720. That tree was to be my gallows; the soldiers, however, were not very proficient at hanging. They strung me up with my toes just off the ground, and then they returned to their ship. They laughed at how they were leaving me there to die an agonizingly slow death as the rope dug deeper into my neck. The rope they used had stretched just enough so that I was able to stand on my tiptoes. God, what a miserable time it was! The leg irons they placed on my ankles weighed me down even more. I would have thought that British marines would be more civilized, but obviously I erred.

As the rope slowly tightened around my neck, I could feel my life slipping away. Though my vision was blurred, I could see the sun setting through the trees. It sank away as the day neared the edge of darkness. My dying took considerable time.

Off in the forest, the young cabin boy had watched in horror. He spent a week or so watching the sea, hoping to be saved. His luck changed when a passing ship that had stopped to ransack my own vessel picked him up. He did not say a word about the treasure or my lifeless carcass hanging from the tree.

Years later, however, he sketched a map of the location of the treasure. By that time, he had become quite the drunkard around town. Everyone laughed at his foolish whiskey-laden treasure-chasing dreams. On his deathbed, he passed the map to a young sailor. That young sailor would later become the father of a William Henry Rhodes. Young William's father would give his son the map, in hope that he might look for the treasure someday. That might have happened had not that bloody civil war misdirected the lad.

Why did I not kill the boy when I killed the others? I have asked myself this question over and over. How could I have been so stupid? I should have cut his throat.

Hanging from that tree, I thought of my sweet Annabelle, whom I had left lying lifeless on the floor of the inn. Before dying, I called to her in the afterlife. I swore to her that my spirit would always keep watch over her broach and no other would ever possess it.

After what seemed an eternity, I could no longer stand. My toes were numb and lifeless, my strength sapped to the bone. I surrendered my life there in the twilight, dangling from the oak that would become my eternal home. Yes, I was hanged and left to rot under the full moon of a cool October night somewhere along the coast of Carolina.

Before long, the buzzards and other scavengers had picked me clean. All that was left was my skeleton and my empty scabbard clanging in the wind against the leg irons. Eventually, even my skeleton fell to the ground and returned to the earth. For three hundred years, my soul has lingered there, watching over the broach. Evil spirits that guard my chest have claimed the old oak tree and its surrounding thick forest. They lurk in the shadows in a world of dark and evil, waiting for me to summon them to do my bidding. They are known as "plat-eyes," and they watch over my treasure. They are an evil lot and do an admirable job of keeping mortals away. The place is fantastically eerie and frightening, exactly the way I want to keep it.

As my final act to protect the treasure and my beloved emerald broach, I placed a curse on the whole lot of it. Whoever held any piece, especially the emerald broach, would also hold the curse, which would follow in that family for generations to come.

Here is where this story really begins. I was quite content until one John Waters and his cousins came and stole the chest, taking with them my beloved Annabelle's broach. I did everything in my power to stop them. I called on every evil demon—summoning them all to the old oak. I was incapable of preventing the theft—because, you see, John Waters was a supernaturally powerful man. The potent gift he possessed was used very wisely and effectively against me. My powers failed because of the gift he possessed; I could not keep him away. It was that do-gooder John Waters and his friends who took my treasure.

So, here we are. A hundred and fifty years or so have passed since they stole it from me. But I will have it back! I will!

As the years have slipped by slowly, I have waited patiently for the right person to help me in my quest. All I seek is the return of the broach. I was able to keep track of its location for a few days after it was taken, but as the distance between us increased, my powers could no longer reach it. Even if I should find the person who has it now, I could not retrieve it alone. You see I am a spirit. I have no powers that would allow me to pick it up, even if it were lying before me. To do this I need the help of a mortal being.

Since the broach was taken by the powers of John Waters, it can only be returned by one of his descendants with those same skills.

Until recently, not one of his descendants has been born with the mark of the serpent, the mark which indicates that this person will have the knowledge and wisdom to make full use of the powers with which his family line has been empowered. Unfortunately, most of his heirs that possessed the gift have been too burdened with the curse to be of any use to me.

I still sense, however, that the broach is very close to the family. There is one now who bears the mark of serpent, and such a beauty she is. Strangely enough, she has the dark hair and green eyes of my Annabelle. She is a loner, a very spiritual girl. She could be the one, the one to find and return my precious broach. At this time, she has no idea of the gift that has been passed down to her. I will keep watch on her closely as she matures to see if and when she will recognize her inheritance. If she does and the time is right, I will call to her, and she will bring me my broach.

As for now, I must be patient. Only time will tell what the future may hold.

PART ONE

Chapter One

The year was 1866. In those days, the farming community of Adrian lay on the outskirts of the river town Conwayboro in the northeastern part of South Carolina. It was a land of piney woods, swamps, black water rivers, and dusty fields, a part of South Carolina cut off from the rest of the world. The Little Pee Dee River with its vast black water swampland bordered the county on the west; the Atlantic Ocean lapped at the beautiful sandy beaches of its eastern border; to the north, the thick lonely stretches of pine forest reached across the border into North Carolina; and to the south, were the dense swampy marshlands of Georgetown County. The inhabitants of the area were rugged, independent souls who would take a stand against anyone who threatened to change their way of living.

Beginning in the sandy pine forest of southeastern North Carolina, the Waccamaw River flows south across the state line into the District of Horry, passing down through Conwayboro and on to the sea at Georgetown. The river is the lifeblood of the area.

Like so many other small communities in those desperate times, the area was recovering from the Civil War. Many of the young men who left their small farms and families to fight for the South never returned. The ones who did return brought with them the memories of having seen their friends and relatives killed or wounded in battle, their bodies buried where they fell. For those who did make it home, the bloody memories would haunt them for the rest of their lives.

One of those soldiers was John Ian Waters, a man deeply scarred from the blood bath he witnessed. John tried to return to a normal life, but his war memories tormented his every waking minute. Working as a crewman on a flatboat, he stayed away from home as much as possible for his family suffered also, victims to his raging outbursts of violence. The vessel on which he labored floated the dark ribbon of the Waccamaw down to Bucksville where it delivered turpentine and lumber. From there it drifted on down to Georgetown where the crew picked up stock items for the stores of Conwayboro.

Leaving his wife, Letsy, and the children to keep the farm, he traveled the river for weeks at a time only to return home full of whiskey and meanness. This man was not the same pre-war John that his family and friends had known. Evil had possessed him. That war had taken a good man and turned him into a whiskey-swilling demon.

John would sit on the edge of the boat and stare into the dark water as the vessel slowly moved along. At night he would escape into the darkness to reason with his demons. The others on the boat knew to leave him alone when his mood turned dark. At times, unable to bear any longer the war stories the other men would recount, John would slip away to his bunk where he would try to close his mind to the evil that gripped his soul. Whiskey flowed freely on the river, and John used it to help with the maddening nights. It had become his crutch.

He possessed a special talent of a supernatural nature, passed on to him through his Scottish bloodlines. His internal struggle with this gift turned him into a man possessed. He would often curse his father for passing the torment down to him. He couldn't understand why he wasn't normal like other men. This cross he was destined to carry had become a burden that ate at his soul. He knew that he had, at some point, lost control. The dark side of these powers was taking over, and he was helpless to stop it.

According to his father, his family had come from the highlands of Scotland. John's father told him stories of the ancient one, an ancestor, who had been a great Druid priest. On the day that he died, the story goes, the clan gathered around his lifeless form. They watched his soul leave the body and inhabit the body of a small boy standing nearby. As the boy grew into manhood, he found that he possessed powers the others did not. This gift was passed on and his children, too, were blessed (or damned) with the powers.

In the late 1500s, the Scottish Parliament outlawed the pagan religions and accused innocent people of witchcraft. They were subjected to horrible inquisitions at the hands of so-called "Godly" men. Eventually, many learned to pretend to follow the new religion, but deep in caves and in other secret places, they would gather and practice the old ways. Eventually, the group was forced into hiding in the Scottish high country. Realizing their days in Scotland were numbered, they decided to send a few families to the New World to carry on their beliefs.

On board one of the many ships that came into Georgetown were John's ancestors. The elder of the group was the carrier of the gift. Having escaped persecution back in Scotland, the Waters family found their way up the Waccamaw and settled near the town of Kingston (now known as "Conway"). They hoped for the peace and freedom to practice their own spiritual beliefs in their own way.

John and his siblings were born into a world of secrets. It was forbidden for the children to talk with anyone outside the family about the old religion. In hiding, the family still found ways to practice what had been in their blood for centuries. John's mother and father knew the moment he was born that he would be one of the gifted.

The old black slave woman that helped with the birth was gripped with fear when the infant boy slipped from his mother's womb. Lizzie had birthed a lot of babies but seeing the caul over his face, she knew he was special.

"Oh hep' us Jesus," she whispered. "Da chile's head be covered wit' da caul! Oh, sweet Jesus be wit' him."

She delicately wiped the thin membrane away from his little face; cleaning him up, she wrapped him in a wool blanket and passed him to his mother. His father, entering the dimly lit room, brought the candle close in order to see his son. Taking the infant from his mother, he cradled him in his strong, gentle arms.

"We will bless him with his grandfather's name, John Ian Waters." Watching little John stretch his arms, his father recognized the birthmark on his right hand—the sign of the serpent.

"Maggie, our son has the mark; we have been blessed. It's the mark of the old ways; he has been chosen." The sign of the serpent represented knowledge; the boy would learn quickly and later in his life would become a seer. Little John not only possessed the family gift, but also possessed the powers that came from the caul that covered his face at birth. He would possess special powers for divination and healing. The spiritual powers of this child would go far beyond what his father imagined. The old religion ran deep in his blood.

As the old black woman started to leave, she turned to John's father.

Raising her hand to heaven and closing her eyes as if in prayer, she said, "Massa' Waters, dat boy, he be special. Dat caul be meanin' he be able to see da udder side. He gwine be called on all his life by da spirits."

She hastily left the little cabin. Climbing into the wagon that waited, she turned and looked back with obvious fear in her eyes.

As the years passed, his father accepted that the day was approaching when he would have to start teaching John and telling him the old stories and ways of his ancestors. In his son's tenth year, John's father had taken sick and was very weak for most of the winter. Lying in bed as he battled his sickness, he realized his own mortality. Knowing it would take several years to instruct John, he felt the child was old enough to hear the telling. He told John that he must keep the old religion alive, and he must also keep it within the family. He must never use this gift for evil—for if he did, the dark side would haunt him forever. He taught John the stories of the old people back in his ancestral Scotland.

On clear days, the father and the son would sit outside under the trees, the man lying on a cot. They would spend hours talking and learning about the gift. Within two years, John was able to use his gift in many ways but was still too young to understand just how far-reaching his powers actually were.

His father never returned to good health. When John was twelve, the elder Waters gave up the struggle and passed over. His dying left John alone as he tried to understand fully this gift and the powers he possessed.

On one occasion, the local minister stopped by for a visit. John's mother, fearing he would find out about their pagan beliefs, removed all pagan writings and objects before inviting him in. She remained nervous and beside herself even after he left. Worried about the repercussions of anyone finding out about their beliefs, she decided to sit John down and ask him to abandon the old ways. She felt to let them die would be best. The old ways would forever be their secret, the secret of the mother and her son. Even then, John understood his mother's fears and agreed with her wishes. They spoke no more of the old ways. Occasionally, though, John would experiment with the gift but only when his mother was not around. For the most part, he put his gift away, respecting his mother's wishes.

As he grew older, he started spending more time in town or with his friends. He was a very handsome young man with light reddish-brown hair that was thick and wavy. He had his grandfather's bright green eyes, so light they seemed almost transparent at times. He was good-hearted, always willing to help others. He was a hard worker, never one to complain. Not a soul ever had a bad word to say about him.

A sociable lad, John enjoyed especially the company of older men who would gather in front of the local mercantile. Here he would often find himself involved in heated discussions over the concerns of slavery and politics. It was a contentious issue at the time, and opinions were split evenly in this portion of the state. Few of the people he knew were actually slave owners themselves, but that had little bearing on their positions on the subject. Most felt the real issue was states rights and resented the politicians from the northern states telling southerners how to run their lives. Personally, John didn't cotton to slavery, believing a man should tend his own fields.

He liked black folks and accepted them as he would anyone else. He would sit for hours listening to their stories, which he found intriguing. In their company, he first learned about the root bags, haints, or spirits that inhabited the swampy low lands, and other such folklore with which their culture was filled. Many of them recognized that John was different, but just how he was different escaped all but a few. Those few, however, sensed his spiritual powers.

Chapter Two

Maggie Waters wrapped the fresh baked bread in a linen cloth and placed it in a basket. She stepped out on the front stoop.

"John," she called out. In a few minutes, her son came out of the barn with his horse bridled and saddled. She had asked him earlier if he could deliver a basket of food to an elderly woman who was down in her bed sick. John was more than glad to make the trip; it gave him a chance to get away from his chores. On his way, he stopped to talk to a friend, the overseer of a big plantation. One of the nearby field workers, an old gray-haired black man, looked his way.

"Don't yo' be dat boy what be born wit' de caul?"

Turning his head quickly, John asked, "What'd you say, Mister?"

The old man leaned against the pitchfork to rest a bit. "My old woman done hep birth yo'. She be tellin' me all 'bouts it but dat be a while back. Yo' be knowin' what dat caul means?"

John eyed him for a few seconds but said nothing. The old man sensed immediately that John didn't want to discuss the power. He tipped his hat to the boy and continued with his work. John resumed the conversation with his friend then bid him goodbye.

Slapping his rein lightly on the rear of his horse, he continued on his way. As he trotted away, John again glanced over at the old black man, and their eyes met. John tipped his hat as he passed. The old man grinned and nodded knowingly. This was the first time anyone, other than his family, had ever mentioned the caul. He wasn't sure what to make of what the old man had said. His mother had told him about his birth and the strange covering over his face, but she was not familiar with the local beliefs of the Negroes. John would ask the old woman that helped birth him.

The following day, John rode to the old woman's house. The foreman permitted him to talk with old Lizzie and directed him to the big house where she and a young Negro girl were polishing silver. Lizzie stepped cautiously out the back door. Studying each of her steps carefully, she came down to where John stood and took his hand. She had to be older than Methuselah he thought.

"Miss Lizzie, do you know who I am?"

"Why, I sho do, I's be knowin' yo' since yo' birth. Yo' be young John Waters. I hep bring yo' in dis worl'." A big smile covered her face as she held his hand. For a moment they stood, just looking at one another.

"Miss Lizzie, my mama told me about the caul that covered my face when I was born. She tried to explain it to me but I never really understood; maybe you can tell me more?"

Lizzie walked over to a wooden bench and sat down, "Come here, boy, and sits down here wit' old Lizzie."

Without diverting his eyes from the old woman, John sat down beside her. She took his hand again and then spoke up. "I's can feel it in yo'. I feels da spirit flowin' from yo' hand and it be powerful."

John glanced carefully around and then spoke. "Miss Lizzie, you know about me, don't you?"

"Ye'sir, Mr. John, I knows all 'bout yo' secret, but what yo' be needin' to know from me is dat yo' gots two secrets," she said, holding up two bony fingers. When yo' be born wid dat caul o'er yo' face, Gawd be blessin' yo' wid' da special sight and I's nos dat yo be holdin' udder powers. I's know yo be seein' da spirit world. Yo' can see dem an' yo' can speaks wit' dem too. Has yo' seen som' a dem haints yet?" she asked, laughingly.

John squirmed around on the bench nervously. "I've seen some things that I can't explain."

Lizzie laughed. "Not to worry, boy. Dey is not be wantin' ta hurts yo' none. Dey jest be a comin' to yo' cause yo' can see'em. Jest yo' be takin' care o' yo' secrets, cuz yo' be havin' a special gift. Yo' gwine learn what ta do wid yo' sight. It be comin' to yo', natural like. Den yo' gwine be talkin' to 'em, too."

This was not enough for John. He wanted to know more, and she could tell he was disappointed.

"Nows don't be worryin' yo' self up ober dis. Yo' gwine learn hows to use de spirit. It jest be takin' some time. Yo' be learnin' soon 'nuf." She gave John a reassuring pat on the hand as she slowly stood. John could hear the groans of old age.

"Nows I bes' be gittin' back to work. If'n I slacks off wid da house dey might be tinkin' bout puttin' me back in dem fields and I's jest too old fo' dat kinda work."

"Thank you, Lizzie. You take care now, and I'll see you again soon, maybe?"

John helped her back up the back steps so she could return to her work.

A couple of days later, he got word that she had passed on. He was glad he had the chance to speak with her but had really wanted to talk even more.

Chapter Three

John and Letsy met at a community picnic down on the river one spring. It was, I guess you could say, love at first sight. John was so shy in the beginning; all he could muster was an adoring gaze and a little smile, but it was enough. Soon, thanks to Letsy's outgoing personality and interest, John found his voice. Touching her hand the first time, they both felt a connection. It was as if they had known each other for years.

Because Letsy was only sixteen, John needed her father's permission to court her. Letsy wondered if he would be able to summon the nerve to ask her father. It took some time, but John's love was all the courage he needed. He got her father's blessings.

Letsy knew he was different from the other young men she had been around. They would spend hours together talking while her father kept a close eye on them. John would share his views on political issues, and she would listen intently. He was passionately against slavery, a position that her father didn't exactly like. His daughter, though, was taken with John. The boy had a good heart and reputation, and so Letsy's father gave them his blessing. They were married, and soon after, the first child came along. Lavenia became the apple of her daddy's eye. The next few years would bring three more children: Franklin, Hallie, and Thomas, stair-step children, one right behind the other. A fifth child would be born, but much later. The new family lived a good life on their small farm and, in the beginning at least, had lots of love.

When the Civil War broke out, many of John's friends and neighbors signed on to fight for the Confederacy. They couldn't wait to join the local militia. All they talked about was killing Yankees and how it would be over in no time, and they'd be back home.

John wouldn't have any part of it. He didn't want to leave his family. He wasn't a slave owner and didn't feel the same way about the war as many of the others. He and Letsy had four children and a small farm to tend; he didn't have time for any war.

Eventually though, he felt guilty. His neighbors and friends were constantly talking about the battles their sons and husbands had taken part in, and that type of talk created even more pressure for him. Every day, word arrived about the ones who had fallen. Finally, the pressure became too great. Unable to ignore it any longer, John, too, went to war. Letsy was heart-broken by his decision, but she understood what he had been going through.

Yancy Johnson, a close friend, was home on leave at the time. So when Yancy returned, John went with him as a private in the South Carolina 26th Regiment, which consisted mostly of men and boys from Horry County.

When time came for John to leave, Letsy couldn't bear it. She kissed him good-by and disappeared into the house to cry. She dare not shed a tear in front of him.

When the war ended in the spring of 1865, John came home a different man. Alcohol now controlled his life. When he came home from having been on the river for weeks, he would stay drunk until it was time to return to the boat. Letsy tolerated his bad habits because she lived in fear of him. She made every effort not to aggravate him for she had learned he had a spiteful dark side. Ever since his return, he had become very abusive to her both physically and mentally. She had started to question her love for John. She prayed every night that he would change, hopefully before her heart hardened and she no longer cared if he even existed.

Many times John wouldn't return with the supply boat. He'd stay over in Georgetown, later telling Letsy that one of the ships had not arrived, and that he had to wait for the next boat home. Rumors circled that he had a mistress in Georgetown, and he spent most of his time with her when he was away.

John did love his children, and he loved Letsy, but guilt was eating at him inside. He had retreated within himself where the darkness was slowly taking over. He was no longer the kind man she had once known. He rarely took part in the day-to-day work around the small farm, much less spend any time with her and the children. For some reason, he had lost the ability to show his love. He was no longer the peaceful, compassionate John Waters that everyone had once known. A part of him had died, and Letsy feared he would never be the same again.

Sometimes he managed to remember the children on his trips down the river and brought them little gifts. Once, after a special trip to Charleston, he came home with shoes for all of them.

Letsy worked hard to take good care of their home and the children. Many nights, after the children were down, she sat in her chair by the window and waited for John to come home. His dinner was always prepared and waiting. If she fell asleep before he came in, he would curse her and wake the entire family. He had become an unpredictable tyrant; Letsy never knew what might push him over the edge. John's struggle within was making their life impossible.

Even after five children, Letsy had kept her beauty. She had poise, and even amidst her hardship, she carried herself proudly. She ruled the home when John was away, and the children obeyed her every word. They were closer to their mother in part because they feared their father. John never knew how to tell his children that he loved them. He was cold and withdrawn in their presence. Everyone in the community thought highly of Letsy, but most by now had lost all hope for John.

Periodically, John would use the supernatural gift to find lost items as well as divine for water for friends. These tasks were simple for him, but he didn't dare let on just how simple. He would often deceive folks deliberately by looking in the wrong places first. After these deceptive attempts, he would then go to the exact location. John would also use his gift in bad ways from time to time, to cheat at cards, for instance. Oh, he'd lose a few times to justify himself, but what he was doing was wrong and he knew it. The darkness had him; he began using the gift more and more in bad ways for bad men. His precious gift slowly became a tool for evil. He no longer even cared that he might lose it.

Letsy spent most of her time alone, living in her own little world. She dreamed of traveling and having nice things. She constantly starved for adult conversation. She especially liked hearing the news from town. The Civil War had been over for two years, and the influx of businesses to Conwayboro brought new faces to the area. Letsy was curious about all of them. On occasion, she would clean the children up and dress them in their Sunday clothes, hitch up the old mule to the wagon, and drive into town. She always made these trips on her own, as John never showed any interest in accompanying her anywhere.

Occasionally, she and the children would stay the night with her cousin, which allowed her the opportunity to vent to someone the hardships she was living. Returning to the farm the next day, John would be angry, claiming she had been gone too long, that she had left him without food.

Chapter Four

On a hot afternoon in late August, Letsy was alone with the children at the small farmhouse. She was in the garden picking the last of the beans when she glanced through the fence. On the other side, she noticed two long legs; her eyes slowly followed them up the body until her sight fell upon the rough face of a stranger. He was tall and lanky, maybe in his late twenties. His hair was dark brown, sprinkled with gray and hadn't been cut in some time. The sun touched the auburn highlights of the hair that fell down to the stranger's shoulders. Such a handsome fellow he was, Letsy thought. The only men she had seen in weeks were a few of the local farmers who had passed and waved.

She gathered her skirt and stood up. "Can I help you, stranger?" she asked in a sharp curt voice. She was damp with sweat, and her hair stuck to her neck. She wasn't in the mood to visit with anyone.

"Ma'am, I've been walking for days trying to get to the coast. I sure could use some food and water and maybe a place to sleep for the night."

Letsy eyed the man with suspicion. His clothes were dirty, his shoes worn out; he needed a bath and shave. She wasn't about to let a stranger in her home, especially around the children, who were, by this time, staring at him from the porch. The children waited to hear what their mother would say. Knowing how she was about strangers, they expected to hear the words "move on."

Letsy, wiping the dirt from her hands, spoke rudely. "Exactly where are you coming from?"

"Ma'am, I been walking south ever since that damn war ended. It's just taken me awhile."

Letsy spoke sarcastically. "Well, I'll say, since it's been over for two years. Stranger, you'd best get on down the road. I've got children to look after and don't have the time or enough extra food to mess with the likes of you."

She turned away, looking up to the porch where her two sons were standing. Her thoughts drifted to that terrible war, how it spared her children, who were just small boys. If they had been old enough to carry a gun, they could very likely be in a grave somewhere far away. If they had survived, she thought, she would pray that some good person would take them in for a meal and rest. Turning back, she saw the stranger was walking away.

"Wait, Mister. Don't go! Please forgive my manners. It's been a hot day and as you can see…" She pointed to the children, "I have my hands full." Cautiously, she added, "My husband is at work but should be home soon." She knew, of course, that John wouldn't be back any time soon. If the stranger was up to no good, she figured, he'd probably move on. For a moment, she felt a little guilty as she searched the stranger's face for one trace of dishonesty and found none.

"Ma'am, I do appreciate this. You're a blessing. I'll take my meal out in the shed and, if it's all right, I'll sleep there also. There's no need to fear me. I just hope your husband won't mind, but if you think he will, I'll keep going."

Letsy didn't respond. She turned to the children and motioned for them to go about their chores. She sent the stranger to the shed, and instructed her oldest boy, Franklin, to get him some water to wash up with.

She prepared a pot of beans along with stewed potatoes and biscuits. The stranger ate on the porch, devouring his meal in minutes. After the dishes were washed and the children were sleeping soundly in bed, Letsy sat down in her rocker to read. She couldn't get her mind off the handsome stranger. Putting her Bible down and walking to the window, she peeked out to see where he might be. To her surprise, he was sitting on her steps smoking a pipe.

"I wonder if he would like to talk a bit?" she thought.

After looking in on the children one more time, she unlatched the lock on the door and stepped out into the night air. She could smell the tobacco, a sweet and pleasant smell that reminded her of her father.

The man, startled, stood quickly and stepped back from the porch. "Good evening, ma'am."

Letsy acknowledged him with a nod. "Can I get you anything before I turn in?" she asked.

"No, I'm just fine. You've been more than accommodating, but I just have to ask you… Ma'am, I don't mean to be gettin' into your business, but I got a feeling your husband ain't a comin'."

Letsy's eyes wandered about for a moment as she tried to decide how to answer. There was something about this man that told her she had nothing to fear.

"Well, you're right, mister. My husband works on a riverboat, and sometimes he's gone for days. I wasn't too sure if I should tell you, but somehow I feel I can trust you."

The stranger removed his hat and bowed slightly to Letsy. "Ma'am, I can assure you that you have nothing to fear from me."

She smiled with relief; she just knew she had judged him right. "Mister, I don't even know your name. You got one?"

"Yes'um, William Henry Rhodes, but they call me Will."

"Will, my name is Letsy, Letsy Waters. I'm sorry I was so rude earlier today, but I spend a lot of time alone, what with my husband working on the boat. I'm always careful about who comes around."

"No apologies needed. I understand."

"So, Will, tell me where you were during the war?" Letsy asked.

"Well, Mrs. Waters," he started.

"Please, call me Letsy," she said.

Will stretched his tall frame out across the steps and looked up toward the night sky. Puffing a couple of times on his pipe, he started. "Well, Miss Letsy, I was in the Confederate Navy. I guess I was better off than those fellows who joined the infantry. I was taken prisoner off the coast of North Carolina in June of 1863. They sent me and the rest of the prisoners to this hellhole of an island off the coast of Massachusetts. It had to be the coldest place I have ever been. I stayed sick most of the time, but even so, I guess I was one of the lucky ones. A lot of the men died from dysentery sickness and consumption. I could never seem to get dry; my clothes, skin, everything stayed damp.

"After the war ended, I was still pretty sick so those Yank's put me in a hospital for a while. I'll have to say, I did get good care in that place. After they released me, I figured it would be a good time to see the northern part of this here country, and so I stayed there for a time. I found work in different towns; it wasn't much, enough for food and lodging but not much else. They didn't cotton to giving a Johnny Reb a decent job.

"Wasn't long before I started getting home sick for Georgia. A friend of mine down in Savannah has a steamboat, so I wrote him asking for work. He wrote back and told me that he would be coming into the port of Georgetown around the first week of September, and if I could get there, he would give me a job working on his boat. So, here I am, trying my best to get there before September. That's how I come down this here road and walked up to your fence. When I get to Conwayboro, I'm hoping to catch a boat down the river to make Georgetown."

Letsy listened intently to Will as he revealed his future plans. She thought about the journey he had been on and what still lay ahead of him. In a way, she envied him. He had seen so much of the country, while she had been dreaming of just being able to go to Georgetown or even Charleston. One day, after the children were grown, she was going somewhere; maybe John would even take her with him on the boat to Georgetown. But deep inside she knew she would go no farther than Conwayboro.

Glancing over at Will's face, she picked up a walking stick by the steps and started to scribble in the sand. He was her age, but the war had left its marks on him. He seemed older. He looked comfortable leaning back against the steps, relaxed, as if he were sitting on his own porch. He was handsome, and she could sense his loneliness. His gentle manner and polite conversation began to arouse feelings in her that she had suppressed for longer than she cared to remember. She was awakened by the thought of a man, a warm body, his arm around her shoulder, holding her close and safe. She craved a small amount of intimacy, but her moral senses quickly returned and her emotions were suppressed. Looking back down at the sand in front of her, she asked softly, "Will, have you ever been on the Waccamaw?"

"No, ma'am, I haven't, but I'm sure looking forward to seeing a different river."

"Well, I'm here to tell you it's a beautiful, mysterious river, but I'll warn you! There are outlaws that lay in wait for folks, so you best keep a sharp eye out."

Pulling his jacket back to expose his belt, Will smiled. Letsy could see the butt of a pistol sticking out of a holster. She was a bit surprised, and for a few seconds, a little uncomfortable. He could sense the sight of the weapon bothered her, so he took it out of his belt and handed it to her.

Reluctantly, she took it from him. A strange feeling came over her. The weight and the feel of the hard steel gave her a sense of security she hadn't felt before. The gun strangely intrigued Letsy. She couldn't help but wonder how many good men it might have killed.

"What kind of a gun is this, Will?'

"That's an 1860 Colt Army."

"Have you had to use it lately?" Letsy asked seriously.

"No, and I hope I don't have to."

Letsy passed it back to Will, and he slid it back into his belt. "I'll keep a sharp eye out for any roughnecks on your river, Letsy. I promise."

"How did you get a gun like that Will?'

"After I got out of that Yankee hospital, I found a job cleaning out stables. One particular morning, I was told to clean out a stall in the back of the barn. When I got there, I found a saddled horse. Its rider was lying up against the wall, drunk. He told me he was some famous cavalry officer, naming all the battles he had been in. He claimed dozens of horses were shot from under him and that he was some kind of hero.

"While I cleaned, he talked and talked. I guess all he really wanted was for someone to listen. When I finished, he stood up and reached into his saddlebag. He pulled out the pistol and handed it over to me. Said it was a gift, a token of his appreciation for not telling the stable owner he had been using the stall on a regular basis. He even gave me some cartridges to go with it. I wasn't sure what I was going to do with it but knew I better keep it hid. He told me he didn't know if he'd be back that night or not, but it was nice to know he would have a clean stall to pass out in. I gave him a leg up onto his horse and off he went."

Letsy laughed, shaking her head.

Will laughed, too. As he tapped his pipe against the bottom of his black boot, the burned up ash sparkled as it fell to the ground.

Letsy stood with her back to him, looking out toward the shadowed woods. Fireflies blinked everywhere. She imagined a little girl who used to chase them in the yard of the little house down near Toddville. In many ways she wished she were that little girl again. She hadn't seen the old home place in many years. Oh, how she missed her mama and daddy! They both had passed on several years back. Her mother could not stand being without "Pap," as she called him. Six months after his death, she joined him. Now, all Letsy had were the children and John.

Chapter Five

Snapping back to the present, Letsy began talking again for she wanted to keep the conversation with the handsome stranger going. She had been starved for company until now.

"I think the happiest I've ever seen people around here was when those two Union boats came up the Waccamaw and dropped off a passel of Yankee soldier boys. We hated them, but it was a Godsend. The war was over anyhow; Georgetown belonged to the Yanks, and so they started sending boats up the Waccamaw to search for deserters and bushwhackers. There had been a lot of murdering and robbing going on in this area. This is such an isolated part of the country; I'm here to tell it was a dangerous place before those Yankee boys arrived, and I honestly have to say I was glad to see them come."

They both sat in silence for a while looking out into the darkness. The woods hummed with the sounds of the night. Off in the distance, an owl hooted closer and closer to them. Then he faded into the night and all went quiet. She turned to Will and smiled—knowing he would be gone in the morning and her life would return to its normal routine.

"Will, have you made arrangements to catch a boat in town?"

"No, I'm just going to have to see what I can work out when I get there."

"I've got a friend who can help you," she said excitedly. "When you go to the docks tomorrow to catch your boat, look for the Bertram Belle, a small steamboat. You can't miss it; it's painted blue. The old captain is a fellow by the name of "Bertram Johnson." He carries lumber and a few other items down to Georgetown. He and my daddy were real good friends. Tell him I sent you. He might put you to work on your way down, but you'll be taken care of. There are lots of legends about the river and its people. If Bertram has a drink or two, you might get him to tell you a few."

A fleeting thought about her old slave friend Blind Jolene ran through her mind as she looked up at the stars. She laughed out loud.

"What's so funny, Miss Letsy?" asked Will.

"Oh, there's a place down the Waccamaw called "Old Woman Lake." Tell Bertram I said for him to tell you about Blind Jolene. Poor old Bertram is scared to death of her. I don't know why; she's long dead. She passed away a few years ago. She could do magical things." Her eyes sparkled as she spoke of Jolene. "She was really something."

Letsy chuckled again. "Old Bertram swears she's still out there. He says you can hear her chanting, doing that 'voodoo stuff,' as Bertram calls it. He also claims if you look real close, you can see a fire burning outside her old cabin. So, Will, if you believe in ghosts, you might get to see her."

"How did you come to know this Jolene, Miss Letsy?"

Letsy began pacing back and forth in front of Will, dragging her stick along the ground behind her like a small child would a doll. Her mind had taken her far away before she finally spoke.

"When I was a little girl, my daddy would take me fishing on the river. One really hot day, we rode one of Daddy's mules, for miles it seemed, until we came to a well-used fishing spot. He told me not to go far out of his sight. But you know how children are, and I was always one to explore beyond my boundary. I saw a patch of water lilies with the prettiest milky white blooms; I could smell their sweet fragrance from where I stood. They were just floating on top of the black water close to a fallen tree half submerged in the river. I just had to have one. I waded through the shallow water until I was knee deep, standing right in the middle of the beautiful green pads and white flowers. Their sweet fragrance drifted up around me; I tell you, it was intoxicating. I reached down to pick one without seeing the cottonmouth sunning itself on the fallen tree. Before I could jerk my hand back, he bit me right there."

Letsy held her hand up and pointed to two little scars just above her little finger.

"What happened then, Miss Letsy?" Will questioned.

"I started screaming for Daddy. He came running down the bank in a panic. He grabbed me up, pulled his gun, and shot the snake dead. He carried me up on the bank, laying me down on the sand. He did his best to comfort me, but we were pretty far down the river. He knew I'd never make it home alive, and so he started praying. Suddenly, I was jerked up into the arms of this old black woman. I have no idea where she came from; it was as if she just appeared out of nowhere. She had no eyes, just big scars where eyes used to be. All kinds of jewelry and funny looking things were hanging around her neck and from her clothes. I'm not sure if I was more frightened by the snakebite or the old woman. She told my father to follow her, which he did without hesitation. He was willing to do anything to get me some help at that point; he also sensed that this strange woman was somehow the answer to his prayers.

"As we passed into the dark swamp, she was moving as smoothly as if she were floating. Not once did she stumble on a cypress knee or sink into the black mud. We came to a skiff pulled up on a bank. She got in and laid me across one of the wooden seats. Sitting down next to me, she motioned for my daddy to get in and paddle us across. Daddy was real excited. As he stepped in, he accidentally pushed the boat off, leaving the paddles on the bank. As the boat glided away from the muddy bank, we stared helplessly back at the paddles. Getting ready to go back for them, Daddy already had one leg over the side when Jolene told him to keep his seat. As if pulled by some invisible power, the boat glided to the other side of the river where it slipped right in to a hidden canal. I lay there watching the dense tree tops pass above, the tall, moss-covered cypress that lined the shallow passage. Though still conscious, I was beginning to feel the effects of the venom. I heard the splashing of another snake as it fell into the water, like someone slapping the water.

"Soon the canal opened into a beautiful hidden lake. As the boat continued across the dark water, I caught sight of a cabin just ahead of us in the shadows at the edge of the swamp. The boat bumped up against the bank; Jolene took me in her arms and headed toward the cabin. Daddy tied the boat to a cypress knee and followed.

"I heard her tell him that she could help me but only if he would not interfere with what she was about to do. Reluctantly, he agreed and then backed away. She laid me down outside on a pallet made from moss next to this huge pot of some sort of boiling stew. I don't know to this day what she was cooking up, but I know it smelled terrible. She went into the little cabin and came out with a couple of clay jars. She placed them next to me on a small table. Then she placed candles around the pallet and lit each one. She told my father it could be a long night, and so he might as well get comfortable. She warned him again that if he interfered, her efforts to save me might fail.

"As the sun set through the cypress trees, the darkness descended on us. The pain increased, and then the fever hit me. She rubbed the contents of the jars on the bite while mixing up something in that pot of stew. She poured a little of it into a small clay bowl, and then she made me drink it. Lord, I thought I'd lose my stomach, it tasted so bad! It took awhile, but finally I settled down. In the flickering of the fire and candles, she started chanting and making a kind of groaning sound. Moving her body like a snake, she danced around the fire. She took a handful of white powder from a gourd bowl and threw it into the fire. Flames and sparks burst up into the night sky. About this time, Daddy had decided he had seen enough and was going to take me away from that place. But he couldn't move; she had some power over him that kept him seated just where he was.

"Suddenly, everything got real quiet, not a sound could be heard, not even the wind. It was so still that I could hear my heart beating in my chest. Even the sounds of the night creatures hushed. Then out in the distance I heard a little voice. It sounded like a little boy. He was calling out as if searching for someone.

"Jolene called to him by name saying, 'Elijah, my li'l Elijah, here we is. Over by da cabin, come to me boy I needs yo' hep.'

"The voice came closer and became clearer, calling Jolene.

"'Jolene, where are you?'

"Once again the fire flared up. Sparks flew upward to the treetops. Then the ghostly shape appeared right beside me.

"'Jolene, why have you summoned me from the other side?' it asked.

"Jolene spoke sadly, 'Li'l Elijah, please hep our li'l friend. Da po chile been bit by da cottonmout. She in pain an' it be alls I kin do to keep her soul wid' us.'

"Through the tears and pain, I could see this beautiful blue light. It hovered all around me and above me, as if it were looking me over.

"Jolene spoke again, asking him for help, 'Please Massa Elijah, hep' me keep dis chile's soul ground' to dis place. I's knows I's lets yo' down befo', but please hep me keep her soul wid' us now.'

"The little voice spoke again, 'Jolene, I won't let you down. I will help you. You were always there for me. Don't you worry; I won't let her soul get to the other side.'

"The blue light slowly faded into the swamp until it was gone. A strong wind came up, bringing with it many strange sounds. As best I remember, it sounded like people talking; they were discussing something, and it just all ran together.

"Jolene was next to the fire, still moaning and rocking back and forth in some sort of trance. My body struggled with the venom until I finally drifted off into a deep sleep.

"The slight touch of a dragonfly resting on my forehead woke me in the morning. The hot coals of the fire were barely smoldering. Daddy was lying up against a tree, sound asleep. I still felt a little strange but immediately looked around for Jolene. I could hear her talking to someone as she walked around the corner of her cabin. She was carrying something. Still a little groggy, I rubbed my eyes to clear my vision, and I swear she was talking to a crow perched on the branch she was carrying. I couldn't understand a word being said, but I know she and that crow were talking. After a few minutes, the crow flew away and she walked over to me.

"'Oh, da baby girl be feelin' better?' She asked.

"I still couldn't, for the life of me, figure out how she could get around so well without her eyes. That woman may have been blind, but you'd never have known it.

"With the sound of her voice, Daddy awoke. He hesitated. I think he was waiting for her to tell him it was safe before he jumped up and rushed over to check on me. After seeing I was much better, he fell on his knees and said another prayer.

"She looked his way and laughed. 'She be gitin' better. Yo' needs be gitin' home, ya' hear? Folks be worrin'. De mos' likely be out lookin' fo' da both o' yo' right now.'

"We got back into the boat. Jolene brought another pair of paddles from the cabin, only, this time she handled them. On our way back across the river, I asked her how she had made the boat move without the paddles the day before. She just laughed, said I was so lost in the fever I must have imagined that.

"This woman intrigued me; she was so mysterious. I had to ask her how she was able to get around without eyes. She told me she'd lived in the swamp so long that she didn't need eyes to see. It was all familiar to her, adding that sometimes a person doesn't need eyes to see.

"I asked her about the events of the night before: the blue light, the child's voice, and the other things I had witnessed. Again she told me I was full of the fever and was seeing things.

"Daddy watched her silently. I knew he was trying to figure out what to tell folks. I believe that he thought he had seen the devil at work. I was just a child, but even I knew she had used voodoo magic to help me. Daddy kept rubbing the cross hanging from the chain around his neck.

"After we got to the bank, Daddy thanked her and offered to pay her or maybe do something for her.

"'No, Mister, I's gots all I needs right here in dis here swamp.'

"Slowly, she started back across the river. I watched as she moved the paddles rhythmically through the dark water. When she was almost all the way across, Daddy turned to leave. But I stood there watching. She turned back, smiling with a big grin, waving goodbye. Holding up my little snake-bit hand, I returned the goodbye. Somehow I knew I would see her again. I didn't think about it at the time, but we never did know her name until years later when I started asking questions about her.

"I have never forgotten that night. I remember my daddy saying, 'God works in mysterious ways.' I think he realized he couldn't tell a soul about what had happened. He knew they'd think he'd lost his head, especially the folks at the church. He just told folks we got lost and had to stay the night in the swamp. Daddy didn't say another word about it, and we never went back to that fishing spot either. I've never forgotten Jolene or that night. She was mysterious; I was fascinated with her. I kept up with her by asking the old Negroes about her. They would look at me with fear when I would bring up her name. She must have been some special kind of witch or voodoo woman.

"I wanted to go and see her again. Before I married John, I hired a man to take me back to Old Woman Lake to visit with her. She had to be at least 90 years old. We sat and talked for a while about that night. When it came time for me to leave, she held my hand tightly, telling me I shouldn't marry John. She said he wouldn't do me right, that he had a wandering soul and some sort of mystical gift that would push him to the dark side. I've never been exactly sure of what she meant by that. I just brushed it off as the talk of an old woman. Now I know how right she was."

Will looked a little confused; he was curious about what Jolene meant by "mystical gift" and a "wandering soul," but he decided against asking her.

"Sounds to me like she might have known what the future was going to bring." Will said hesitatingly, hoping his statement wasn't too insensitive.

Letsy pondered the comment for a moment.

"You know, I think she could see many things that the rest of us couldn't even imagine. She was blind as a bat. She didn't have any eyes at all; her eyelids were completely covered by scars. I keep remembering her saying, 'Sometimes a person doesn't need eyes to see.'"

"How did she lose her sight, Miss Letsy?"

The pleasant smile on her face faded. He could see the question had saddened her. Turning away from Will, tears welled up in her eyes and ran down her cheeks.

"The story I've heard is morbid. She was a slave owned by a cruel, greedy man. He'd purchased her from a plantation down in Georgetown. After she had grown old and wasn't able to work the fields anymore, he put her to work as a nanny for his small son. She just about raised the boy whose mother had died from a fever when he was just a baby. Jolene became the only mother the boy had ever known. The story goes that the child wandered off one day and got lost in the swamp. Jolene was supposed to have been watching him. She let him play in the yard of the big house and found herself a sunny spot to sit. It was mid afternoon, and the warmth of sun soon put her fast asleep. You know how children can be; slipping away from her, he walked off toward the river.

"No one knows how long it was before she woke up, but the old folks say she had always been very watchful of the boy. When she woke, she was frantic and ran everywhere looking for him. Finally, she mustered everyone on the plantation to help her. Night came and still there was no sign of him. Bonfires were lit, and the search went on using torches throughout the night. The boy's father had been away on business in Conwayboro. The foreman sent a rider to find him. When they returned the following morning, the boy was still missing. The father was so angry that he had Jolene chained to a post down by the river. He ordered that she be kept there until the boy was found. Later that afternoon, one of the search parties returned with the boy's body. He had apparently drowned.

"The father went crazy, blaming Jolene's carelessness for the boy's death. He took his rage out on her by ordering the foreman to burn her eyes out with a hot iron rod. As the foreman heated the rod, the father screamed at Jolene that she would never repeat this mistake. He told her, 'You had eyes and didn't use them, now you'll no longer have them. From this day forth, you'll not see again!'

"The foreman picked up the glowing iron rod from the coals. Approaching Jolene, he paused. He glanced over to the boy's father who nodded for him to go ahead with the grizzly task. Four slaves were instructed to grab her arms and legs and keep her down. Another man knelt at her head and pinned it between his knees. As they held her down, the foreman held the hot iron just above her eyes, searing them shut. She screamed until, mercifully, she lost consciousness. She was then taken into the swamp and left on a sand bar, left to suffer and die in the darkness. The old Negroes said her eerie screams could be heard throughout the night. No one knows how, but somehow she survived. They say she learned the mysteries of the river, and that it gave her life. That's all I know about her."

Letsy's story fascinated him. "Miss Letsy, do you wish you had listened to her advice?"

"Yes and no, Will. There have been times in our marriage that I'd never trade. The last few years haven't been good though. I don't know what's come over John. When he came home from the war, all he talked about was the blood and the killing. He told me how those Yankees tunneled under them at Petersburg and set off explosives. Many of the men and boys in his company were killed in the explosion. John was lucky. He said he somehow knew where to go to stay safe. I guess he had an angel looking after him. His officers were amazed at his ability to know when and where the Yank's would attack. He was given several awards for his leadership. But when he came walking down that road, I could tell he was a different man. I guess all the killing and hatred can turn anyone into a devil. He drinks too much, and I know he has a woman in Georgetown. He met her after he started working on the river. Oh, I've heard rumors of her. I just hope and pray that one day he'll change."

Sighing deeply, she added, "But I don't know how to change him."

Half smiling, Will looked at Letsy and said, "Maybe you could call on your old friend Blind Jolene? She might have a cure for him."

Raising her hands to the air in a pleading way, Letsy joked, "Oh, Jolene, can you come and help me with John?" Laughing she added, "If she were alive, I bet she would help."

Letsy had no way of knowing that after Jolene saved her life in the swamp, the two of them would always be spiritually connected. She didn't realize that whenever she called for help, Jolene would always be listening.

Chapter Six

As the stars twinkled in the night sky, Letsy remembered her mother and the many conversations they shared. She cherished those nights when they sat on the porch and talked. Her mother told her about her life, the hardship of childbirth, and of the things a woman needed to know. She told Letsy what to expect when her time came to marry. When these conversations would start, her daddy would find a reason to go to the barn or find something else to do. He had no need, or inclination, to listen to "woman talk," as he called it.

Letsy's eyes welled up with tears as she thought about her parents. For some reason, she felt compelled to tell Will, especially about how her father told ghost stories.

"On cold winter nights, we would sit inside by the fireplace, waiting for sleep to overtake us. Pa would tell all kinds of stories, stories of ghosts and pirates and buried treasure. He sure did have a gift for story-telling. He made them sound so eerie; he would draw me into those stories so deeply that I actually felt like I was there. Then he'd grab my arm and make this scary sound like, "arggh," scaring me half to death. We'd both laugh, and then he'd reassure me the stories were make-believe before sending me off to bed. I really miss those days."

Letsy turned to Will with a sorrowful look in her eyes. "I'll tell you, Will, that is one person I could stand seeing right now, my Pa. I would love to hear one of those ghost stories the way he told them when I was little."

"Miss Letsy, that is strange about the pirate stories. My daddy told me stories, too, but I always believed his were real. Before he died, the only thing he gave me was an old map. He swore on his deathbed that it was a real treasure map. But knowing my daddy, I don't much believe he knew what he was talking about."

Will stood up and reached into his coat. He pulled out a piece of leather, unfolded it, and then laid it down in front of her.

"The whole time I was in that Yankee prison, I was able to keep this hid in the lining of my coat."

It was a beautifully drawn, detailed map with a big X marking a place where a treasure was supposed to be buried.

"Miss Letsy, even if you don't believe those stories your daddy told you, you might be interested in this map."

"I can't say that I believe those stories, Will."

He pushed the map toward her. "I want to give you this map anyway. It's not much, but who knows, someday you or someone you know might take a notion and want to go looking for it. Maybe even your boy Franklin would want to give it a go."

He moved very close to Letsy and spoke in a hushed voice, as if he were telling her a secret story much as her father used to do.

"Drawn on this here piece of leather is a real treasure map. It just happens to be in this here part of the country, too. My daddy gave it to me before he died. He told me the treasure belonged to a black-hearted sea captain, the kind that would cut your throat if you crossed him. It was said that he fell in love with a beautiful dark-haired, green-eyed woman. She was his only love, and that love caused her death. Daddy told me that somehow this treasure was connected to that woman and that the pirate had cursed the treasure. Whoever found it would be doomed for all eternity."

Mesmerized, Letsy gazed at Will as if she were in a trance.

Realizing how well he had drawn her into the story, he reached out, grabbed her arm, and made the "arrgh" sound.

She jerked away so hard her hand struck the post next to the steps. Shrieking, she shook her arm and glanced at Will who by this time was laughing hysterically.

Her face turned red with embarrassment. "Will Rhodes, you had me going."

She laughed, too, knowing that he'd just gotten the best of her. She'd not had a good laugh in a long time. She looked deep into Will's eyes, and for a brief moment, the world seemed to stop. Her sadness passed, and she felt an uncontrollable desire to move closer to him. He had awakened a feeling she remembered from long ago. She was lonely and starved for the touch of a man.

Will sensed the same desires, as he moved even closer to her. Turning his head away from her gaze, he knew he had to say something to break the pull between them. What was he doing? She was a married woman. Her husband could show up at anytime and justifiably kill him for making advances on his wife. Clearing his throat to break the tension, he continued the story about his father.

"All joking aside, Miss Letsy, my daddy did drink a lot. In more than one of his drunken states, he swore if he could find the place on this map, he'd be a rich man. He told me it came from a sailor who traveled with a devil of a man named "Caleb Bland." Judging from the map and what he told me, the place is not too far from here. It's probably about thirty or forty miles toward the north on the coast. I'll tell you straight, I just don't have any desire to be chasing such stories. I really need to get me a good paying job somewhere, maybe on a boat and stay there. Anyway, he was just an old drunk telling stories. I've done about all the traveling and fighting I ever want to do. As far as I'm concerned, following this here treasure map means nothing but more traveling and, most likely, more fighting."

"I guess we all get tired of chasing our dreams and fortunes," Letsy said sadly. "Just simple things mean more than all the gold in the world."

"You are so right, Miss Letsy."

Letsy took the map and scrutinized it a little closer. The leather was soft and pliable, the printing very detailed. Whoever had made it had taken great pains to get it accurate.

"Will, I don't know if I believe in treasure maps, but this might look good hanging on a wall or maybe just a good conversation piece," she offered.

"Do what you want with it, Miss Letsy. It's yours, as a token of my appreciation for the food and place to bed down and, of course, spending time with you, talking."

Letsy and Will's eyes met again. Long dormant feelings were welling up inside them, feelings that hadn't been felt for a long time. He moved a little closer, taking her hand in his and caressing it gently. He moved his other hand up and over her shoulder, brushing her breast as he pulled her closer. Realizing that he had touched her breast, he pulled his arm back and waited for her reaction.

"Will, don't let go," she whispered. "Just keep your arms around me and hold me for a while."

Their eyes met yet again, but this time there was a deepness she hadn't noticed before. His eyes seemed different, as though they had something to say, something that had gone unspoken. His eyes, his touch, the closeness they shared, all combined to arouse in her a passion that had long been missing from her life.

Will, too, sensed something in Letsy. He was drawn to her as to no other woman. His passions, too, were aroused in a way he had almost forgotten. It had been a long time. He wasn't sure but this woman was having a mesmerizing effect on him. At first, he convinced himself he was imagining things, that she was not drawn to him the way he was to her. But her gaze, her presence—he realized that she shared the desire. He took her hand in his, gently kissing it. His eyes returned to hers as the passion welled within him. He moved his other hand up and placed it over her shoulder.

The heat of rushing blood pumped through her body. She hadn't felt these sensations since the early years of her marriage. She placed her arms around him, and they held each other for what seemed like a long time. She gently started to pull away, although her heart wasn't in it. She loved what she was feeling and sensed that he did too.

He continued to hold her but eased his grip just a little. He then moved his head and placed a gentle kiss on her neck. Responding, she shifted herself to face him, to look again into his eyes, to find the reassurance she needed not to pull away. It was there. He held her tighter, placing his next kiss tenderly on her lips. He sought her permission to take it further, and her body yielded, granting him the permission he sought. He again placed his lips to hers, and they kissed, long and deeply.

Neither Will nor Letsy wanted to or could stop what had started. Will's hand again brushed her breast as he adjusted his position. She grabbed it, placing it firmly over her left breast. He began caressing it with the same passion she felt in his kisses. The heat between them had reached proportions neither of them could remember. They enjoyed each other's touching and caressing for what seemed like hours before Will rose from the stoop, pulling her up with him. She nodded toward the barn; they walked slowly toward it while holding each other in the shadows of the night. She could no longer resist the desire to be close to a man, this man.

Entering the barn, she thought to herself: "I pray the children don't awaken, let me have this moment. I have no idea what I would say to them, but I don't have the strength or desire to stop what is about to happen."

Soon Will's gentle kisses and touch pushed those thoughts to the back of her mind. The passion took control; there was no going back.

Slowly running his hands down her back, he carefully unbuttoned her dress. As it fell away from her body, her cotton slip partially revealed her breast. Will reached up and pushed the slip off her shoulders, which left her completely naked. He gently touched her, first on the shoulders. He then moved his hands up to her face until he held her, with one hand on each cheek. Her soft skin and the clean smell of lavender caused him to tremble. She could smell his freshness, his lips tasted of the tobacco that intensified her desires. She was driven by a need, the need to be a woman.

She unbuttoned his shirt, running her hands over his chest as she kissed his skin that was warm against her lips. She unbuckled his belt and slowly unbuttoned his pants until they fell to the floor. As he lay back on the dusty hay, he pulled her down on top of him. Through the heat of raw and passionate love, they became one.

Pulling herself together, Letsy felt the pangs of guilt as she dressed.

Will pulled her back, whispering, "Miss Letsy, you could leave all this and come with me."

"No, that wouldn't do. I know John hasn't been a good husband or father, but I do love him, and I pray that one day he'll change. I have five wonderful children, and this is the only home they have ever known. I could never leave this farm."

Her hand slowly slipped away from his as she rose from Will's grasp.

She turned cautiously. Slipping into the night and without looking back, she returned to the little cabin, leaving Will in the darkened barn.

He watched her disappear through the door of the cabin. He knew that if he did not leave soon, he might not leave at all. Sometime after midnight, he gathered up his gear and headed down the road leaving through the same gate that he had entered.

Not until the next morning did Letsy realize that he had gone without saying goodbye, but she understood why. She looked down the road to get a glimpse of him, but he had left shortly after making love to her.

Letsy put the map away in her chest and tried to put the memory of William Henry Rhodes away also. She had no way of knowing that the map Will had given her was real and the place marked with the X held a king's ransom.

Chapter Seven

Letsy soon forgot about the map Will had given her as life returned to its normal pace around the farm. She instructed the children not to tell their father about the stranger, suggesting it might spark his anger.

A month or so had passed after Letsy's passionate encounter with Will. The routine hardships continued. Her life had become a struggle, and each new day drove her deeper into depression.

Lavenia, her oldest, had complained about not feeling well and soon came down with a fever. As usual, John was gone down the river so Letsy knew she could expect no help from him. After all the usual home remedies failed, Letsy sent Franklin to town to get the doctor. She instructed the boy to use his father's horse instead of the mule because it would be quicker.

Franklin knew better; his father had forbidden him to ride that horse. He remembered the beating he'd received for riding the mare without permission; he wouldn't touch the horse, regardless of what his mother said. The willow stick his father used on his backside left his legs bleeding. It took weeks for the cuts to heal; the pain still burned in his memory. He saw the devil in his father on that day. His mother had tried to shield her son, but John threw her to the ground out of his way. She was powerless to stop him, and Franklin knew that her failure still haunted her. On that occasion, Franklin came to understand his mother's fear of his father, the man called John Ian Waters.

As Franklin bridled up the old mule, his thoughts drifted to his sister's illness as well as his father's absence. His anger seethed. He felt helpless; the resentment and hatred boiled within. He would never forget what his father had done, nor would he forget his abusive treatment of his mother.

Climbing on the mule's bare back, he reined her up. He felt her resisting his commands. Finally, she turned onto the sandy lane, and they headed for town.

The night engulfed Franklin, every sound caused wild imaginings in his young mind, and his heart pounded from fear. He pushed on through the darkness until he finally reached the outskirts of town. Although he felt a little safer, his sick sister still rested heavy on his mind. He needed to find the doctor. Looking everywhere, he finally spotted the doctor's buggy out behind the local shoe repair shop. Approaching the back door, he heard the muffled sounds of grown men's laughter from inside. He knocked on the door, timidly at first, and then quite loudly when no one responded. The laughter from within turned silent; after a few seconds, the door opened and a tall, bearded man appeared. Franklin could smell the unmistakable odor of whiskey coming from the small room, a smell he had learned to associate with his father. The stench had become Franklin's warning sign whenever his father came home. It was almost always present, but when it was especially strong the boy knew to expect the worst. The pungent odor of burning tobacco mixed with whiskey almost took his breath away.

From the deep recesses of the dark place, a familiar voice spoke: "Franklin Waters. Boy, what are you doing in town this time of night?" It was the voice of Doctor Samuel Pearl.

The doctor sat at a small table with several other men. Glancing around the table, Franklin recognized each one of them. A deck of playing cards lay on the tabletop and a jug of spirits sat on the floor by one of the men. Judge Gordon, who sat in silence fingering his mustache, watched the nervous Franklin as if he were eyeing a criminal standing before his court. Denton Graves poured a cup of whiskey and brought it to his lips; he sighed with enjoyment, and then flashed a big grin toward Franklin. Franklin had heard Mr. Graves was the best attorney in town; still, something about him made Franklin uneasy. The tall bearded man at the table, Slim Baxter, owned the shoe repair and was head deacon in his church. Franklin then realized another man loomed in the darkness behind the door. Sheriff Osborne stepped forward; light from the lantern revealed his face as he placed the cigar to his lips and took a long draw, holding the smoke a few seconds before releasing it in a long wispy stream. Everyone waited for Franklin to speak.

"Doctor Pearl, my sister Lavenia is sick, and Mama needs you bad. Could you please ride out to the house? Please, sir!" Franklin pleaded.

Sam Pearl could see that the boy was trying hard to fight back tears. "Is your father home, Franklin?"

"No, sir, he ain't." Franklin looked down at the dirty floor. He felt the steady gaze of the grown men. What were they thinking of him? He wanted to run out the door and not ever look back. Everyone in town knew his father and how he had turned into a miserable mean drunk.

Without question, Dr. Pearl rose from his seat. "Boys I'm out of the game. Looks like I got doctoring to do. I'll see ya'll next week. Let's go, Franklin."

When he saw the mule, he realized that Franklin wouldn't be able to keep up with the buggy. "Son, I'm going to go on ahead; so I'll see you when you get there. Now you be careful; everything is going to be all right."

As Franklin watched the buggy disappear into the night, a helpless feeling besieged him once again. He felt alone and angry, and he wanted to cry. Fighting his emotions as long as he could, he finally gave in. The contempt he had for his father had turned into rage, a rage he could no longer hold inside. Tears streamed down his cheeks as he whispered the words: "I hate you, John Waters."

Inside the shoe repair shop, laughter rang out; he heard his father's name. He was ashamed of his father, and for the first time, he wished he wasn't the son of John Waters. Wiping his face, he nudged the old mule. As they moved along Main Street, Franklin wished silently his father would drown in the dark waters of the Waccamaw.

Letsy greeted Dr. Pearl at the cabin door. Her fatigue and worry were apparent in her red swollen eyes. The other children were clinging to her like a flock of biddies to a mother hen. The doctor saw that they, too, had been crying.

"Letsy, where's John?" he asked as he walked toward Lavenia.

"Sam, you know good and well where he is."

He looked at Letsy in disgust. "I can't believe that man of yours. Why do you put up with it? He should be home with his family. The man's got no business in Georgetown."

"Hush, please." Letsy whispered. "Don't talk like that in front of the children."

"Well, when I get back to town, I'm going to send a telegraph down there and tell him to get home."

As Dr. Pearl checked Lavenia, Letsy watched intently over his shoulder. As he worked Letsy thought about the horrors the doctor had experienced during the war. John had mentioned seeing him in a field hospital after one of the many battles. He had been busy most of the day amputating arms and legs, stitching up wounds and trying to sort out those of the wounded who didn't have any chance at all. How had he survived that hell and put it behind him? Why couldn't John have done the same?

The concern on Sam's face told Letsy that Lavenia's situation was grave. She was running a high fever and hadn't been able to keep any food or liquids down for the past two days.

Sam turned to Letsy, "I'm not sure if I have anything with me that will help her. Try to keep her comfortable. If we can get this fever to break, we may have a chance of getting her through this. Keep bathing her with cool water. I know you're tired, Letsy, but you need to keep her cool. I'll be back first thing in the morning with more medicine and to check on her. In the meantime I'll send for John."

When Sam Pearl returned to town, he went directly to the telegraph office. Loudly beating on the door, he finally woke the operator. It took five telegraphs before they finally found John.

By the next morning, Lavenia's condition had worsened; the medicine had not helped. Her illness had gone too far. Her little body had fought it for as long as it could. Finally, she just gave up and slipped away.

Chapter Eight

It was too late by the time John made it home; Lavenia had been gone for several days. Her burial had been in the family cemetery just down the road.

Bursting through the front door of the cabin, John found Letsy sitting in a chair holding Lavenia's doll. The other children were busy cleaning and trying to get things back to normal. Letsy hadn't been able to bring herself to even comb her hair. She looked tired, too tired to go on. John sensed immediately he had arrived too late.

He fell to her feet crying, "What's happened Letsy? Please don't tell me I'm too late!"

Through tears, Letsy looked into John's eyes.

"John, Lavenia's gone. She's now with her maker." Her voice was cold and hateful.

John lay on the floor at Letsy's feet and sobbed. The children, who had never seen their father overcome so with emotion, were shocked. Not sure what to do, they looked to their mother for guidance. Letsy motioned for them to go outside for now. She wanted a little privacy with John.

Reaching down inside herself, she mustered the strength needed to get up from her chair. She understood clearly now that she couldn't depend on John; she had to take control of her life and do what was best for her and the children. She no longer feared him. A woman never to show anger, Letsy felt anger and resentment awaken inside her. So many times he had left her bruised and battered. She thought of the humiliation she felt, a reflection she often saw in the eyes of her neighbors and friends.

She had concealed the fact that he also lashed out at the children, especially Franklin. She had learned to draw her anger in, but now she had had enough. Backed into corner, she was ready to fight. The abuse, the whiskey, everything he had ever done to her and the children smoldered like the coals of a long burning fire. He would never hit her or the children again. The late nights coming in drunk, throwing things around the cabin were over. Never again. If she had to commit murder to stop him, she would. Never again. She would not allow John to abuse her or her children any longer. Never again.

She collected her thoughts and waited for John to calm himself; only then did she speak.

"John, I'll not live my life cowering down to you anymore. I no longer fear you. If you ever lay a hand on me again, you'll not wake the following day. I swear I'll kill you while you sleep."

She could hardly believe she was speaking the words as they soared from her lips. Clearly, she was not the same passive, gentle, soft-spoken Letsy. She knew this. John knew it, too.

She continued before John could say a word, his mouth agape. "As sure as the sun rises, you will not see another day. If you don't love the children and me, then you need to be on your way. I'll do what I must to survive; I'm alone now as it is. You're no kind of husband or father. If the whiskey and harlots are the life you wish for, then your comings here must end."

"Now, John, pull yourself together and go down to the cemetery and pay respects to your daughter."

Meekly, John pulled himself off the floor. Turning toward the door, he placed his hat on his head and reached for the door handle. Hesitating for only a moment, he spoke in a weak voice. "Letsy, please forgive me."

Letsy stood stone-cold looking at him. "John, I meant what I said. You need to think about your life." She had no compassion left for him.

He left the cabin and headed down to the cemetery. It was late in the afternoon by the time John walked through the gates. It was the middle of October, and he could feel the season turning. The sun had just set, and a light breeze passed through the cemetery. A slight chill teased, offering relief from the hot sticky summer.

John froze with sadness as he looked down at the fresh mound of dirt.

A small cross stood upright at one end. Both fresh and wilted flowers lay all around. He had picked a few brown-eyed Susans on his way down the road, which he carefully laid down against the cross.

Overwhelmed with guilt, he fell to the grave and grabbed a hand full of dirt. The tears that streamed down his face fell into the fresh soil that now held his first born child. She had always been his favorite, but he never let the others know. He thought about the pretty little shoes that he had brought her from Charleston, the shoes that now adorned her little feet in the grave. He lay beside the grave until well after dark, crying uncontrollably as wave after wave of grief spilled from his soul.

A cold wind blew in from the north carrying leaves and dust with it. He looked up in the night sky; a crescent moon was rising through a cloud. He thought he heard a voice speak to him from the woods. He sat up beside the grave, still clutching the handful of dirt, which had, by now, become imprinted with the mark of his inner hand. He tossed it away and brushed the dirt off. Again, he listened to the far away sound. He opened his mind to the other side to see who, spirit or mortal, spoke from the darkness.

In a sobbing voice, he asked? "Who's there? Are you of this world or the other?"

Then he sensed her. Her. It was Lavenia. "Oh God, no, it's my child!"

The sound of Lavenia's voice pierced him like a knife.

"Pa, I'm sorry I couldn't wait for you, but they were calling for me; it was my time. I've come back now. This will be our good bye. I wanted you to know that I love you, and I'll be waiting to meet you here one day."

Before he could respond, the others came. He was besieged at the grave, surrounded as if he were on trial. He knew them all. Hovering around him, they probed and prodded his mind with their spiritual powers. He tried, but he couldn't block them from entering his thoughts; he was helpless to the intrusions. Not knowing their intentions, he was frightened. He slumped back against the little cross that stood at the head of Lavenia's grave.

The specters moved even closer. He recognized his father even though the man appeared only as a ghostly outline. John was ashamed to have his father see him this way, but he realized very quickly why he and the others had come. During their mortal lives, each one had possessed the powers of the gift. They had come to put him on notice. He wasn't able to move a muscle or say a word, so frozen by fear was he.

Lavenia continued, "Pa, we've come here to try and set you on your way. You have used the gift that was passed to you in evil ways. You must change, Pa. You have to be at peace with yourself and allow the gift to take care of you. I love you so much, Pa, please do this for me?"

One of the specters came closer to John than the rest. Though he was a man the grief-stricken father had never met, John had heard stories of him. This ghost was the oldest of the clan. He spoke in the old language.

"John Ian, you have lost someone very special to you. You are suffering because your heart and soul are lost. You have allowed the dark side to control your life. You must consider yourself now and the power of the gift that you have. My son, you are blessed with the mark of the serpent. Only a few throughout time will ever possess this mark. The gift we have passed to you is strong; you must turn yourself around before it's too late."

Then his father spoke: "John, I am so disappointed in you; I can't believe you would treat your wife and children as bad as you have. Our wives and children have always played an important role in our lives. They are the ones who bear the future, and they must be cared for. It is your responsibility, John. Your ways must change, or the spiritual gift you possess will fade from your life. It has been in our bloodline for thousands of years. It's your responsibility, John. If you continue on this path, the gift will be forever lost to us and our family will pay the price. And it will be of your doing, John Waters! If you allow this to happen, you will be left in the darkness, never to see the light. There are still secrets that you have yet to discover; and you never will if you continue to abuse the gift. You must have peace within your soul for the gift to work. You must take care of what your ancestors have bestowed upon you. This is the only warning we can give you. Beware, my son; if you don't make this change, your place in this family will be lost."

In an instant they were gone, not a trace anywhere, only the wind blowing in the trees. John listened with his extraordinary powers, but not a spirit could be heard. He called out for Lavenia, but she did not answer. He knew then that she had passed over into the light. She was with God, and she was at peace. John realized also what the ghosts meant. He had been reckless with the gift, abusing it as well as himself.

Pulling his coat up around his neck against the cold night, he crawled up onto the grave. He lay back on the cold damp earth and looked up toward the night sky. He held his right hand up in the moon light and studied the serpent-shaped birthmark. Promising Lavenia and the spirits, he swore he would change. He'd be a different man from that day on.

As John carefully considered what had just transpired, his thoughts took him back to his father and the teachings of the old religion. In a low whisper, he spoke in the old language. He hadn't forgotten a single word his father had taught him, and he assured them all they had gotten his attention.

His strength drained from the long trip home, he decided to stay the night in the cemetery instead of walking back home.

As he approached the house the next morning, he could see his children at their chores. As John came near, his children instinctively froze in place, staring at him as he neared the gate.

Letsy met him there, "Well, John, what is your decision?"

Taking Letsy's hand, John bowed his head to her in shame. "Letsy, if you can find it in your heart to forgive me, I promise on my daughter's grave that I will never again touch a drop of whiskey. I will never spend my days away from you and the family again."

"What about your work on the river, John?"

"I still have to work, but every minute that I'm off that boat I'll be right here with you and my children. I promise! I am a changed man!"

John looked away from Letsy, his eyes welling up with tears: "The messengers came."

Letsy, puzzled, looked strangely at John and asked, "What do you mean, 'the messengers came'?"

"Just trust me, Letsy; I'll do right from now on."

Letsy sensed something spiritually moving had changed John during the night. She dared not question him. She would wait and see if he was serious about changing. She didn't say another word, but she had her mind made up. If he didn't change, he would have to go.

Chapter Nine

Changing his ways did not come easy for John. Some days he thought he'd go crazy if he didn't have a drink. He thought often of a bottle he had stashed away in the old stump across the ditch. Many times he had wanted to go for it but had fought the desire by busying himself with work around the place. This usually helped take his mind off what he knew would be his downfall. Still, John did not dispose of the bottle, the temptation, hidden in the stump of a dead tree.

The New Year came, followed by an exceptionally cold and rainy February. The family had been confined indoors for several weeks, and John's nerves were about to get the best of him. All he wanted was one little sip of whiskey; that would calm him. Like a revelation, it came to him, the hidden bottle. Praying it was still there, he put on his hat and coat and told Letsy he was going out to the barn.

Acknowledging him with a smile, she continued reading to the children.

When he stepped into the cold damp air, he turned and looked back at the door as if to return inside. He struggled with his decision. Running his hand across his lips, he visualized turning the bottle up and letting the soothing, warm potion run across his lips and into his soul. The dark side was winning; he stepped down off the porch and walked toward the barn. Looking back to make sure no one was watching, he slipped around behind the barn. Once he was hidden from view, he sneaked over to the ditch. The sky was a cold, hard gray and the wind howled like a banshee.

John pulled the coat up around his neck. He again ran his fingers over his lips. The dark side now had him in its grip.

"God, I hope it's still there," he thought.

The rain dripped from the brim of his hat. He searched the wide ditch for a place to jump across. He hadn't remembered the ditch being this wide before. Finally, he found a spot and made his first attempt. As he jumped, he felt himself stopped abruptly, even before he had left the bank. It was as if he had hit a solid wall. Falling back, he stood up, adjusted himself and tried again. Once again, in mid-flight, he fell back.

Then he felt the presence, a strong spirit just on the other side of the ditch. A thick ghostly fog blocked his view. He could no longer see where the ditch began or ended. The dark side pulled at him. A fiendish spirit encouraged him to try again, assuring him that this time he would make it. Giving in, he tried once more, but something again threw him back. He found himself lying face down in the mud.

Using his powers, he asked silently, "Who are you and why are you stopping me? I've not called you, so why are you here?"

He listened for an answer. He heard her laugh; then as the mist began to take shape, she appeared on the opposite side of the ditch.

"Yo' don't needs to call me. I's bin here fo' sometime. I keeps watch over Miss Letsy. I's be here to hep her an' not yo', my friend."

John sensed he was alone with this spirit. No others were present. "How did Letsy call you up? She doesn't possess such a craft."

"She jes' calls. Dat's all she needs do. She calls me back dis summer, an' I's be here since den. Yo' see, John Waters, Letsy an' me be connected. I hep save her life when she be a li'l chile, so we fo'ever connected in da spirit. I be hep'n her keep yo' in line."

"So... you must be Blind Jolene? She has told me about you, how you saved her life. But why haven't I felt your presence before?"

She laughed a loud guttural laugh. "John Waters, yo' thinks yo' be dat pow'ful wit yo' magic? Yo' cain't sees if'n yo' don't knows how to see. Yo' be blinded by yo' thirst fo' da potion hid here in dis here stump. I kin tells yo', if'n yo' don't change yo' ways, yo gonna lose yo' powers. I tells yo' now, don't yo' be cross'n over dis here ditch. Da bottle be here, but if'n yo' crosses over and drinks of it,' yo' gwine be lost fo'ever!"

John sat in the mud, his head resting in his hands. Using the gift to calm himself, he thought just how stupid he must look. Why was he letting the dark side torment him so? Looking down at his muddy clothes, he muttered, "Now am I a sight for sore eyes. What in the world am I going to tell Letsy? She'll think I've lost my mind."

He looked back across the ditch to see if the old spirit was still there. She wasn't, neither was the mist. For a long while, he sat there in the cold going over and over Blind Jolene's words, the words of Lavenia, and his ancestor's ghost from the cemetery. After more than an hour, he brushed the mud off his clothes as best he could and returned to the house.

Once inside, Letsy wanted to know where in heavens name he had been to get so muddy. Silent for a moment, he pondered whether he should tell her what really happened. "Letsy, I was trying to jump that old ditch and fell."

Letsy looked at him in disbelief. "What are you doing jumping a ditch out in the rain and cold?" As she said it, she realized he was hiding something from her. There is no mistaking the look of a guilty man.

"Letsy, come in the bedroom with me for a minute. I've got something I have to tell you."

She handed the book to Franklin and instructed him to continue reading. She followed John into their bedroom and closed the door behind her. "Well, John, what is it?"

"Letsy, I have a confession to make. I went out looking for a drink. I got to feeling so confined, I felt like if I didn't get out I'd go crazy. I had a bottle hid; it's out there in that hollow stump across the ditch."

Sitting down on the edge of the bed, he felt completely lost, ashamed. It was all he could do to look up at her.

"John, I know you've been having a hard time of it, but you've come to me and we'll work it out together because I love you."

John leaned over and placed his elbows on his knees. Rubbing his hands together, he looked down at the floor. His mind drifted for a moment, away from the room, away from Letsy to his earlier conversation with Blind Jolene.

"Letsy, there's some things that you can't help me with. It's a part of me that I have to reckon with, but I am working on it." He chuckled a little, thinking of his attempts to jump the ditch, and then looked at Letsy.

"Letsy, tomorrow morning I want you to go over and get that bottle and bust it up for me. It'll tempt me forever as long as I know it's there. I want to leave that part of my life behind. This is really hard for me. Can you understand?"

She sat down by him on the bed and said, "John, you know I'll do it for you, but I think it's better for you to do it yourself. I'll go with you, but, Honey, you've got to do away with it yourself. It has to come from you."

The next morning the sun was bright, and the rain clouds had moved on. John and Letsy both went out to the ditch. While Letsy waited, John easily jumped the ditch. Reaching down into the hollow stump, he pulled out the whiskey bottle and held it up to his face. With a quick glance at Letsy, he took it by the neck. Then, with a short hard swing, he smashed the bottle against the stump. The shattered glass fell all around the log; the smell of the whiskey filled the air. He glanced back at his wife.

"I did it! I just smashed a fine bottle of sipping whiskey. Letsy, I didn't think I could do it, but I did!" Reaching down, he picked up some of the pieces of glass. As he held them in his hand, he knew he had done it the right way.

"Are you having regrets?" Letsy voiced across the ditch.

"No, can't say as I am, at least not right now."

Chapter Ten

As the long winter turned to spring, John occasionally began attending church with Letsy and the children. Still, she sensed that he was struggling with something, something he hadn't told her.

As they lay in bed one night talking, she told John about the visit that she made to see Jolene before they were married. She asked him what Jolene had meant when she said that he had a "dark gift?"

John's body tensed. "I never knew Jolene. Why would she say such a thing?"

"I don't know, John, she was holding my hand, and she just said it."

John realized what Jolene had done. By touching Letsy's hands, as he often did, Jolene had been able to probe his mind with her powers. She had apparently learned a lot about him in this manner.

"John, here lately I've been paying a lot of attention to the way you've been acting. I think you're keeping some kind of secret, something that you don't know how, or don't want, to share with me."

John rolled over to face her. Brushing her hair back from her face, he kissed her on the forehead. "You're right, Letsy, I do have a secret." Now he would tell her about his gift; he would share with her the many secrets he had kept for so long. He longed to unburden himself.

"I don't know how to tell you without your getting upset."

Letsy sat up, leaning back against the headboard. "What ever it is, John, I'll try to understand."

Taking a deep breath, he began to tell her about his family secret. This telling, which would go on only when they were alone, continued for days until he had told her all that he knew.

In the beginning, she wasn't sure if she believed him or not; she had never heard of such things. As time passed, he explained in a little more detail until she finally came to accept it.

Once she understood her husband's powers, she was adamant that he would never use any of them on her. John, respecting her concern, promised that would never happen. In the following months, John told her even more about his powers: how he knew things that others didn't and how he could communicate with spirits.

Folks in the area began looking to John for guidance. He now used his gift to do good deeds for his neighbors and friends. He became, once again, the man that Letsy had fallen in love with before the war. John was doing well with the supply boats; everything was going his way. He had been promoted to first mate, and the extra money came in handy, especially with all the children growing up.

Even though life was going well for Letsy, too, she would find herself standing by the fence occasionally, recalling the stranger who had stopped for the night. She would forever hold those moments close to her heart. She wondered how he was doing, and she hoped that his life was good.

Chapter Eleven

Autumn approached. With the days growing shorter, the small farming community prepared for the coming winter. A slight chill hovered over the land as the sun sank in the west, spreading a final burst of purple and red against the darkening sky. Inside the little cabin, Letsy stood in the front room, the flames in the fireplace bravely pushed back the shadows into the corners of the room. The wife was preparing the evening meal. Delicate in stature, she moved with a strength and purpose that belied her fragile appearance.

John and the children came in after a hard day of chores and seated themselves at the long table in the center of the room. Moving quickly, Letsy and Hallie began filling the plates with food from the iron pots suspended over the hot coals on the hearth. When everyone had been served, John bowed his head and gave thanks for the meal.

A hush fell over the room as the first distant sound came to disturb the silence. Then, faintly, the muffled sound of horses' hooves on the sandy lane leading to the little house became louder. Letsy lifted her eyes questioningly to John; their exchange of glances needed no words. John rose from the table just as the night riders came to a stop at the low picket fence surrounding the house.

"Hello, the house," came a low-pitched voice from the gathering darkness. "You in there, John?"

John walked toward the door as the frightened children rushed to their mother's side. He lifted his hand in a gesture to allay their fears as he approached the door. Lifting the latch, he went outside and closed the door behind him. The only sounds Letsy and the children could hear were the inaudible murmurs of the men and the restless movement of the horses. In a few minutes, John, pensive, returned to the dinner table.

Letsy waited for John to tell her what news the riders had brought. After a few seconds, her curiosity got the best of her. "Well, John, what did they want?"

"Oh, it was my cousins Everett and Levi. They wanted to discuss some business. When the children are down, I'll tell you all about it."

Looking around the table at the children, he smiled to let them know everything was fine. "Let's grace this fine meal your mother has prepared."

Hallie spoke up with a spoon in hand, "Pa, we already blessed it. Remember, before the riders came?"

"Oh Yeah, we did; now I remember." John exchanged looks with Letsy, not sure how he was going to tell her about his cousins' plans.

After dinner, when the children were in their beds, John and Letsy went out on the porch. The moon, half full, was just showing itself above the dark tree line. In three or four nights, it would be full.

Letsy knew whatever news the men had brought that night was troubling John. He had changed so very much since she had laid down the law. He now had become almost a saint, and before he did anything, he first discussed it with her.

John spoke very seriously. "Letsy, Everett and Levi have asked me to help them find a treasure. I know its crazy, but hear me out before you say anything. I told them I wouldn't do it unless I had your blessing."

Letsy crossed her arms under her shawl and listened as John told her of Everett's proposition.

"Everett tells me that he met a man awhile back, down at Bucksville. The man had had a little too much to drink and was spouting off about a treasure buried somewhere near here on the coast. The fellow told him that his father had given him a map showing where the treasure was located, but he had given it to some woman he had met. Everett says the man must have had it a long time because he was able to tell him about it in detail, as if he had it memorized. The place is not far from here, and

Everett thinks it's worth looking for. There may be nothing to it, but who knows. That fellow may have been telling the truth."

Letsy thought instantly of the map Will had given her. Surely, it couldn't be the same map.

"John, is that all that Everett told you?"

John could sense something strange in Letsy's voice, but he dared not try to read her thoughts. He continued, "He said this fellow was traveling down to Georgetown with old man Bertram Johnson."

"Where is this so-called treasure supposed to be, John?"

"Everett says it's up around Little River, north of here on the coast, just before you get to North Carolina. I'm seriously considering helping him out if you don't mind me being gone for a little while. I know it'll only take us a few days to ride that far and return."

Letsy's mind was still on Will. She couldn't help herself. She wanted to know more about this man that Everett had run into. Could it have been Will?

John could sense the tension in her. There was a reason for all of her questions. John studied her, resisting the urge to read her thoughts. She seemed in another world.

"Letsy, what are you thinking on so intently?"

"Oh, just that Everett, you know, he's always up to something."

John knew that wasn't what had stirred her. There was something else.

Letsy's gaze returned to John. Shaking her head from side to side, she then referred to Everett and Levi in a sarcastic manner: "All those two do is stay in trouble, not so much Levi as Everett. I just don't trust him!"

As she turned away from John, her thoughts again went back to Will and the map he had given her. Her mind raced back to the night they sat on the porch, talking and laughing, enjoying each other's company and the passionate moment they shared. The memory was sweet and enduring, his touch and how he gave her life again. Her mind just wasn't with John at this moment.

"Letsy, are you listening to me?"

Startled, Letsy turned to John. "Yes, I hear you, John."

Letsy felt guilty, but she couldn't tell John about Will. She feared, too, that John might try reading her mind. Surely he wouldn't; he had promised he'd never use the gift on her.

She tried to come up with some way to tell John about the map. He wouldn't suspect anything if she just told him about it. The strong urges she had felt that night with Will would remain her secret. Reaching deeply inside herself, she mustered all her courage and told John about the stranger who had come by asking for food and shelter for the night. She told John that the man had given her, in payment for her kindness, a map before he left. The rest of story was hers alone; John had no need to know her secret.

John wouldn't use the gift with Letsy. He knew it would be a self-serving invasion against which she was defenseless. John had so much control over his powers that he was able to turn them on and off just as if he were opening or closing a door. He knew, too, that if she ever felt he was reading her, she'd never forgive him. He never blinked an eye or questioned her about the stranger staying over night. Who was he to be upset with Letsy for helping a stranger after the life he had been living in Georgetown?

"Do you still have that map, Letsy"?

"I think so, but I'm not sure. I'll have to go and look for it. I'll be right back." Letsy rushed inside to the chest where she had hidden the map.

John sat looking out into space, knowing deep in his heart that there was more to Letsy's story about Will than she had told him. He fought the urge to open that door; if anything happened, it was now in the past. Besides, he couldn't blame her. After all, it was his fault she had been lonely. The blame for whatever may have happened lay with John himself, and he knew it.

Filled with excitement, Letsy frantically started digging down to the bottom of the chest. There it was, the map Will had given her. Holding it to her face, she felt the soft leather against her skin. She remembered those brief moments together and how special he was to her.

She silently mouthed, "Will, maybe there is something to this map." Letsy returned to the porch, handing the map to John.

John took the map and studied it. He felt it meticulously with his strong hands. Suddenly, he saw the past in quick spurts. The vision kept appearing: a beautiful beach, an island, a young boy hiding. With tears running down his dirt-stained face, he was afraid someone was going to harm him. A dark man appeared; uniformed soldiers hanging someone from a tree, a vicious evil man, dressed in black. Evil! Evil! John threw the map on the porch, breaking the connection to the past. His breathing was labored, and he had started to sweat.

Letsy could see John had seen something. "John what is it? What did you see?"

"Oh, nothing to be concerned about. Just a place on the coast is all; real pretty place." He managed a little smile for Letsy. "I believe this may be the same place Everett was speaking of."

Letsy could sense John felt a strong force from the map by the way he caressed it. She also saw the fear in his eyes before he threw it down. He couldn't fool her; she had lived with him too long. She knew he was hiding something.

John picked up the map again, but this time he intended to see just how evil this man dressed in black could be. He saw ruthless and senseless murders, a ship in trouble, people crying and screaming, drowning in the ocean. He knew if he went after this treasure, he'd face a very strong and evil force. He ran his hands slowly over the map several times, as if in a trance. After a few minutes, he laid it down and turned to Letsy.

"Letsy, I get a feeling there might be something to this. I know you don't think much of Everett, but for some reason I have a good feeling about this. The gift is calling me to this search. I know I can't keep any of the treasure if it really exists, but I'll enjoy the hunt. You know I've never had a chance to use the gift to find anything like this before."

Letsy's low regard for Everett was difficult to hide. He drank a good bit and had a reputation for getting into fights and such. She knew his mother worried about him all the time. The sheriff had been out to the house a few times looking for him. She wasn't too excited about John going anywhere with him.

"Letsy, how do you feel about me helping them and using this map to do it? I think this might be the same place."

John realized even if they did find any treasure, he couldn't take one piece of it. To do so would mean he would possibly lose his precious gift. It was the adventure of the search that intrigued him.

With a worried look, Letsy turned away from John. She knew he had seen something sinister. She also sensed that this was something he really wanted to do. Hesitantly, and against her better judgment, she said, "John you have my blessings. Just be sure to come back to me the same way you leave."

Although Letsy's memories of Will were sweet, her love for John was deep. She and John were soul mates; he was the father of their children. They were destined, she knew, to live out their lives together. Even after all the years and children, she still felt butterflies in her stomach when John looked at her in that certain way.

John took Letsy in his arms and held her. "I love you so much, Letsy, and always will." This man was the John that Letsy had fallen in love with.

Chapter Twelve

The next day, John waited anxiously for his cousins to arrive. In the late afternoon, he heard the horses coming up the road. The children, who had gathered around Letsy, now stood in silence as they watched their father. Reassuringly, he promised to be back in a week. "But if we're not, go and find the sheriff and tell him where we've headed. He should be able to figure about where we would be."

Franklin already had his father's horse saddled and tied out back. Letsy had filled a bag with enough food for a week. John reached for his coat and hat from the wooden pegs by the door. He then turned to Franklin. "Son, bring my horse around and fetch the saddle bags."

"Yes sir, Pa!" The boy was gone in a flash.

John went into the bedroom. He knelt down and pulled the rug up at one corner revealing the wood floor. Sliding his knife between two of the planks, he lifted a loose board. Reaching into the darkness, he pulled out a leather bag tied tightly with a small cord. He opened the bag and checked its contents. Satisfied that everything was there, he tied it up, stuffed it under his coat, fitted the board back into place, and then replaced the rug.

Over the years, John had collected the items he needed for his root bag. It contained all he would need for dealing with both the spirit world and the living. Some of these items had come into his possession through a root doctor down in Georgetown. The other items were magical tools of the old ways given to him by his father, items actually passed down from his ancestors in Scotland. Those were his most precious.

"Letsy," he said turning to his wife, "I'll be careful, and I promise to be back within a week. Just be watching the road for me."

He knelt down before his children and opened his arms to them. All but Franklin wrapped their arms around him. Keeping his distance, Franklin didn't feel the need for such a show of emotions, especially with his father. John stood up, and then reached out to shake the boy's hand. John recognized some distrust still deep inside his son.

"Franklin. Son, you're in charge until I return. Ya'll mind your mother, now. I'll be back in a week."

Everett and Levi Waters sat on their horses waiting for John. Burt Jordan, a good friend who was courting the Waters boys' sister, had come along as extra help. Burt was a little younger than the others. John didn't know him nearly as well, but for some reason, he sensed he might cause problems along the way.

The three spoke politely to Letsy as she walked out to the porch. She nodded in reply and told them to take care. Nevertheless, Letsy's disdain for Everett was very apparent to everyone.

John came out and dropped the latch of the door behind him. Stepping over to his horse, he glanced back at Letsy. He paused, brought his foot back down from the stirrup and walked over to his wife. Hugging her tightly with both arms, he kissed her on the forehead.

Letsy felt tears welling up inside but fought them off. She knew John would be back, but fear settled in her stomach, nonetheless. She couldn't let the children sense the fear; she had to show them she believed in him and believed that he would return sober and in one piece.

In a moment, the restless prancing of the horses ceased. Then the sound of pounding hooves on the sandy lane faded away into the distance.

The four men rode at a fast, steady pace. Soon they turned off the dirt road onto a side trail that was not much more than a well-worn path through the dense forest. They headed cross-country toward White Oak Swamp. As darkness fell, a waxing moon rose in the sky. In a few more nights, it would rise in all its full glory. Still, it afforded them their only light, occasionally penetrating the canopy of tree limbs overhead and dimly reflecting off the sandy trail. The riders rode in silence. Three of the riders, driven by their lust for treasure, pushed on through the darkness.

The fourth, however, wasn't interested in the wealth that he could never possess. John's quest would take him into the spiritual world and what he might encounter on the other side in the darkness.

Everett knew that crossing the swamp would be dangerous, but it would be faster than traveling to Conwayboro then turning up the Waccamaw. Because he had spent most of his life stumbling around in the swamp, Everett led the group. He knew this swamp well. Most of his income came from trapping and fishing in this very place. He sold whatever he could in town and spent most of the money on whiskey and gambling.

Although he knew how to pass safely through the murky morass, even his knowledge of the swamp was hindered at night. Not sure of exactly what lay ahead, he felt it best to wait until daylight to attempt the main swamp crossing. Arriving at the edge of the swamp, the men, therefore, looked for a place to camp.

Once across White Oak Swamp, Everett figured they wouldn't be far from the road they'd take to Red Bluff. There they would cross the Waccamaw. From there on, it would be even rougher riding north toward Little River. Everett had only been up that way once or twice, and so he wasn't real sure what the conditions would be. He wasn't even sure if he could find any good trails to follow. He had heard stories of men getting lost in the area, never to be found. They would need good instincts, and some luck, to make this journey successfully.

Chapter Thirteen

Levi and Burt gathered up some firewood. After a short time, they had coals hot enough to boil water for coffee. They poured up a cup and started remembering old times. Everett pulled out a bottle of whiskey and offered the men a drink. John refused and told them the whiskey had to go; he wanted every man to be alert. They all laughed at the idea of staying away from the bottle.

John, visibly upset, stood up. "I'll be going home now, boys. I see you're not as serious about this as I thought."

Everett stood, taking John by the arm. "John, we were just having a little fun. A few sips won't hurt."

John jerked his arm out of Everett's grip. "I can't begin to tell you boys what might be out there. You can't go taking this trip like it's some kind of game."

Looking directly at them and pointing his finger in their faces, he told them, "The powers I have can make you rich men, if there really is a treasure. I can't take any of it for myself, but if you want me to continue, you best put away the bottle and listen to what I'm telling you or maybe none of us will return home!"

As the men quieted down, John silently contemplated this gift, which at times, seemed to have the devil's hand in it. He questioned why he alone of his siblings had been blessed with the powers. He sensed also that one of his own children would be blessed but had no way of knowing which one it might be. As of yet, he hadn't seen any evidence of the gift in any of them.

Everett soon ended the silence between them.

"John, Mama told me you had some kind of spiritual powers. She said you could find things people had lost. How'd you learn to do that stuff?"

Before John could answer Levi chimed in, "Yeah, I heard you found Billy Moore's pocket watch, the one his daddy gave him."

Glancing a second or two at Levi, John drank down his coffee. He then cast a cold distant stare back to Everett. In the flickering light of the fire, Everett's pale green eyes appeared translucent, giving the illusion that he could see behind them into John's mind. An illusion to be sure, as John's eyes, not Everett's, were doing the probing. Everett's mind was an open book as John's powers worked their magic.

"Everett, I can't really explain it. Let's just say it was something I was born with. We're all born with certain natural gifts. Like you for instance, you're a natural when it comes to living off the land, staying in the river swamp for weeks at a time, surviving the elements and such.

"When I was a small boy, strange things began to happen. I could hear voices, like someone was whispering to me. I thought they were real. I would lie in bed at night and listen. It was kind of like I was eavesdropping on someone else's conversations. I finally figured out that the voices were those of dead people, spirits that couldn't rest. I recognized some of them, people I knew were long dead.

"When I turned ten, Daddy took me aside and told me about this special gift I had inherited from my ancestors. They left their homeland in Scotland to escape the persecution and ignorance that existed there. The family came here looking for a better way of life. They came into Georgetown, traveling up the Waccamaw to the far reaches of this God-forsaken land.

"He told me many stories about our ancestors. They were good hard-working people, afraid of nothing. The church in Scotland had accused them of practicing witchcraft. Knowing they'd be in danger if they stayed, the family decided to come here to this country to preserve their beliefs. They were your people, too, Everett. A few years after Daddy died, Mama called me aside and asked me not to practice the old ways for she was afraid some of the puritans in the area would find us out. So, I have kept it inside of me; I told not a soul. Your family didn't possess the gift, but they did practice the old religion. They, too, gave it up for fear of being found out. People just don't understand the pagan way, so they fear it, and because they fear it, they eventually kill it."

John reached for the coffee pot and poured a little into his cup. He could see he had touched a cord in Everett. Apparently, Everett had never known the history of his own family until now.

John continued with the story. "As I grew older, I learned more and more of the powers I had. I learned they could be used for evil as well as good. I mastered them so well that I could use them whenever I wanted. I could even turn them off if they got to be a burden. Now, I've been able to use some other mystical powers, too, those that I learned about from the Negro root doctors down around Georgetown. They taught me about the "root" and how to place a hex or give the evil eye. The burdens that come with all these powers have led me down the wrong path so many times that I don't care to venture there anymore."

Burt leaned against a log and stared at John through the flickering fire. He had a hard time believing what John was saying, but if it were true, it would scare the hell out of him. He sure didn't want the other men to sense that.

Finally, the young man managed to summon up enough courage to ask John, "What did you mean when you said, 'what might be out there'?"

John met Burt's stare, which caused a shiver to run up Burt's spine that made him very uncomfortable. Truthfully, he was scared of John. The heat rising above the fire distorted John's features giving his face, Burt thought, a demonic look. He could see John's jaw muscles tighten.

"You see, Burt, when we get near to the treasure, I'll be able to see and hear things that you boys won't. My powers will let me sense what's happening on the other side, in the spirit world.

"I'll be able to tell if the spirits are good or evil. Most dead folks I've come across are just out there wandering around. They don't want to harm a soul. But there's a lot of evil spirits, too. They're the ones I'll need to be aware of."

By now, Burt was thinking John was flat out crazy. He didn't voice his skepticism out loud for he preferred that John not know just how crazy he thought he was. They weren't going to run into any spirits and such. They just needed to find the treasure, dig it up, and then they would be rich men. Not saying a word out loud, he was far braver in his thoughts.

John turned to Burt. "Burt, there have been a lot of times that I, too, really thought I was crazy. I've seen things and heard things that would drive many a good man out of his mind. And just so we understand each other, I would appreciate it when you have something on your mind just say it to my face."

Burt dropped his cup, spilling his coffee in his lap. "Damn, John. How in the hell did you know what I was thinking?"

John laughed. "This gift is not just for talking with dead folks." He cocked his head a little and looked Burt dead square in the eyes.

"I know a lot more about you than you'd like. You're easy reading, boy!"

John turned his attention back to Everett and Levi. "If there is a treasure, you can bet that it's guarded by its owner, and by that I don't mean a mortal. He'll be of the spirit world; he'll be able to call on other demons to help him protect his treasure. If he's a strong spirit, he'll be able to cast spells. I can't begin to tell you boys what might happen. I won't even know myself until we get closer. Little by little, I'll be able to feel his presence. That's why you have to lay off the whiskey and stay alert. This ain't a game. You could just as easy become one of them if you don't listen to me. I hope you boys know a good prayer because you'll be needing it when we get there."

Everett had no doubt that John was serious. "I'm sorry, John. I didn't realize that you had all those powers and could do all that."

John's face saddened, and his voice broke a little. "Sometimes I wish I couldn't. This thing has been a mixed blessing. Without it, I'd probably be in a grave in Petersburg, Virginia, with my friends who didn't make it."

The guilt ate at him. During a battle, John knew where not to be; the gift had helped him survive. On that bloody day at Petersburg, the day the Yankees dug those tunnels and blew his entire unit up, he knew beforehand. He never forgave himself for not speaking up.

John sat back down and gazed into the fire. "Everett, you and your brothers were with the tenth under Bragg, isn't that right?"

Everett angrily threw a stick at the fire. "Levi and me is all that's left. Jasper died at Stones River and James fell at Kennesaw Mountain. We couldn't even bring 'em home. They're laying a long way from here in some unmarked hole."

The hate was apparent in Everett's eyes. "You know, I don't hate them blue bellies; they were fightin' just like us. I'll tell you though, I'd like to have shot some of our own officers. They didn't anymore know how to lead men than I do. My brothers were just boys. Jasper was fifteen, and James had just turned seventeen. Neither one had ever even kissed a girl. They had so much life ahead of them. Mama has never got over Jasper. He was her baby. When Levi got hit in the leg the day after James was killed, I knew if I didn't do something she wouldn't have a single son left. I grabbed Levi and we hid out. We surrendered to the first Yankee patrol that came along. Hell, the war was about done for anyway. We only stayed prisoners for a few months."

Levi held his mangled leg up, grinning like a possum. "They thought I was going to let them cut my leg off. I told them Yankee doctors, leave it be. If I died from it, it'd be God's will. I'd be needing it for working the fields when I got home. It may not be pretty, but I can still walk on it."

The men laughed, but silently under their breath, they each thanked the good Lord they had made it home in one piece.

Breaking the silence into which they had all retreated, John asked Everett to tell him more about the treasure. Biting a chaw of tobacco off a plug, Everett told John about the whiskey joint he had been in down near Bucksville. Pieces of the tobacco were still sticking out through his lips as he talked.

"I met this here feller one night in one of my hangouts down Bucksville way. I think his name was Will Rhodes. Well anyway, this here Will fellow tells me he was on his way back to Georgia. I believe he said Savannah. He was trying to hitch a ride down the river with Bertram Johnson. He was trying to make his way to Georgetown so's he could meet up with a ship headed back home to Savannah. Anyway, he and the old man had been in the whiskey pretty heavy. We were all drinking and talking when Bertram started going on about pirates and stuff. Then this Will fellow, who was pretty well on his way to an all night drunk, told us he knew where there was a treasure box.

"With him being as drunk as he was, I was able to get a lot of information out of him. For some reason this night I wasn't as drunk as the rest, and so I paid close attention to what he said. I remembered the whole story, but the rest of the boys didn't. So when I got back to Conwayboro, I figured I might just try and find this treasure box. I studied on it a long time before I decided to give it a try."

Everett grinned real big, slapping his leg. "And here we are going treasure hunting! I talked Levi and Burt here into helping."

His expression turned very serious. "I knew I'd need you, John, more than anyone. When Mama told me that you had some kind of special gift, that you could find lost items, devine for water and such, I figured you just might be able to help us. I had no idea you could see spirits and such."

John thought for a few seconds about the map Letsy had given him. Standing up, he walked over to his saddlebags. Reaching inside, he pulled it out. "Everett, I got something here I want to show you."

John laid the map out on the ground. Everett, Levi, and Burt gathered around to get a better look. Their jaws dropped when they realized exactly what John was showing them.

Everett lit a match so they could get a better look. "Well, would you look at this. John, where in the world did you get this map?"

"Letsy had it."

"How did Letsy come by it?"

"She said that some stranger stopped at the house last year. She gave him food and water, and he gave her this map for payment."

Everett wanted to know. "When last year?"

John thought for a moment. "I think it was in August."

Everett laughed. "And I bet his name was Will Rhodes. That's about the same time I ran into him down at Bucksville."

John and Everett looked at each other in disbelief. A big smile formed on Everett's face. Turning, he spit tobacco juice into the fire. "Now, ain't that strange, boys? Looks like we pretty well got it made with this here map."

John folded the map and placed it back in his saddlebags. "No, maybe we don't. We still got to get there, and we don't know what might be lying in wait for us."

Everett's meeting with Will and Letsy getting the map seemed to both of them more than a coincidence. The smile vanished from Everett's face. John could sense his fear but said nothing. The men returned to sit in silence by the fire until sleep overtook them.

Chapter Fourteen

The next morning, the men were up early. After coffee and a little food, they set out through White Oak Swamp. Fall was in the air. Still, it hadn't been cool enough yet to run the snakes into their holes. Mosquitoes were also plentiful. As the men led their horses through the muck and still waters, duck weed and mud coated their pants legs. The moss and twisted vines that hung from the trees slapped their faces as they passed. After several hours, they came to the main water passage where the current was much faster. The water grew blacker as green plants that had been floating on top disappeared. For a short while, the swamp took on the appearance of the river, but that didn't last for long. The muck and weed returned as the four men headed out the other side of the swamp. Everett knew right where to go. John was impressed at Everett's ability to maneuver through the endless maze of cypress knees protruding up through the muddy water.

After several hours, they were finally able to mount their horses and ride. The sandy path they followed soon opened onto the main road north toward the North Carolina line. The riders would follow this road to Red Bluff where they would cross the river. Many travelers would be coming and going along this main road from Conwayboro into North Carolina.

By mid-afternoon, they had reached the turn off to Red Bluff. John pulled his horse to a stop. "We better stop and rest these horses for a while."

Moaning with stiffness from riding, John slowly dismounted. Everett snickered at John as he struggled to dismount.

"You laugh, cousin Ev', but I haven't spent most of my life running from the law on the back of a horse. You're far more accustomed to sitting for long periods than I am. Anyway, how far are we from the ferry?" John stretched his back and rubbed his rear.

Everett looked off down a narrow sandy road and pointed toward the east. "I believe that's the way, a few miles down around the bend. There's an old fellow by the name of Solomon who runs the ferry. If we pay him a little extra money, he won't tell anyone we crossed, just by chance anyone is following us. I don't really think anyone is. I know I haven't told a soul." Everett glanced at Burt and Levi.

"Hell no, no way. I ain't breathed a word of this," they both said in unison.

Everett trusted no one and didn't want the whole town knowing he was after buried treasure. Sure enough, if word got out there would be men after him that would kill for any amount of gold.

After the short rest, John slowly began climbing back in the saddle. "Everett, let's cross the river, ride for another hour, and then camp. My old bones and rear have had about enough for one day."

As the men approached the ferry, not a soul was visible. John sensed something was wrong. They cautiously walked their horses to the river's edge. The rays from the late afternoon sun cast a golden hue on the trees on the opposite side of the river. The dark water had taken on a glassy cast as it barely moved on its southerly course. An eerie silence floated across the water's surface. Not even the sound of insects could be heard, much less sounds of human life. The quiet was deafening. They sat on their horses, four abreast, looking across the river for any signs of the ferryman. The ferryboat itself was tied on the opposite side of the river. John thought that a little strange since most of the traffic on the road was usually north bound.

Across the river, the dense underbrush almost hid the road that led away from the river. The tall, pale cypress trees cast long shadows on the water, which was low for this time of year. The white sandbar beaches that melted into the water's edge turned the sand to gold as it mixed with the black water.

The afternoon sun would soon be setting. If the old man didn't show up, the riders would have a problem. Not only would they get wet crossing the river, but it would cost them a lot of time. Nightfall would soon be on them.

Everett hollered out, "Anyone over there?" There was no response. He tried again, "Old man Solomon, you over there?"

John walked his horse over to the ferry shed and rang the bell; still no response. He rang it again.

Then across the way at the edge of the swamp, an old Negro woman appeared. She was one freakish looking creature. A sort of mist surrounded her. She walked to the ferry and started pulling on the rope that returned the boat to their side of the river.

"I's comin'. Jest hol' yo' horses. It be hard on dis old blind woman pullin' on dis here rope."

John watched the old woman as she rhythmically pulled on the rope. Only as the boat came closer to the bank did he recognize her. It was Blind Jolene. John held tight to his saddle to calm his mount as even the horses got a little jumpy at the sight of her. He thought it better not to say anything to the others. If they knew she was a spirit, he knew they'd turn tail and ride like hell.

By now the river had taken on a completely different appearance. The late afternoon sun barely penetrated the smoky mist that now covered the river.

As the ferry neared the bank, Everett asked the old woman where the ferryman was.

"Oh he be down da riber workin' on a boat. He be askin' me to hep him out." After she spoke, she let out a hellish laugh, which echoed through the river swamp.

Everett turned to look at John. "What do you think, John? Is she right in the head?"

"Oh, yeah Everett, she's right in the head. You can bet on that," he replied.

Burt watched her every move; John could see the fear in his eyes. He was so scared his knees trembled, and his hands shook like a man with a drinking problem.

"Welcome to de ferry, my friends," the woman said.

John couldn't help but feel that she was looking right at him, in spite of her blindness. They began a silent conversation.

"Jolene, why are you here? Is there something wrong with Letsy or the children?" he silently questioned.

"Oh no, Mr. John. Dey be fine. Yo' know she be prayin' fo' yo'; she be a part o' yo'. She knows yo' be on a hard journey. I comes to give yo' warnin', yo' be headin' fo' troubles. Da treasure yo' be huntin' be da property of a bad, bad spirit. He be havin' lots o' powers, John Waters, so's yo' best be ready. I hopes yo' brung yo' Bible. Yo' might wanna start readin' dis very night."

As they crossed the river, Jolene sang an old spiritual. The men said not a word.

On the other side, John let the others walk their horses off the ferry. He then pulled out money to pay her, but she wouldn't take it. "Jolene ain't taken' money for hepn' folk like yo', John Waters. Anyways, what I's gonna' do wit money where I is? I gots all I needs."

Everett, Levi, and Burt had already started up the trail, leaving John behind with the old woman.

"John Waters, yo' gots yo' root bag too, I hopes? Yo' gwine be needin' it too, fo' dis journey."

"I do, Jolene."

She stood on the ferryboat, looking down into the darkness of the water flowing beneath the ferry. " Mr. John, I cain't hep yo' no mo'. From here on, yo' be in the land of Caleb Bland. It be his treasure. Gawd be wit yo'."

As John started to ride off, he turned around to take one more glance at Jolene. She had vanished. The mist was gone; the river was again glassy, as the setting sun reflected off its surface. John noticed an old boat pulled off in the bushes. As he passed it, he saw old Solomon lying in it peacefully. John figured quickly that Jolene had done her magic on the old ferryman so that she could get her message to him. He thanked her silently for the warning.

Chapter Fifteen

The men rode on in silence. The only sounds were the muffled pounding of the horses' hooves on the sandy trail and the gentle squeaking of leather harnesses and saddles. The heavy breathing of the mounts was punctuated from time to time by a harsh snort. Twilight had finally caught them. From the dark forest pressing in from either side of the trail came the distant haunting sounds of a screech owl accompanied by the usual chorus of cicadas, crickets, and the steady hum of mosquitoes around their ears.

John pulled his horse up, stopping the rest of the men. "Boys, this old man needs a rest. Let's camp here for the night. We'll need a good night's sleep. Tomorrow may be a rough day."

Everett agreed and Levi and Burt offered no argument. They were all ready for both food and sleep.

Levi was a pretty good cook. Before long, he had cooked up some side meat and warmed over the biscuits. "Boys, if I had a little better set up here, I could really put out a spread of food."

Poking a little fun at Levi, Everett said that Levi had always helped their mama with the cooking. "He'd make a fine wife for some feller," he joked.

All Burt wanted to talk about was Sarah, Everett and Levi's sister. To him, she was the prettiest girl around. He was real careful not to talk too openly about her though; he knew that Everett might cut his throat if he said anything suggestive or even vaguely improper.

Burt was still a little spooky about this venture, especially now that he knew John could read his every thought. He was so full of questions that he rattled on to the point of aggravation. Everett finally lost his patience with Burt, telling him to either shut up or go home.

"No way! You think I'd go back and cross that ferry by myself with that old crazy looking hag running the thing?"

John spoke up, "She's most likely gone by now, Burt. I'm sure old man Solomon is back running the ferry."

"No way. I'm staying with you boys. Besides, I told you I'd help."

John still felt that Burt was going to be a problem, and he was hoping he'd ride back to town, but no such luck. Burt was full of piss and vinegar when he talked about things. When it came to getting the job done, though, he was hard to find. According to Everett, Burt was simply spineless.

John feared Burt would hold them up, and any delay could be a real problem if they got into a fix with this spirit Caleb Bland. John knew that a spirit could easily possess a man like Burt. Spirits always picked on the weakest one in the bunch.

If Burt was going to stay with them, John would have to do something to alleviate his fear. He finally decided that he'd have to prepare a little "root" for Burt. Later that night when the boys were asleep, he'd put it together and hide it in Burt's coat. Burt wouldn't even know it was there.

They each found a comfortable place to lie down. After a few minutes, three of the men were snoring. Very quietly John sat up. Opening his bag, he pulled out the ingredients he would need: a little piece of High John the Conqueror root, a sprig of five finger grass, and a little gofer dust. The dust was special, for he had taken it from Lavenia's grave. He had gone out the night before they left, waited for midnight. Then saying a special prayer for her, he took a small bottle of dry dirt from the top of the grave. The dirt was only to be used for good purposes.

John quietly slipped over to Burt. Picking a few hairs from the young man's jacket, John added them to the mix. Then he wrapped the mix in a small piece of leather and tied it up tight with a thin strip of cord.

He lightly lifted the flap of Burt's pocket, and then he slipped the pouch deep inside. "This root," he whispered softly, "will give you nerve—nothing to fear now, young fellow." John then moved quietly back to his spot and lay back down. Burt never even knew.

Before John closed his eyes, he looked up at the stars twinkling in the night sky. He thought about Letsy and the children. Were they safe? He said a silent prayer for them.

Off in the woods, a screech owl called repeatedly. Every call grew louder as the bird came closer to the camp. John knew that this could be a bad omen. He'd have to put a stop to it, using a trick one of the root doctors had taught him. He lifted his hand, pointed his finger in the direction of the owl, and scribed a small hex in the air. At the same time, he spoke beneath his breath: "Silence and be gone." Immediately, the owl fell silent. John listened for a while longer to be sure the owl had gone. Feeling safe, he lay back against his saddle and drifted off to sleep.

Throughout the night, many spirits visited him in his dreams. He tossed and turned and was unable to get the rest he needed for the following day's ride.

One of these dreams took him back to the war. He saw himself lying behind a stone fence. It was night. The bodies of dead and dying soldiers lay out in front of him on the open field. Some of these were men he had known all his life. The night was cold. Heat from some of the still warm bodies rose in smoky columns that lingered above the field. Then, in the light of the moon, he watched as their souls rose up from the mounds of lifeless flesh. Some seemed to vanish into the night. Others seemed to stop at each body as if they were searching for their friends. This was not the first time John had witnessed this phenomenon. He watched as one of them slowly came toward him. It was Yancy Johnson. A part of his head had been blown away; his left arm dangled from his body by a thin piece of flesh. His skin was pale blue, and his eyes were red like fire. He was the walking dead.

"John Waters, is that you?" it asked, as the spirit reached out with its good arm to touch John's shoulder. "Man, I thought I'd never see you again. I need some help friend. Can you help me?"

John recoiled from his touch. He screamed out both in his dream and into the night where the four travelers slept. The next thing he knew, Everett and Levi were shaking him, trying to wake him up. "John! You okay? You were lying over here just a screaming."

"What was I saying?" John asked.

"Something about Yancy Johnson," said Everett.

"Yeah, I saw him and the others, all of them, my friends lying out on a battlefield—dead! Yancy came right up to me and touched me. God, he looked awful. I haven't dreamed about Yancy in a long while. When I joined up, Yancy was home on leave. He returned to Virginia, and I went with him."

John added, while tears welled in his eyes, "He looked so real. I can still feel his hand on my shoulder." John looked at his shoulder—a bloody handprint stained his shirt! The others backed away in horror.

"John, is this part of this gift thing that you have?" Everett asked.

"I'm afraid so, Everett."

With his finger, John touched the print; the blood was still wet. "God in Heaven, I've never experienced a dream so real before."

Wiping off his finger, he grabbed his canteen and poured water all over his shoulder to wash the blood off his shirt. The water had no effect. The print stayed.

"I've always heard that aggravated blood won't wash out.

Reaching for his saddlebags, he pulled out the extra shirt Letsy had packed for him. He then tore the stained shirt from his body and threw it on the hot coals. To their horror, the fire roared to life, and flames rose high into the early morning darkness. The smoke from the flames formed the shape of a man, contorted and screaming in agony. The screams were deafening; covering their ears, the men jumped to their feet and turned their backs to the fire. Then there was silence. The flames subsided, and the fire returned to only red hot coals as the smoke floated away. With sighs of relief, the terrified men gathered their courage and returned to their places by the fire.

As daybreak approached, John stoked the fire and put on a pot of coffee. He felt drained from the dream-filled night. He didn't get the rest he needed, and he figured he probably wouldn't until this journey was over. He sensed an ominous presence all around the camp. Was his lack of sleep making him imagine things or was it his power? Perhaps the old spirit knew they were coming. Was the dream his doing? John didn't know.

He thought of Jolene's warning about being in the land of Caleb Bland. What kind of spirit was he going up against? Was Bland so powerful that he could call up any dead soul? John concluded that Bland had read his mind; that meant the old spirit now knew his weaknesses, and he'd use them against him. Whatever he tried, John would have to keep his wits about him.

Burt and the others had walked off into the edge of the woods to relieve themselves. When they returned, John handed them each a cup of coffee then poured his own.

"Drink up, boys! There's nothing like hot coffee to get a day started off right."

Chapter Sixteen

As the sun rose, storm clouds nearly covered the sky. The sun would show itself momentarily then disappear. A light rain started, and the wind picked up. The day was not looking good. This was the gale season, and there was no telling what kind of weather might be headed their way.

After biscuits and coffee, the four men saddled up and started out.

About mid morning, the clouds began to clear, and the sun came out briefly. Before long, the rain and wind began again, this time with a vengeance. Searching for shelter, they spotted an abandoned hunting shack back off the road. They tied the horses under a big spreading oak tree that provided the animals a little shelter. They hadn't seen a single traveler on the road thus far. With the weather like it was, they figured anybody with any sense would hole up somewhere, just as they had.

The shack was dusty and covered with spider webs. A family of mice had a small nest in the old bed that still stood at one end of the shack. It was the only piece of furniture remaining.

John stood with his arm resting on the windowsill, looking out into the dense forest. The rain was heavy, and he could see almost nothing. He was in deep thought about what had happened during the night when, suddenly, he saw something move at the edge of the woods. He strained his eyes to get a better look, but with the wind-driven rain, it was hard to see clearly. After several minutes, the wind let up enough for him to get a better look. It looked like a wild hog rooting around at the edge of the trees. It then turned and faced the cabin. Startled, John saw that the hog had the head of a human. It stared in his direction for a few seconds and then disappeared. It had to be a sign that the spirits had found them and probably knew they were coming for the treasure.

In folklore, plat-eyes are spirits that can take on the form of animals. A headless hog is a sure sign that a plat-eye is around, but a hog with the head of a man? John looked down at his shaking hands. He had heard the old black folks talk about the plat-eyes, but this was his first sighting. These were the spirits of the pirate crewmen that dug the holes for the treasures. They were murdered afterward, usually by the pirate captain so that only he would know the location of the plunder. Often, the attendant pirates were thrown into the hole on top of the treasure to be buried with it. The captain would then cover them up in their eternal, but opulent, grave. Folklore was that the dead pirates' souls would rise up and become plat-eyes. Their spirits would guard the treasure by scaring off anyone who tried to find it.

John thought it best not to say anything to the other men about what he had seen. He reached inside his coat and pulled out his small Bible. Opening the front cover, he read the inscription: For my husband, may the spirit of the Lord walk with you, Love, Letsy.

Knowing that something was going on, Everett cautiously watched John. Everett was no fool: John was frightened by something.

Turning, John looked Everett in the eyes. "You much into reading the Bible, Ev?"

"Every now and then, Mama makes me listen to her. I never did learn much reading, just enough to get me by."

Burt and Levi were sitting quietly in the corner of the room. They, like Everett, sensed it was time to be serious.

John opened his Bible to Psalm 91. "Listen up, boys! There are a couple of verses here that I especially like. They seem to give me strength when I need it. 'He will cover you with feathers, and under His wings you will find refuge; his faithfulness will be your shield and rampart. You will not fear the terror of night; nor the arrow that flies by day'."

John continued to read as the others sat in silence. After he finished, he put the little Bible back into his pocket. The room was silent. No one had noticed that the rain had stopped. The sun was again having its way, peeking through an opening in the clouds. The rays that flowed through the window painted a golden glow on John's face, as if the Lord himself had taken notice of his reverence.

He stood up. "Let's ride boys; we got a lot of time to make up."

Chapter Seventeen

Pine forests rose from thickets of myrtle, briars, and saw palmetto. Trees hung heavy with moisture from the heavy rain. The woods were so thick you couldn't see five feet off the trail. Occasionally, the riders would find themselves in a clearing on sandy ground, but soon they were back into the thick of the forest, struggling to follow the trail. Every so often, they would come upon a depression with crystal clear water bubbling up from the bottom. These water holes were filled with lily pads, duck weed, and a few other strange plants. As far as the men were concerned, this land was useless; only a fool would think of living in these parts.

Finally, they stopped at one of the water holes to rest a bit. It was much larger than the others they had passed; large cypresses lined its edge and gray moss hung like ragged cloth from the limbs. The water was clean and clear, just as the others had been, and it, too, was covered with lily pads and duckweed. It looked as though someone had spread a green blanket over the cool surface. They could see in the distance more pines against the sky. The dry land they were on was barely inches higher than the swamp itself.

John climbed from his horse. Wiping the sweat away from his forehead with a handkerchief, he suggested they rest for a while. Everett gave no argument. The horses needed a rest anyway. "I reckon a rest would suit me just fine. Levi, you and Burt take the horses over and let them have a little water."

Everett, sensing John's preoccupation, asked in a low voice, "What's going on? You sure are acting strange."

"Everett, we're not alone. We've had company ever since we left the shack."

"What do you mean? Nobody knows what we're doing."

John looked Everett dead in the eyes: "Everett, this here company we have is not of the living."

"John, what the hell are you talking about?" Everett muttered.

He smiled wryly and said, "Yeah, Everett, 'hell' is a good word. Now I've known you all your life, and I know you can keep your head. I'm telling you this might be hard on those two over there. Levi might be okay, but I don't feel too sure about Burt. He's the one I'm most concerned about."

John knew he could trust Everett. "It's important that you fellows follow my commands."

Hesitating for a minute to swat the gnats away, he continued: "I'm going to be pretty busy keeping my powers focused on what's going on around us. We can't afford to have one of them lose his nerve."

Everett listened intently. "I understand, John. You can count on me."

"Well, when we get a little closer to the treasure, I'll have a long talk with them. These here spirits that are following us are what they call 'plat-eyes.' I've been listening to them. They're a rough bunch. They're not aware that I can hear them, and I want to keep it that way; it gives me a bit of an advantage."

John's eyes drifted out over the swamp to the piney woods. They penetrated into a world that Everett couldn't even imagine.

Softly John whispered, as if to no one, "Yes, I hear you."

Everett could hear nothing but the humming and buzzing of insects. He sensed, though, that John was hearing and even talking to something or someone.

Breaking the silence between them, Everett spoke in a nervous tone, "I've heard stories about such ghosts but never imagined I might get to see one." Pulling his tobacco pouch out, he stuffed a big wad in his mouth. "You know this stuff helps calm my nerves. Yours might need a little calming, too. You want a chaw, John?"

"No, never have cared for it."

John studied his surroundings for a moment. He rubbed his rough hand over his bristly face, and he thought how good a shave and bath would feel.

Turning his attention back to Everett he said, "From here on out, I'll take the lead. Let's try and keep close, and keep your eyes open, back and front. If anything's close, I'll know, so don't worry. I'll warn you when I think something bad is about to happen."

Everett called his brother and Burt over. "Listen up now! From here on out, we've got to pay attention to John and follow his orders. I don't want any joking around. Things might get a bit hairy. John's going to take the lead for now, then myself, then you, Levi. Burt, you bring up the rear."

Burt spoke up with a smirk, "Yeah, boys, that's me, an ass! I'm even bringing up the ass end of this damn fairy tale goose chase."

John grabbed Burt by the shirt and pulled him up close. "Now, you listen, and you listen good! If you want to go back, just get on your horse and go. But if you are staying and you want to see home and your sweet Sarah again, you better pay attention to everything I tell you." John threw him back against his horse.

Burt's voice was shaking. "Jesus, John, you don't have to get mad. I'll be fine. You just tell me what to do, and I'll do it. I'm sorry. I guess I'm just a little nervous about the whole thing."

It was obvious that John was becoming a little edgy. He had been concentrating on what might lay ahead, trying to listen to the other side, but the boys kept interfering with his thoughts.

John took the lead. The others fell in as they had been told. Horses and riders followed one after the other closely. The day was ending, and dark clouds again gathered overhead. John wanted to get as close as he could to Little River before they stopped for the night.

After they had ridden for some time, the wind suddenly picked up. The men were certain there would be rain again before long. The wind grew stronger, and the wildly swaying branches and vines dangling overhead presented a real danger. The men pulled their collars up snug around their necks.

The forest seemed alive. Vines reached out toward them. Occasionally, young pines snapped. Their tops yielded to the wind and fell to the ground.

The nervous horses jumped around so much that the men had trouble controlling them. They had slowed almost to a crawl when a strangled scream rang out over the constant shriek of the wind.

John could feel the presence of evil. "Whoa!" John called out, "Are we all here?"

The darkness had closed in on them so completely that no man could see the others.

"Everett?" John shouted.

"I'm right here, John." Everett answered.

"Here, John," Levi responded.

"Burt?" John called out but there was no answer. He called several times, still no answer. "We have to go back, boys," John said.

They carefully picked their way through the darkness in the direction from which they had just come. In a few minutes, they heard the sound of a horse's heavy breathing and restless movements.

"Burt?" John called again. "Where are you?"

"Help me!" came the strangled cry.

John dismounted. Holding on to the reins, he splayed his arms about, as a blind man would do. As he flailed around, he brushed against Burt's legs hanging down from the trees and vines overhead.

"Hold on, Burt. I got you."

John held Burt up by the legs while Everett rode up beside him and tried to untangle the vines. One was wrapped around his neck like a noose, strangling him. Everett unsheathed his knife and cut the vine from Burt's neck and threw it to the ground. As the cut vine hit the ground, it appeared to come to life, slithering into the undergrowth like a serpent. In just a few seconds, Burt was free but still shaken.

"Damn, John, I could have sworn that vine was alive! I swear it kept getting tighter and tighter. Did you see what it did when it hit the ground?"

"That was just the beginning, boys. It'll probably get a lot worse as we go on. Remember, you didn't really see what you thought you saw," John explained. "The spirits are playing with your minds."

After allowing Burt to recover for a few minutes, the four started out along the trail once again. When they reached a small clearing, John checked to see if the others were all right. Burt was doing better, and John felt confident the root bag was working.

The weather, however, was getting worse. They decided it was just too dangerous to continue. The only shelter was under one of the big oaks.

Huddled together, with the horses providing some break from the wind and rain, they waited, miserable and impatient, for some sign that the storm was letting up. Burt's neck began giving him a lot of pain, and his voice was almost gone.

After about thirty minutes, John decided they'd make the best of the big oak and stay the night under it. They removed the saddles from the horses, which they tied close by so they could hightail it out of there in minutes if necessary. It would be a night of cold biscuits and no coffee. The four found themselves sitting side by side, backs against the tree, their saddles in front of them. They had draped their rain slickers over themselves in a futile effort to keep dry in the driving rain.

The darkness and blowing rain made it almost impossible to see. The wind continued, accompanied by a pounding rain that eased infrequently. Hours later, their weary bodies succumbed to their overwhelming need for sleep, and the four miserable men slept deeply, in spite of the rain.

Sometime during the night, John came wide-awake! The rain had stopped, but the wind was still blowing. The horses were a little spooked, maybe from the wind, he thought. He strained to see if an animal might be around. He looked under the horses' bellies and into the woods. He listened with the gift. They were out there, just outside the realm of the living. Many spirits had gathered around them. Through the shifting of the horse's legs, he could see ghostly forms. The night was so dark he had a hard time making them out.

The moon that broke through the clouds cast its pale light around the oak. John was horrified. It was the same nightmare; the spirits were his friends who had died in the war. They were reaching out to him with blood-soaked hands. Many, floating toward him, had missing legs. Their clothes were ragged; pieces of the cloth blew in the wind and floated around them in slow motion. They kept coming closer. John couldn't take it any longer. The old guilt raged through him. Why hadn't he died too? His thoughts raced back to that day in Petersburg. He knew the explosion was coming; why hadn't he tried to convince the officers to move the men? Leaving the others behind, John had saved himself. The explosion blew a large crater in the ground and killed many.

After the explosion, the Yankees stormed over the edge—a very bad mistake. The Southern boys rallied, picking off Yanks at will. The killing was gruesome.

Hoping to muffle the cries of the spirits, John covered his ears with his hands. He glanced up into the tree; he could see more of them sitting on limbs. Their eyes were deep black holes with intensely red centers, which gave them the appearance of demons. John turned his head away and closed his eyes. Fear had gripped his soul; he started to question his abilities. He soon realized that the evil spirit had found his weakness: the guilt he lived with daily. It ate at him like a disease. For a moment, he thought of the whiskey bottle Everett had in his saddlebags. His will power was tested as never before, and he knew the evil spirit was its master.

Was he getting into something here that would haunt him for the rest of his life? John was responsible for the others, and he knew he couldn't bear any more guilt. He should've told Everett "no" when he came to the house.

He prayed for help from God. He even called on his ancestors for the courage to continue. From the dark recesses of his memory, he tried to remember some of the ancient prayers, but they remained hidden. All of his efforts seemed in vain. There was no response from any of those upon whom he called.

Finally, he accepted that he alone held the power. This was his test. He had turned away from the evil ways as his ancestor's had told him. Now, he must prove he was worthy of the gift. If he believed strongly enough in himself, he could vanquish even the dead spirits that had ascended on him from hell. Turning back toward the ghostly specters, he summoned all his powers. Focusing the strength of his gift, he quietly cried out.

"Be gone, you God-forsaken lot. Leave me, or I will send you even deeper into hell!"

Then in an instant, as if they had never been there, they were gone! Had he succeeded?

He knew that the demons had been called up by the powerful spirit that guarded the treasure. He realized he must be in control, at least for now. He now understood that he could accomplish this only if his confidence was strong, and only if he let the magic of his powers flow.

Pulling himself together, he entered a trance. He drew from all the powers of his ancestors. Boldly, he told the spirits that he was not afraid.

"This message is for the master of this haunting. I am not afraid of you. I hold more power than you realize. Whatever evil you put before me I will defeat. I will find this treasure, and your evil will not stop me!"

Still in deep sleep, the others didn't realize the turmoil John was in. He knew he must protect them. If they lost faith in him, the rest of this journey could be fatal. John let his head fall back against the tree. He was exhausted. He closed his eyes and fell back to sleep.

Far off on the coast, sitting under his oak, the spirit Caleb Bland listened. "I know you are coming, John Waters. Rest assured I will be waiting for you. We will see just how powerful you really are!"

Chapter Eighteen

In the wee hours of morning, the howling wind had died down to an occasional sigh as the storm finally was spent. As a pale light flooded the eastern sky, the men stiffly mounted their horses and slowly moved out.

Breaking out of the forest, they rode into a grassy meadow. In the distance stood an abandoned barn. John wondered why in the world anyone would want to live in this God-forsaken place.

Riding up to the old barn, the men decided they would rest and give the horses a chance to graze. After a breakfast of jerky and biscuits, they settled down for some much needed rest. They found some dry hay in the barn on which to sleep comfortably.

John and Everett figured they were not far from the coast, and so before going to sleep, they studied the map closely. Unless they found a dry land bridge over to the island, they would have to cross a marsh. With the cold, wet night behind them, neither of the two men looked forward to that prospect.

Levi questioned, "You fellers do know where we are, don't ya?"

"I've got a good idea," John said with confidence.

"This is what they call 'Frink's Neck.' It lies between Little River and the Atlantic. Now there's a trail around here somewhere that will turn north, but we don't want to go that way. According to this map, the trail we want will turn off and go east toward the inlet. It shows some kind of path over to the island. We may just luck up and find a land bridge over there after all."

The urge to sleep was unbearable. John found a spot near the door so he could hear if anyone rode up. He pushed the hay up thick, and laid his tired body down. The rest of the men were sound asleep in a matter of minutes. The storm had made the trip hard on them all; they were exhausted from fighting the wind and rain and from the lack of sound sleep.

It seemed like hours had passed when John sensed a shadow covering his face. He cautiously peeked out through tightly squinted eyes to see what had caused it. He hoped it was just one of the others up and moving around.

It wasn't!

An old black man standing above him pointed a double-barreled shotgun at his face. John couldn't figure out how he had managed to enter the barn without warning, not even the slightest disturbance in the air. Could he be one of the spirits?

The old man's face was covered with a full gray beard that concealed his features. Tobacco had stained the beard down from the corners of his mouth. A single tooth protruded out over the bottom lip. His eyes were hazel, almost a yellowish green. His skin had the look of well-tanned leather. Obviously, he had spent most of his life working out in the sun. He was a small man. In some ways he reminded John of an old dog he once had. It, too, had only one tooth. When it could no longer eat, John had to shoot it.

"What's yo' boys be doin' in de hay barn?" the old man demanded. His accent was of the Geechee patois, common in the area around Charleston. His voice awakened the others. John put his hands out to let him know they meant him no harm.

"We give out from traveling through the storm. When we saw your barn, we reckoned it'd be a good place to sleep for a while. We'll be going now if you'll just let us saddle up. We can be gone in no time."

The old man eyed the four men suspiciously; he turned and leaned out the door, spitting tobacco juice outside.

"What's yo' boys a doin' dis fer up de neck? De ain't no place to go but to da inlet o' da ocean. If'n yo' a goin' to Li'l Riber, yo' be on da wrong side de swamp."

John spoke up before anyone else could. "I guess we're lost then. We'll have to back track."

The old black man laughed so hard he spewed tobacco juice down his beard.

"Yo' boys a thinkin' I's be a mite dumb o somein'? I know'd why you be comin' up dis fer. Yo' not the fust an' yo' not gonna be de last. Da ones dat come befo', de never did come off dat spit o land. Der be bad goins' on dere."

"Why do you think we came here?" John asked, hoping to get a read on the old fellow.

The old man turned and looked at John; he looked through him and not at him, somewhere beyond the time and space they occupied. John tried, but the gift couldn't penetrate his thoughts. Something was blocking John from reading the old man's mind.

The man motioned for them to follow him outside. They all stood, brushed off the hay, and rounded up their belongings. In the sunlight, it took a minute or two for their eyes to adjust.

It was a beautiful afternoon; puffy clouds adorned the cerulean blue sky. The wind was blowing softly, and for the first time, they could smell the salt air. It was by far the prettiest day they had seen in awhile. John asked the old man how far they were from the coast.

"Not fer, Cap'n, but yo' gots a bunch o marsh 'tween yo' an' dat dere beach. Yo' boys come on up to de house. Blue be cookin' fish stew. Since all me tooth done fell out, stews 'bout all I kin et."

They eagerly lashed up their gear and followed the old man into the woods. He followed a well-worn white sandy path. Gradually, the terrain began to change. Big live oak trees draped with Spanish moss lined the way. Saw palmettos grew as thick as grass beneath the trees. Wild grapevines hung from the branches. Some, as thick as a man's leg, grew from the ground. Like giant veins, they traveled the trunks of the old trees and then spread out to the tips of the limbs. Resurrection fern covered some of the trunks, and the tops of the great branches were draped with Spanish moss as they reached outward.

Suddenly, a pungent odor mixed with the unmistakable smell of salt air drifted in. It was the marsh they could smell, with its pluff mud bordering the canals. Burt wrinkled up his nose. Having never traveled to the coast, he had never encountered the briny ocean air.

Then the path opened; it was one of the most beautiful places they had ever seen. They gazed in awe, out over a sea of marsh grass as it swayed with the breeze. It was hypnotic.

As the high tide receded, the dark gray mud glistened in the afternoon sun; little crabs scurried around from hole to hole. Sea birds flew overhead. A few birds at a time dropped to the exposed sandbars to rest, standing first on one foot and then on the other. The changing tide exposed oyster beds that lay in the mud.

Across the marsh, was a small island covered with young oak trees, brush, and sea oats. Tall pines that permanently leaned from years of ocean wind protruded up through the lower growth. Near the center of the island, the canopy of a large live oak tree dominated the sky. The south end of the island looked like it might be connected to the mainland, but it was hard to tell without actually getting closer. The four men could hear the faint sound of waves as they crashed on a beach they could not yet see.

The path opened into a clearing where a small shack stood. An old black woman with braided gray hair came out. Wiping her coal black hands on her apron, she seemed excited to see visitors. A grin so huge it parted her lips came to her face. She had the pretty white teeth and gums as blue as indigo.

"Jobe, where in de world yo' finds des folks?"

The old man turned to John. "Folks call's me Jobe, Jobe Vereen, an' dis here be my wife, Blue."

"Blue, dey was sleepin' in de hay barn."

"Well bring'em on up so's old Blue can gets a good eye at 'em."

Levi whispered to John, "You don't think she's sizing us up for stewing, do ya?"

John chuckled, "You think they're tired of fish stew maybe?"

Everett's eyes widened at that thought.

John introduced himself and the others.

Blue shyly came down the steps and shook each hand. "Oh, I's so glad der be folk 'round. I's gots a fish stew a cookin', an' I hope yo' boys gots yo' hungrys."

They all chimed in, thanking her for the invite. They would be happy to have a meal with them. Without a word, she hurried back into the shack.

John had not seen a shack the likes of this one in a long time. Back in the days when he was staying in Georgetown, he would ride out to the back country to visit his old friend Daniel. Daniel had been a long time acquaintance and the only root doctor John trusted. Daniel's house was painted the same colors: a bright white with the door and window frames a brilliant blue, the brightest blue he had ever seen. The old Negroes believed the blue color could keep the spirits at bay.

The best he could tell, this house had one big room and a smaller room, most likely the sleeping place that was off to the side. It had been built on stilts, three or four feet off the ground.

Jobe motioned for them to put their gear down. "Yo' kin tie yo' horses in de pen wid da mule; she name be Mary. She old too, jes' like me an' Blue, but she be a goodun'. She not gonna pay 'em horses no mind."

The afternoon quickly passed, and John was beginning to worry. He needed to know if there was a way across to the island. He watched as Jobe pulled up some chairs underneath a large oak tree. You could tell the old couple spent a lot of time sitting in this place. John could picture Blue with her straw broom sweeping the fallen oak leaves away. They had a fire ring of shells; the ground around had been walked on a great deal. It was obvious a lot of dancing had taken place near this fire. Jobe bent over to pick something up off the ground. As he did, a small cloth bag fell to the end of the string that secured it around his neck. John recognized it immediately as a root bag.

So, that's why he couldn't read his mind earlier, he thought. He's got protection. I wonder why. Could he know something about the spirits on the island?

John walked over and joined Jobe under the tree. Jobe sat with his legs crossed and his hands in his lap, chewing his tobacco and staring out across the inlet toward the little island.

He spoke up. "Set yo'self down here, Mr. John, an' talk a spell. We be talkin' wit dem udders in a bit."

John sat down next to Jobe. He needed to ask if there was a way over to the island, but wasn't sure just how to do so. The two of them sat quietly for several minutes. Then, all of a sudden, Jobe spoke up. "Dey's be a way to de isle, but yo' gotta go befo' de tide be comin'. Wit de moon full up, the old sea be comin' up a lot mo' den it do wit no moon."

"How'd you know what I was thinking, Jobe?"

"I jes knows. I knows yo' be a special man, too.

"I be show'n you da way, but only to wher' de path to de isle be startin'. No way Jobe be goin' to dat isle wit yo'. I be comin' back here an', we be lightin' da fire fo' yo'. Den Blue n' me, we be setin' up all night waitin' fo' yo'. Ifn' I sees yo' in de mornin', I be shoutin' Hallelujah! But if'n yo' don't make it back, den I knows he done take some mo' souls. Kin I keep yo' horses if'n yo' don't come back?"

John told him yes, but he knew he'd be back.

Jobe explained that the horses wouldn't do well on the island, but they were welcome to take the old mule.

John went over to the others. He told them that Jobe knew a shallow place where they could walk over to the island and that he would show them where to get across.

"We can't take the horses; the footing is just too tricky for them. Jobe here has offered to loan us his mule, but I believe we can handle whatever we find without old Mary. Between the four of us, I think we can carry it back.

"Remember, when we leave here for the island, you boys got to listen to what I say. Do exactly as I tell you and obey every command I give. If you don't, some of us may not come back!"

Blue's voice rang out from the house, "Come et!"

Jobe glanced back to the cabin. "I speck Blue's ready fo' us. Let's be getting' yo' bellies full afo' yo' start out fo' de isle."

Jobe stood; slowly he straightened his back and groaned. "It sho' be hard gettin' ol'. Every day I wakes up wit a new hurtin' some'ers. I be thinkin' de hags be hangin' on da bed post of a'night."

John couldn't help but laugh. He'd not heard the phrase "hags hangin' on the bed post" for some time. He recalled one of his trips down to Georgetown. He'd gone out to Daniel's place to buy some herbs and other things for his root bag.

When John arrived, he found Daniel heading over to a shanty where some old woman lived. Inviting John along, Daniel explained the woman was very old and there was no telling what brought the hags down on her.

She wasn't able to sleep at night because the "hags were hanging on her bedposts." They were telling her lies and keeping her awake all night.

When John and Daniel arrived at the shanty, the old woman was lying in her bed on the front porch. The bedposts appeared to have been cut off. She was tossing and turning, calling to Jesus. Several men were standing around in the yard watching as if it were some kind of show.

Daniel asked one of the men what had happened. "Mr. Daniel, Ms. Eula here and Ms. Cora, who be livin' down da road der, dey be's arguin' bout somethin', I don't knows what. Alls I knows is Ms. Eula's not be closin' her eyes fo' days. She done be up all night fightin' dem hags. She made me move da bed outside da house an' cut off de bedposts so's they don't have a place to roost. I don't knows what mo' I kin do, so I sends fo' yo'."

Daniel walked over to the porch where Ms. Eula was. "Ms. Eula, does yo' thinks someone be puttin' a root on yo'?"

Ms. Eula turned her head toward Daniel and let out an awful sound. She shrieked like she had a demon in her.

John stayed back. He knew it wouldn't do for him to get involved with the spirits that had taken up residence on Ms. Eula's bed. He watched Daniel real close though, taking in everything he did.

Daniel walked around to the back of the house. When he came around from the other side, he was holding a root bag.

"I found it! It was under the back steps." It was a bad one because you could smell it, like it was rotten.

Daniel started chanting and dancing around. Holding the root bag, he danced his way over toward the river. Then he threw it in the river where the water would destroy its power. He then told Ms. Eula to bathe right away in a bath with wild basil leaves. The bath would also protect her from any other root placed on her. He also told her she'd better make peace with Ms. Cora.

As Daniel and John rode back to his house, Daniel explained to John how he had worked this magic. John would return many times for more lessons on the workings of the root.

Jobe took his place at the head of the table, and the rest of the diners found seats down both sides. The table was long and narrow and, clearly, many a meal had been served at it. Jobe said the blessing, and then they all helped themselves to the stew. It was the best fish stew John had ever eaten.

By late afternoon, after they had finished eating, the sun was hanging real low. The heat was now unbearable. Even though it was October, it was still hot and humid. The men checked their gear, and they borrowed two shovels from Jobe.

Jobe set out in front, leading them along a narrow path that followed the shore of the inlet. They walked through heavy underbrush for about thirty minutes until Jobe stopped.

"Dis be it fo' me. From here on out, yo' be on yo' own. Wes' be lookin' fo' yo' in de mornin'. Jes keep on dis here path an' it takes yo' to de isle. Now der be places where yo' gwine hafta muck through de mud. Take care now yo' not git sucked unner'. It be grabin' holt a yo' an' not be lettin' go. Now be sho' yo' gets over fast-like befo' de tide be comin' an' parts o' de path gwine be unner da water. Now gets on over befo' it gets too dark to see. God Bless yo', John Waters."

John shook Jobe's hand and thanked him for all he had done. He could feel Jobe's energy rushing into his body. There was more to Jobe than met the eye. John sensed he was a wise and powerful seer. Jobe hadn't revealed his knowledge of working root magic to John. He didn't have to for John perceived it just by listening to him and touching his hand.

Chapter Nineteen

The four men made their way through the marsh. As much as possible, they stayed to the high ground. Dark was setting in, and the tide was rising quickly. No doubt the path would soon be under water. For the most part, the path was sandy, but eventually they came to the gray pluff mud. The mud had a slick, sticky texture, and with each step, it held fast to their legs. Soon they were covered with mud, having to pull each other free from the muck. They stopped briefly to light the torches they had made before leaving Jobe's. The light pushed back the darkness effectively enough for John to see that they were nearing the island. Another hundred feet or so, they would be safe from the tide.

When they finally reached the higher ground, they stopped. The moon that had by now risen above the ocean cast its pale light across the water. The glowing white sand of the beach shimmered in the moonlight, a luminescent path into the distant darkness.

"Everett, ya'll listen up!" John warned. "If you mess up now, it could cost someone their life. No matter what you see or hear, you have to remember, it can't hurt you as long as you do what I tell you. This demon will try to break you down. His plat-eyes may appear as horrible monsters or even someone you know. You've got to remember they aren't real. Everett, get the map out and let's have a look one more time so we can be sure we are going in the right direction."

Everett pulled the map out of his shirt and laid it on the sandy ground. They all gathered around. Everett held the torch close so they could study the map.

"Levi, hold this light so I can use my hands," Everett directed.

He handed the torch over to Levi then brushed the fine sticky sand from his hands.

Pointing to a spot on the map, he said, "I think we're here." Hearing no response from John, he looked around to see if he was listening.

Everett's fear rose when he realized that John had wandered away from them. Adjusting his eyes to the dark, he finally spied John standing just at the edge of the darkness. He was gazing off into the distance, his arms dangling down by his side. Faintly silhouetted against the night sky, he appeared ghostly. He just stood there; he didn't move or make a sound. Suddenly, from out of nowhere, a gust of wind blew up against John, as if to push him back. The force was so strong, it almost knocked him to the ground.

Everett jumped up, ran to him, and grabbed him by the shoulders. "John! What's wrong?"

John's eyes slowly moved toward Everett. Levi and Burt sat motionless, their fear evident by the expression on their faces.

"Boys, this is going to be a long night. We won't be needing the map anymore; I know which way to go."

"How you know that, John?" asked Burt, the fear evident in his shaky voice.

"Never mind how I know, Burt. Just believe me that I know the way. Our host waits and he knows we're here."

Everett glanced over at the other two. He thought to himself, "What in heaven's name have I got John into?"

John swung around like a man possessed; he grabbed one of the torches and stuck it into the ground. He pulled a long red cord from his bag. Then he closed his eyes, as if in prayer. He concentrated on the cord. He began tying little knots along its length. With each knot, he jerked it tightly until he had seven knots. Holding it over the smoke of one of the torches, he spoke indecipherable words in a language none of the others understood. John finished this strange ritual by tying the cord around his neck like a necklace.

"Now listen! We're starting off into that brush line over there, and I suspect it's going to be hard getting through, but once we're inside, I'm sure it'll thin out a little. We've got to stay within reach of each other as we go. You're going to see and hear things that'll scare the hell out of you. Whatever you do, don't forget that none of it's real. It's all just these spirits here trying to stop us. They'll try to get to you—because if they do—they have a good chance of stopping me."

John attempted to remain calm, but there was no way to conceal his excitement. The others picked up on it easily, causing them even more fear.

John's demeanor reminded Everett of a holy man he knew who preached about fire and brimstone. The preacher may have been a man of God, but he sure had the look of evil. Everett wasn't too sure whose side John was on either.

"One more thing now. Once we enter the brush, don't say a word. Don't open your mouth for any reason. None of this stuff can hurt you if you keep your mouths shut; remember, whatever you see can't harm you if you do as I say. When we get to the treasure, I'll show you where to dig. No matter what you see or hear, don't stop digging."

"John, what could happen if one of us did speak?" Levi asked.

"I was hoping you wouldn't ask, but now that you have.... If you open your mouth, these demons could enter your body and possess it. If that happens, it would have a physical body to use to fight me. Your body would be mortal, but it would be controlled by the spirit, which would give it the strength of several men. These things have unbelievable spiritual strength, but in order to use it physically, they have to take control of a real living body. As long as none of you gives them that chance, I believe I can match them with my powers."

None of them noticed that it was a beautiful night; the moon hung in the sky and covered the island with its pale, eerie light.

John's thoughts fleetingly turned to Letsy and the children. He said a little prayer for his family and one for himself and the others as well. He then set off, leading the group into the spirit-filled darkness.

He held the torch as if it were a flag he might carry into battle. He hesitated, and then turned around. He held his finger to his lips to remind the others to stay silent. He used his arms to push the thick brush aside. The others followed closely. After fighting their way through for several yards, they found themselves under a low canopy of small oaks and myrtle trees. It looked like a cave. Light from the moon that penetrated the small openings overhead caused shadows to move about on the wind. It was one of the eeriest places John had ever seen.

He pressed on, holding his torch high. The men were so close together that when John stopped, they all bumped into each other. He could hear them breathing, panting behind him like men who had just run a mile. His own breath, he then realized, was as labored as theirs.

Then the sounds of the spirit world began. Voices mumbled off in the distance. Ghostly faces appeared in the dark recesses of the canopy. The spirits talked directly to each of the four men, trying to get them to speak. Two of them appeared as Everett and Levi's dead brothers; crying, they asked why they had been left behind. Their woeful plea for help was horrible—and worse yet—it was working. Everett and Levi were about to break down.

Sensing their weakness, John turned. He reached out and held onto both of them, calming them. They held strong; not a word was said or a cry heard.

Suddenly, Burt started flailing the torch from side to side as if he were fighting something. John glanced down, seeing dead men all around. Rushing to Burt's aid, he slapped his hand tightly over Burt's mouth. John sensed the boy was about to scream. Burt's eyes bulged with fear; John held his hand tightly over his mouth. Finally, John felt Burt's body relax under his hold. Slowly he released his grip, which allowed Burt's body to slump to the ground. The assaulting spirits melted into the dark shadows of the night, vanquished, at least for now.

John sensed that the spirits had begun to fear his supernatural power. They were actually afraid of him—something he never expected—and this was good.

The men regrouped behind John and pushed on. After several minutes, they found themselves before a very large oak tree. The trunk was as big around as a wagon; its limbs stretched out in all directions. The light of the moon cascaded down through the branches, bathing in unnatural light the Spanish moss that swayed slowly in the slight breeze. Looking at the tree, John could see plat-eyes, perched on the limbs, waiting for their master's orders. They watched John's every move; they were ready to defend the treasure buried below. These demons were the worst John had ever seen. Taking turns, they swooped down toward John, trying to break his concentration. Each time, John would turn them away with the wave of his hand; his powers were unbelievably strong on this night. The demons' mouths were open; their howls and screams were deafening. Everett and the others held on to each other, forming a little circle at the base of the tree. With their eyes closed and jaws locked so tightly a pry-bar couldn't have opened them, they trembled in unison.

John began to circle the tree. He held out his arms as if he were a blind man looking for something. Then he stopped. He stood for a moment, listening to some sound the others could not hear from the spirit world. Turning to the men, he held his finger once again to his lips as a warning.

He reached for his bag and pulled out a corked bottle containing a yellow powder. Walking in a circle, he poured the powder behind him. When he finished, he had drawn a large circle. He directed the others to step into the circle.

He then spoke quietly, reminding them not to reply. "Whatever you do, don't step from this circle until I tell you its time. You'll be safe inside this circle. The treasure is right under you, and I'll be right here with you. Now start digging. No matter what happens, don't open your mouths and don't stop digging until you find the box."

John stepped back but stayed within the confines of the circle. The other men started to dig. Almost instantly, lightning and thunder erupted violently; the wind picked up with gale-like intensity. The tree came alive—swaying in the howling wind. The others looked at John for reassurance. He nodded his head affirmatively and motioned for them to keep digging.

One of the demons tried to penetrate the circle. As it reached the outer edge, John used his powers to throw it back away from the men. His spiritual strength was even more effective than he himself had imagined. These demons were not mortal, but his obvious ability to control them was surprising. Only now was he really certain that they were protected within the circle.

As the men continued their work, John periodically reminded them that he was there protecting them and to keep their minds on the digging.

They were drenched in sweat, but they continued at a hard and furious pace. Levi paused long enough to glance out of the hole. Startled by what he saw, he nudged Everett and Burt to take a look. There stood a figure so scary in appearance it had to be the devil himself. He was tall and lanky with long black stringy hair. His mustache and goatee were neatly trimmed, but his skin appeared as rotting flesh. His eye sockets were dark; eyeballs glared like hot coals. His clothes were ancient. The topcoat and pants were black as the night; he wore a white French style shirt with ruffles on the chest and cuffs—covered with blood. Silver buckles and studs adorned his boots as did heavy iron shackles. Everything about this man spoke of evil, especially the large group of plat-eyes hovered around him.

The demons continued to approach the circle but were pushed back by the invisible force emanating from John's presence. They were no longer able to reach even the edge of the circle before John's powers threw them back. Twisting and screaming in agony, they retreated into the profane darkness.

Suddenly, Everett's shovel hit something solid. At that instant, the demons began to scream at an even higher pitch. They flew around the circle frantically as they tried to find a way in. Then the wind stopped, and the screaming was silenced. The demons outside the ring vanished.

Off across the inlet, Jobe and Blue sat by their fire and watched the little island. Jobe could sense that it had started. "I prays fo' dem boys. I hopes we sees dem in de mornin'." Acknowledging her feelings, Blue closed her eyes and nodded.

John eased into the hole. The silence brought an eerie, disturbing feeling to him. Slowly he brushed the sand off the top of the box, where written in beautiful lettering, was the name Captain Caleb Bland. Whispering an apology to the spirit of the evil captain, he grabbed the box. As he started to lift it from its resting place, the sound of metal clanging against metal caused him to drop it. He glanced up to see the others staring in horror at something above him.

He looked up to see the skeletal remains of a human body hanging from a branch. As the scabbard struck against the leg irons still locked around the ankles, it produced a rhythmic clanging.

John stood up quickly. Pointing toward the hanging corpse, he shouted,

"I know you're here, Bland! You know now that you can't stop me. This treasure belongs to others now. There's nothing you can do. You have no power over them or me. You may as well go back to the other side where you belong. You have nothing to guard any more. It's gone forever."

The screaming rose up again. The wind raged and tore the body loose from the tree. It fell down toward John, striking the treasure box. As it hit, it faded away quickly.

John lifted the box out and handed it to Levi and Everett.

"Take it! Take it now! Help me out of this damned hole, and fill it in quickly."

The men worked furiously until they had placed every shovel of dirt back into the hole. John lit a match. As he put the match to the yellow powder, he mumbled something, as if in prayer. The powder flared up all around them. The bright flash of yellow light and acrid smell of sulfur burned their eyes. The smoke and odor were awful, reminiscent of those battlefields long ago. After the smoke and fire had cleared, John, with the box securely in hand, led the others out of the circle.

The island was quiet now. Lighting a torch, he then led them away from the old oak tree. As they moved out to the first clearing, John told them they could speak again. Between the digging and the terror of the demons, they were exhausted. Exhaustion, however, didn't stop Everett from wanting to open the box immediately. With shaky hands, he pried the lock open with his knife. As he slowly pushed the lid up, the men simultaneously dropped to their knees around the box. They were not disappointed, for it was filled with jewelry, plunder that had been stolen well over a century before. Right on top was a beautiful emerald broach.

John started to reach for it but stopped, his hand just inches away. To touch or possess any of the contents would have ruined his powers forever.

Everett noticed that John was taken with the emerald. "Take it, John; you've earned it."

"No, Everett, I can't. I'd lose my powers if I took any of it."

He felt weak. The night had been long, and his fatigue was apparent. He sat back, away from the treasure and the others. As he looked up into the night sky, he wasn't sure if this had been what he expected. The trip had brought up a lot of issues he had forced from his mind long ago. As he watched the three men admiring their bounty, a dark and eerie feeling came over him that he could not understand.

Meanwhile, back at the old oak, Caleb Bland materialized. He fell sobbing to the ground where his treasure had been buried. Quickly the sobbing ceased, and rage took its place. Standing up, he called on all the demons of the dark side. With them as allies, he mustered all the powers they controlled, and he cast his dark spell.

"Whoever holds my emerald will forever be cursed, and such curse will remain with his descendants! In the name of Evil, this spell be cast!" He slowly faded back to the other side. There was no doubt, however, that he would not rest until the emerald broach was returned.

John stood up and wiped the sand from his clothes. He looked out on the horizon. The sun would soon be up. They needed to get back to the mainland. Looking out across the marsh from where they had come, John could see the glow of the fire where he knew, Jobe and Blue waited.

"Everett, that box of jewels is yours now. Do whatever you want with it," said John.

Waiting for the tide to recede, the group found themselves again struggling to keep on the path back to the mainland. The gray mud that sucked at their feet and legs nearly swallowed their boots. In due time, they crossed the land bridge and headed toward Jobe's place.

John paused to look back at the island. The rising sun cast rays up into the sky. The brightness of the morning belied the events at the oak tree a few hours before. Although the new day would quickly erase the darkness and the evil it held, it would have no effect on Bland's curse!

As John followed the others toward the little cabin, he swore, "I'll never, ever go back to that place or any place like it; I'm finished with evil. There was enough evil last night to last a lifetime. I'm heading home!"

The men walked into the clearing at Jobe's. The old man and Blue came out and greeted them with smiles and blessings. Jobe took John's hand and welcomed him back with excitement. "I's so glad yo' boys comes back. We set up all de night prayin' fo' yo'."

Everett placed the box on the ground and opened it. Reaching in, he pulled out a few pieces of jewelry. "Jobe, this is for you, a gift of thanks for showing us the way and feeding us."

Jobe stepped back from the box. It was apparent he didn't want any dealings with what lay in front of him. He grabbed hold of his root bag. Rubbing it between his fingers, he drew a hex sign in the air in front of Blue and himself. John knew he was trying to protect them from something.

"No! No gifts," Jobe insisted. Again Jobe drew the hex sign in the air. "Yo' boy's gots to go now. If'n you stay here wit' dat box, yo' be bringin' bad tings down on Blue an' me."

Jobe glanced over at John, who by now was saddling up his horse. He knew it was time for him and the others to leave. The fear he saw in old Jobe's eyes made him suspect that something was very wrong with this treasure. Jobe knew it. They both sensed the evil, and they sensed, too, that wherever the treasure went, so went the evil.

Picking up on this fear, Everett wasn't sure what to do or to say. "John, what the hell's wrong with that crazy old darkie? Did I offend them?"

"No, Everett, it's just their way. They're a little spooky. Now let's get out of here."

The men mounted their horses. Everett, Levi, and Burt rode out ahead. John stopped and turned to Jobe. "Jobe, you think what we did was wrong?"

Jobe looked out to the island, his yellow eyes sparkling in the sunlight. Holding on to John's hand he looked him in the eye. "Let me say dis, Mr. John, dat bad spirit, he ain't be done wit yo' yet. I tells yo' now, right where we stands, don't yo' be touchin' dat treasure! Let dem udder boys keep it, but don't yo' o yo' family be takin' nary a piece of it."

John understood that Jobe was pleading with him. "Don't worry, Jobe, I won't touch any of it." John nudged his horse and rode out.

Chapter Twenty

For hours, Letsy watched from the sandy road for any signs or sounds of a rider. The early evening air brought a chill. She went inside to get her shawl then quickly returned to her vigil. In the sky, the first stars appeared. Curiously watching their mother, the children sat outside on the steps. They sensed her anxiety. As night approached, Letsy told the children to go inside to get ready for supper. After one more glance down the road, she returned to the house. If John was not back by morning, she had decided that she'd go into town and tell the sheriff. He'd surely send some men to look for him.

Without a word, she went over to stir the soup simmering over the fire. She lifted the black pot and carefully carried it over to the center of the table.

"Hallie, bring the bowls and spoons over and set the table."

Hallie slowly maneuvered around the table as she gently placed a spoon beside every bowl. The silence was eerie. After several minutes, Hallie couldn't stand it any longer. "Mama, do you think daddy will be home tonight?"

Letsy sensed the children were feeding off of her own fear. Turning to them, she forced a confident smile. "Now don't you children worry one bit about your father. He's fine and he'll be home soon."

Their fear brought back memories of the bad times. Letsy recalled the times John came home drunk, scaring the hell out of them all. She was well aware that the children, too, remembered those times.

Looking out into the dark, Franklin stood at the window. The full moon had already traced its short path to the western horizon, which allowed the night to envelop the little house in darkness. He strained to see any movement. He could see nothing but dark shadows and the faint reflection of light on the ground from the windows of their cabin. He had grown angry because his mother had to worry so much. He had even thought of how he might kill his father if he came home drunk. John's drinking had caused the whole family fear and worry for too long, the boy thought, as he slammed his fist against the wall.

With tears in his eyes, he turned to his mother and vowed, "Mama, if he's drinking I'm gonna kill him. He's let us down for the last time."

"Franklin! You will never speak like that again! You'll do no such thing! He may not be perfect, but he is your father. Now all of you, you gather around. We're going to say a prayer for him before we eat."

They gathered in a circle and held hands as Letsy led them in the Lord's Prayer.

During the prayer, Franklin thought about what he'd just said about his father. This last year or so, his father had become a changed man, that was true enough. He hadn't been drunk at all, and Franklin could see that his mother was much happier. He felt really guilty, and silently he asked the Lord to forgive him for having blurted his comment out. Franklin was only twelve when he began shouldering the burden of being the man of the house in his father's absence. He loved his father but still carried a deep anger for him. When John was drinking, he'd put Franklin down; nothing the boy did was good enough. Franklin never talked back to his father, and he never cried in front of him. He'd just hold it all in, slowly building the resentment and anger he now possessed.

Ironically, Letsy had decided that if John did come home drunk, she might kill him herself. After all, she had made him that promise. As she prayed, the thought went through her mind. She begged forgiveness for such an evil thought. Was she losing her mind? Letsy feared that one day Franklin might explode and do something he'd later regret. She was determined to help them work it out.

They sat down and served up the soup. Letsy helped Nellie with hers. As the children ate, Letsy looked around the table at their faces. She missed Lavenia, but often wondered if God had taken her to bring John back in line.

Hallie was ten when Lavenia died. She realized that with Lavenia gone, she'd have to help her mother more. Letsy soon found she could always depend on Hallie. If John's drinking or Lavenia's passing had any profound effect on her, it wasn't apparent.

Thomas was seven, a boy without a care in the world. He was the prankster in the bunch. For some reason, he had never allowed his father to worry him the way Franklin had. But then John never treated Thomas the way he had Franklin. Maybe he was just too young when John was at his worst.

Nellie was three years old, the youngest of the five. She was quiet and shy. She had come into the world with hardly a whimper, never cried much and was rarely sick. Letsy had given birth to her while John was away in the war. She arrived during a storm, and Franklin had to go to a neighboring farm for help. Letsy had gotten pregnant while John was home on leave. It was probably the worst time in the world to be with child. With the war going on, getting the things she and her newborn needed was hard.

Nellie loved to play by herself, and Letsy often heard her talking and playing with imaginary playmates. She sometimes told her mama about a strange black woman that watched over her. Letsy passed it off as the product of an active imagination. At times she even offered detailed descriptions of the big black woman, right down to the bead necklaces and charms she wore around her neck.

Letsy wondered if Nellie, too, possessed the gift. Could she be talking about Blind Jolene? Her brothers teased her and called her a "little witch" even though the children had no actual knowledge of their father's gift. John and Letsy both felt it was better not to tell them.

As they ate their soup, the children kept glancing at the empty chair where their father sat. Hallie set a bowl and spoon, just in case he might make it home. After supper they all gathered around the fireplace. As she held Nellie in her lap, Letsy read verses from the Bible, a nightly ritual. The children, as always, listened intently.

Suddenly, Nellie interrupted her mother: "I see Daddy riding his horse, Mama."

Letsy told her, "Hush now! It's not polite to speak when your mother's reading."

Nellie pleaded, "But Daddy's coming! Daddy's here!"

Thomas laughed. "Little witch Nellie thinks Daddy's home, ha, ha."

Letsy put the child down and walked to the door. She had the strongest feeling of a presence outside. She hadn't heard any horses, and she knew that John would call out before coming in.

Nellie followed at her mother's side. Then pulling at her mother's hand, Nellie said, "Mama, it's just Daddy."

Letsy retrieved the shotgun from the corner. The children were all visibly upset, except for Nellie. Letsy stood right in front of the door as she told Franklin to open it. Franklin pulled the door open.

Looking like death, John stood before them. Letsy quickly put the gun down and helped him into the house. His appearance left little doubt: it had been a hard ride.

John sat down at the table. Letsy filled a cup with coffee and dished up some soup. He just sat real still for a moment before picking up his spoon.

"Letsy, I'm so tired I don't even know if I can eat."

He asked Franklin, "Son, would you please go out and tend to the horse for me? I don't believe I have the strength to lift the saddle off her back."

"Yes sir, Pa."

Franklin quickly ran outside where he found the old mare by the fence. He led her into the barn and then lit a lantern so he could better see what he was doing. She was all lathered up. It was obvious she had been ridden hard and needed a good rub down and some feed. He unhooked the girth and gently slid the saddle off her back. Free of the weight, the mare shook herself and sprayed sweat and foam all over him. He opened the stall door, removed the bridle then slapped the horse on the rear. The mare slowly walked into her stall, and he closed the door behind her. Franklin then went to the feed bin and filled the tin bucket to the top. Pouring the corn into the trough, he spoke gently to the tired horse.

"There you go, girl. Now don't eat too fast, you might get colic."

He then went out to the well, hauled up a bucket of water, and hung it inside the stall. While the horse ate, the boy brushed her until she was almost dry. He stayed with her for a while to be sure she was okay.

He pulled the saddle blanket from under the saddle and hung it over a railing so it could dry. As he hung the bridle over the horn of the saddle, he noticed the saddlebags were still strapped on. He untied them. Almost unconsciously, he looked into the saddlebags. He noticed a cloth bag. Curiosity got the best of him; he wanted to see what was in that bag. He slowly pulled it out of the saddlebag. He then held it up to the light of the lantern. He had just started to untie the bag when his mother came in.

"Franklin? Son, what are you doing?"

"Nothing, Ma."

"Oh yeah, what do you have there?"

Searching for a quick answer, he stumbled with his words. "Er… I… Ah…."

"You'd better let me have that, son, and you come inside. It's late."

Franklin handed the bag to his mother. As the strange cloth bag was passed from his hand to his mother's, he sensed it contained something secret, something he would always wonder about.

Once inside, Letsy took the bag into the bedroom and closed the door behind her. She knew Franklin was curious about what was in the bag, but she wouldn't allow it. None of the children needed to know about that bag.

John was still at the table eating the last of the soup; he looked as if he had aged ten years.

Franklin walked over and sat by him. "Pa, are you all right?"

John turned. He placed his hand on the boy's shoulder. "Son, I'm fine, just worn out. It was a long trip. I'll get a good night's sleep and be fine in the morning." John knew his family was worried about him.

Franklin wanted to know where his father and Everett had been, but John wasn't going to tell the children about the nightmare he had experienced. Even a lie would be better than the truth.

"I'll tell you kids about it tomorrow; I'm just too tired tonight." He'd have to make up a good story if they pressed him. "I also have some good news about a job."

Franklin accepted that for now, but John knew the boy would quiz him tomorrow.

Calling them all to his side, he again assured them that he was fine. All he needed was a good night's rest.

Out of the blue, little Nellie spoke up, "Daddy, I knew you were safe."

"And just how did you know that, Honey?"

"The old black woman told me."

John glanced at Letsy questioningly; she shrugged her shoulders and shook her head. She was as puzzled as John was. John lifted Nellie up on his lap. "Honey, the next time you talk with this woman, you've got to let me know. Okay?"

"Yes Sir, Pa. I sure will. Do you want to talk with her, too?"

"Well, maybe. Now you and Hallie get to bed."

John surmised that Blind Jolene had visited with Nellie, and that meant he'd have to have a talk with her. He certainly didn't want Nellie learning about the gift at such a young age. If she had the powers, he would teach her how to use them in due time.

Letsy made sure the children were tucked in before she returned to John at the table. He was deep in thought when she returned, but he smiled and took her hand.

"Letsy, I'm so glad to be home. I missed you so much. I know I'll never do anything like that again."

Looking down, John searched for the right words. "Before I tell you about the trip, we need to discuss Nellie."

Letsy spoke in a whisper. "You know what? She knew that you were here long before I did. She knew it was you outside the door. How could she have known? You didn't call to the house like you normally do."

Letsy wasn't ready to accept that her daughter might have the gift.

"John, I don't want her teased and laughed at. Thomas and Franklin already tease her so much that they make her cry. They call her a 'little witch'."

John closed his eyes and rubbed his face with his hands. "I'm going to need some guidance with this. When I've rested, I'll deal with it."

Too tired now to tell Letsy about the trip, he pleaded, "Do you mind if we just go to bed now? I've got a lot to tell you that you'll find hard to believe. But it'll have to wait till morning. I just don't have the energy tonight."

Letsy was fine with that. She knew he needed to rest. Taking him by the hands, she pulled him from the chair. As he stood, she pulled him against her tightly. Kissing him softly, she then led him to their bedroom.

Chapter Twenty-One

In the morning hours just before dawn, John tossed and turned and talked crazy. Letsy listened in horror to the things he said. Finally, unable to take anymore, she woke him. As she touched him, she could feel he was covered with sweat.

"John! Wake up. Honey, wake up!"

John sat straight up, screaming, "Go away! Go away!" He realized instantly he was home, safe in his bed. It was the same nightmare, the dream about Yancy Johnson.

Letsy got up and went into the main room where she stoked the coals in the fireplace. She added a few pieces of wood, which helped the fire slowly come to life. She wrapped her shawl around her before she went outside to get water. When she returned, she found John sitting at the table. He had dressed and was pulling on his boots.

Letsy filled the coffeepot and placed it over the fire. In a bit they were outside on the porch watching the stars fade from the sky as the sun began to have its way. The coffee tasted good, and for a moment, the husband and wife were at peace in each other's company.

Letsy cradled her cup with both hands; the heat from it helped to keep them warm. As the steam floated up around her face, her nostrils filled with the comforting smell of the coffee. The chill of the morning brushed against her bare neck and sent shivers through her body. She pulled her shawl higher to ward off the morning cold. She watched John as he sipped his coffee. Softly, she moved close and wrapped her arm around her husband's waist. Pulling herself close to him, she could feel his warmth and strength. He then hugged her close. With her head against his chest, she fit perfectly under his arm. She felt his heart beating in unison with her own. They were soul mates. Their paths, surely, had crossed many lifetimes before.

"I just love this time of the morning," John said, "right before the sun rises, when the sky is between the night and day. Everything seems to stop for just a moment, even the spirit world, as if they are taking a moment to reflect." Letsy eased from his hold and seated herself on the top step. Feeling cold, John stepped into the house to get his coat. When he returned, he sat down beside her.

After a minute of silence, he asked, "Would you like to hear about what happened?"

"Of course, I want you to tell me everything."

John proceeded to tell her about the trip. She listened intently, in absolute amazement at the adventure he had been through. Now she realized why he had been so tired when he came in. She found Blind Jolene's role in the saga particularly interesting.

"I wish I had the ability that you have, John. I'd really like to talk with her again, not that I'd want to take on what you did. I'd have run like a scared chicken."

John put his arm around her and pulled her close. He thought back to the time she told him to leave, after Lavenia died.

"I don't think so, Letsy. You'd have stood your ground. I know. I've seen you stand up to evil before."

They had both been through an awful lot. All John wanted now was to stay close to home and be with his family. He recalled his meeting with Clyde Smith on the road a while back. Smith owned a lot of timberland and had been looking for a foreman to run one of his crews. John told him he didn't know much about timbering but knew he could learn. He desperately wanted off the boats. Timber had become a booming business in the area, and there was plenty of money to be made. He knew he had one more river trip to Georgetown coming up, but he had already decided he would quit after that trip and take up Smith's offer.

He reasoned to Letsy that with this job he'd be closer to home and wouldn't be gone for days at a time. She was real pleased with the idea; having John home every night sounded wonderful.

She pulled her hair back, and with one swift motion, she made a bun and pinned it in place. With a contented smile, she looked over at John.

"Well, John, it is Sunday, and the Good Lord has blessed us with a beautiful fall day. If you'll take the children to church, I'll prepare dinner. We can eat out under the big maple."

Letsy's mention of eating under the big tree brought memories of Jobe and Blue and the fish stew they shared under those big, moss-draped oaks. Jobe's warning of a curse on the treasure came to mind also. John prayed Jobe was wrong.

Meanwhile, Letsy had gone inside to get the children up and ready for church. After breakfast, they were off to church; humming happily, Letsy stayed behind to prepare dinner. She rarely ever missed preaching, but this Sunday was different. She wanted to do something special for John.

Chapter Twenty-Two

Around the children, John neither spoke of the magical power he possessed nor did he practice any magic around the house. He would always slip off to a secret place away from his family for the invocation of the spirits and such. He felt it was best that way. Besides, Letsy was not especially open to the idea of lost souls wandering around the children. It frightened her to think of what he saw during these conjuring sessions. She also knew that his magic might scare the children. John actually had several secret places deep in the pine forest that surrounded the cabin. There he found the solitude he needed. He never used the same place twice for he feared someone might see him.

After Sunday dinner, he whispered to Letsy that he had something to tend to and that he would be back in about two hours. She knew he was going to call up Jolene. She put the children to work washing the dishes. This gave John the chance he needed to disappear without the children noticing.

He walked out near the edge of the woods. He was careful that the children were not watching him as he quickly stepped behind a large pine tree. Looking back one more time, he melted into the shadows of the forest like a phantom. Pushing bushes aside, he fought an undergrowth of briars until he finally found a suitable clearing under a stand of towering pines. The afternoon sun cast slant rays of light that resembled polished swords thrust through the trees. The rays abruptly stopped as they hit the ground. Pine needles carpeted the forest floor, soft and comfortable under foot.

"This looks like a real good place," he thought to himself as he sat down on the soft blanket of pine straw. Closing his eyes, he concentrated on Blind Jolene. From deep in his mind, he summoned her from the spirit world. He was very careful not to let his mind wander from Jolene during this time. Some unwanted spirit could easily slip through the veil if he was careless. After a few minutes, he opened his eyes and found himself completely engulfed in a damp mist. He could only see a few feet into the forest, but he felt the presence of a spirit. He dared not move; at this point he couldn't be sure this was Jolene. He remained motionless. The mist that floated up around him caressed him gently.

He then spoke, "Jolene, are you here? Is this mist of your doing?"

He heard a deep-throated laugh. It was she; she was all around him but did not show herself.

"John Waters, I's be glad to sees dat yo' be safe, affa yo' journey to de isle. Now tells me, what yo' wants wid Jolene?"

"Jolene, have you been visiting Nellie?" There was a long silence.

"What if'n I has?"

"Jolene, she's young, too young to understand this gift. I'll decide when it's time to tell her, and I'll teach her how to use it. I don't mean you any disrespect, but now is not the time."

Jolene began slowly to materialize.

"John Waters, yo' cain't be waitin' fo' too long; yo' never nos' when yo time might jes' run out. She must know 'bout da' gif'."

"What do you mean, 'my time might run out'? I don't worry about my fate anymore. I still have plenty of time. Anyway, she needs to be a bit older; right now she's a mite too young to understand."

By now Jolene had fully materialized. She seemed as human as John, as she had seemed that day on the ferry. John's attention was drawn to the beads and jewelry hanging from her neck and wrist, so many bracelets he could hardly see her wrists. Wrapped several times around her head was a red cloth. Braids of long black hair, decorated with beads and brightly colored pieces of cloth, hung down her back. She had two leather pouches hanging from a plain rope tied around her waist—her root bags. She was quite a sight he thought.

"None o' yo' magic kin tell yo' when yo' maker be comin'. He be comin' at yo' do' wit' de shroud o' death. Dat we knows. Death be sho' as night an' day. Yo's might soon be comin', John Waters. But, befo' dat day, yo' gots to tells dat chile o' de power what be inside her. Don't yo be lettin' that chile thinks she be crazy. Da' dead be comin' to her an' she not be knowin' what she 'posed to do. Yo' gots to tell her."

"Jolene, I promise when she's a little older I'll teach her the way of the gift. Please don't visit her again. Please wait until I've had the chance to teach her the ways; then you can visit all you like."

Jolene moved closer to John. "Dat be fine wit me, John Waters. I be leavin' de chile alone fo' now 'cause I knows now yo' be doin' what needs be done. Afore I leaves dis place, I gots to tell yo' sumpin' dat be impo'tant. Dat treasure yo' boys done stole, it be cursed. It be bringin' yo' nuttin' but troubles."

"But I don't have any of the treasure. Everett and the other two took it all. I knew better. I knew what would happen."

"Did yo' not knows it be cursed? Did yo' not feel da dark powers flowing off it? Dat be da last ting da evil pirate what owned it do, makes a curse on it, he do. I's sho be hope'n yo' not be havin' nary a piece o' it!"

"No, Jolene. I gave it to the others, didn't touch it at all. I just hope the others don't have bad luck from it."

"Yo' not havin' control over what dey be doin', John Waters. Now, is we done wid dis talkin'?"

"I guess so. I've said what I needed to say."

Jolene drew in close to John once more.

Pointing a long, bony finger in his face, she warned him, "Don't yo' be waitin too long o' it be too late." With that said, Jolene disappeared and with her, the mist.

Chapter Twenty-Three

On Monday morning, John left Letsy and the children standing at the fence. They watched as he disappeared down the dusty road. He was meeting his riverboat for the last time, his last trip down to Georgetown. He was looking forward to the new job. Knowing he'd be at home every night lifted his spirits.

Hoping to hitch a ride into town, John hung around the crossroads for a while. He saw a wagon coming his way; he knew immediately it was Tom Porter. If he rode with Tom, he'd get a real ear full of religion. Checking his pocket watch, he realized he'd have to ride with him, for time was pressing.

As Tom approached, John waved his hand in the air. "Tom, could I catch a ride with you on this glorious morning?"

"Praise be, John Waters, I'll be glad to share my seat with you."

John pulled himself up onto the seat. Tom slapped the leather reins on the rear of the big mule. "Get up, Molly." The wagon was loaded with firewood; so Tom didn't press her too hard. They moved slowly along the dusty road toward town.

Tom wasn't a real talkative man, though he'd always discuss religion if given the chance. John tried his best to keep the conversation off that subject, but somehow Tom got started. He spent the whole trip to town trying to convince John he needed to be saved. It did make the time pass more quickly. He spoke of all the bad goings on and told John they were the workings of the devil. He kept asking John if he had been saved. If he hadn't, Tom kept reminding John, "he'd surely one day pay for not accepting Jesus into his life. Tom was your typical fire and brimstone believer, a good Baptist. John allowed him to go on without any argument, just an occasional nod or grunt of agreement. Poor Tom didn't realize that John probably knew more about the Bible than most of the preachers in the area. Just because John practiced the old ways didn't mean he was ignorant of modern beliefs. John found comfort in all manner of spiritualism, something Tom's narrow–minded beliefs forbade.

John wasn't an openly religious man. He was very selective about with whom he would even discuss God. Going to church had always helped relax his mind. It was his safe house, his place of peace. Sometimes he would sit in the pew and wait for everyone to leave so he could be alone in the church, just he and the Lord. Often enough, he sat for hours and sorted things out with God's help.

When they finally reached town, John jumped down from the wagon, shook Tom's hand, and thanked him for the ride. Tom just had to get in the last word before John walked away.

"John, now you think on what I've been preaching. The Good Book says only through Jesus will you be allowed into heaven. When you decide to make that choice, I'll be right there to pray with you."

John thanked Tom again. Tipping his hat, he turned and walked down the street toward the river. He thought to himself, "This is my last trip down this damned river. Letsy, soon I'll be home every day, and your worries will be over."

Chapter Twenty-Four

On Tuesday morning, Letsy watched the children run off down the road to the little schoolhouse. She wanted her children to get a good education so they could have a better life than she had. She was determined that her children would have every advantage available to them.

Around mid morning, she was out sweeping off the porch. Wrapped in her shawl to keep warm from the chill, she worked vigorously. The sun slowly warmed her enough that she removed the shawl, laying it over a chair. She continued sweeping, humming a song that her mother used to sing to her. She had stopped to move the chairs around when she noticed a rider approaching. As he neared, she could see it was Everett. Her first thought was, "Oh Lord, I hope nothing has happened to Everett's mother." The only time Everett ever came around was when his mother was sick or needed help with something.

Everett nervously climbed down from his horse and greeted her. "Good morning, Miss Letsy."

"Morning, Everett. John's not here. He's gone to work on the boat."

"Yeah, I know, I saw him yesterday when they were shoving off."

She searched her mind for reasons that would bring Everett around when he knew that John wasn't at home. She didn't trust Everett, and so she kept her distance. He kept looking away and then back at her. He acted a bit strange, even for him, she thought. It was as if he wanted to say something but was having a hard time finding the words. She sensed there was something different about him.

Holding her broom in one hand and shading her eyes from the bright sun with the other, she spoke first. "Everett, what you got on your mind?"

Everett cleared his throat, fiddled with the reins. Reaching up and rubbing the side of his horse's neck, he finally spoke.

"Letsy, I know you don't like me much. I guess I've never given you much reason to, but I'm not as bad as you think. I just get a little wild and mean at times. On that there trip I took with John, my eyes were opened; just being around John, seemed to bring out another side of me. Ever since we got back, I been thinking about going somewhere and starting over, changing my ways and such." Everett looked at her pleadingly, as if he was trying to convince her of this change.

"I just can't stay here any more; I need to move on. I hear tell of some wide open spaces out west. I been thinkin' I might just head out that way maybe. My mama's not real happy about me leaving like this, but Levi won't leave her and Sarah, well, she's a grown woman and can take care of herself now. I just need to go somewhere and start over. Do you understand?"

Letsy listened as Everett poured his feelings out to her; he was totally unlike the Everett she knew.

"Before I leave, I wanted to give you something. John helped all of us. Thanks to him, Levi's got enough gold to take care of everybody, that is, if he keeps his mouth shut. Me, I'm taking my share with me."

He reached into his coat pocket and pulled out a folded piece of cloth. Before I go, I want you to have this. I could tell when John saw it he wanted it, but he wouldn't take it. Said he might lose all that special magical power he has. Now, he may not be able to take any of it, but you can."

Everett unfolded the cloth and exposed the most beautiful piece of jewelry Letsy had ever laid eyes on. Dropping the broom, she crossed her hands over her chest. "Oh, my lord!"

A huge green emerald broach sparkled in the sunlight as though it were lit from within. A dozen sparkling stones were embedded in the gold setting around it. Letsy was speechless.

"Take it, Letsy. It's yours. Call it a gift from John through me."

She looked up at Everett, then back at the broach. Hesitantly, she reached out with her right hand and gently took it from Everett. She held it up; she was captivated by its brilliance, hypnotized under its spell. Never in her wildest dreams had she imagined that she would ever hold a piece of jewelry like this. Words could not express her astonishment. Quickly, however, she came to her senses and told Everett, "No, I can't take it."

"Sure you can. Now keep it. It's yours." Everett turned away and climbed back on his horse. "Tell cousin John thanks for everything." Turning the horse, he rode away. Soon there was nothing but a small cloud of dust on the road.

As Everett disappeared, Letsy felt a slight chill in her left heel. The sensation rose slowly through her foot and traveled steadily up her leg. It entered her spine and continued its upward movement. She shuddered as it moved further up into her neck, finally stopping deep in the back of her head. As suddenly as it had started, it was gone. She felt strangely vulnerable to some eerie force. Never before had she such an unsettling feeling. Somewhat disturbed, she sank down on the steps to collect her thoughts. It was all she could do to keep from crying.

Again conscious of the broach in her hand, Letsy held it up to the sun. Slowly turning the broach around, she watched it glisten in the sunlight. The strange chill faded completely from her mind. She was lost in the beauty of the emerald broach.

She knew John wouldn't approve of Everett's giving it to her. Her mind raced. Should she keep it? She certainly couldn't let her husband know if she did. What in the world would she do with it? After agonizing over the decision for what seemed an eternity, she hurriedly went into the house to their bedroom. She wrapped the gift back in the cloth and placed it in a little box that she buried deep in her cedar chest. John would not be home for at least three or four days, and before then she could figure out what to do. She could tell him, or she could just leave it hidden. If she didn't tell him about the broach, how would she ever enjoy it? She wrestled with the thought. The only secret she had ever kept from her husband was her encounter with Will. The idea that telling him would mean that she couldn't keep it just didn't make sense. After all, if John hadn't helped them, none of them would have any of the treasure. She had begun the slow and dangerous process of rationalization.

All of her reasoning, however, failed to include the most important factor, a factor about which she was completely unaware. The treasure, especially the emerald, was cursed! Unwittingly, she had enabled the curse of Caleb Bland to find them!

As darkness approached, Everett rode toward the Little Pee Dee River. It would take a day or two to get there, but he had plenty of time. He felt good about having talked with Letsy, as well as his decision to give her the broach. He had wanted to make peace with her, and giving it to her was his way of doing so. He, too, had no idea the treasure had been cursed. Neither he nor Letsy knew that they would all pay a grave price for having taken it.

As he rode, he sensed he was being followed. His senses, honed by living in the wilds for so long, were not to be doubted. The sun had set an hour or so earlier, and the darkness consumed him. He felt a little spooked, as if the shadows were coming alive. Suddenly, three riders approached him from the darkness. He reached to draw his gun, but they were on him before he could get it out of his holster. The riders had cloth bags over their heads. Everett couldn't tell who they were but thought he recognized one of the voices. They pointed their guns in his face and demanded his share of the treasure.

"I don't know what the hell you boys are talking about. I don't have any money or treasure," he replied.

"Yeah, you do Everett. Your good friend Burt Jones told us all about it."

Everett's thoughts switched immediately to Burt. He was a spineless son-of-a-bitch. He should have run him off the first time he came around.

"Burt's crazy. He's just telling stories."

"No, we don't think so. Now give us what you got," one of the men demanded as he placed his gun to Everett's temple.

"What'd you boys do to Burt? How'd you know he got a share too?"

The rider in front of Everett's horse spoke up. "We got all he had, left him in the swamp wishing he'd never seen any treasure."

"Is he dead?" Everett questioned.

"No, he ain't dead, but it'll be awhile before he's back to normal." They all laughed.

Everett looked more intently at the rider in front of him. He now recognized the voice.

"You can wear that mask all day, Snake Brown, but I know who you are. You ain't nothing but a yellow bastard, and that's all you've ever been. You ran off and hid early in the war while the rest of us paid. Now you want to take something that ain't yours."

Everett kicked his horse hard. Momentarily, he had freed himself of the riders. The next thing he knew his back was on fire; a split second later he heard the sound of the gun. Falling from his horse, he lay on the ground looking up at the night sky. Peacefully, the distant stars flickered above as life seeped from his body. He thought about his mother losing another son: two in the war and now him. But his time had come, and he knew it. The dark angel was near. His last vision was that of the three hooded men standing over him. Close up, another gun fired. Everett's mortal body jerked uncontrollably on the ground, shot first in the back and now the head.

A local farmer found the body the next morning. He was taken home and buried in the family cemetery. His mother was so heart-broken she took ill. Three weeks later, she died. Darkness had descended upon the entire family.

Sarah, after her mother died, was left on the farm alone with her only brother, Levi. Eventually, she ran off with a stranger from Charleston.

Burt Jones recovered somewhat from the beating the three men had given him, but he was never the same. When he discovered that Sarah, the love of his life, had left with a stranger, he slipped into a deep melancholy. He was never a very strong-willed person. A neighbor found him hanging from a rafter in his barn.

As the dark curse continued weaving its madness, Levi, too, fell into despair. He could no longer work because of the pain in his bad leg. He slowly drank up, and gave away, his part of the treasure. He never thought about paying off the mortgage on the farm with his share. Instead, he used the money for whiskey until it was all gone. He even stopped planting. He was forced to leave after the bank foreclosed on the mortgage. The farm had been the only home he'd ever known. Before long, some gentleman dandy with connections to the bank had the house and land.

Levi moved in with John and Letsy for a while, but that didn't last long. After a few weeks, he moved to a shed down near the river. His health was generally bad, and the old battle scars were taking their toll. By now he could hardly walk on his injured leg. Confined to either his bed or a chair most of the time, he fell even deeper into the bottle. John tried, but nothing he could say or do could help Levi now. He stayed drunk, said it was the only way he could deal with the pain.

One day Levi managed to get himself down to the river for a little fishing. He found himself an old stump on the bank next to a deep fishing-hole. Sitting down, he tossed his line out into the black water. He pulled a bottle from his coat and turned it up for a long swig. "Better save a little for later," he thought. Replacing the cork, he stuffed it back in his coat.

After a few minutes watching his line floating on the water, he pulled the bottle out again, downing the remainder. Gazing at the empty bottle, he knew he'd have to go and beg someone for another. He threw it into the river and watched it slowly float away. The bottle partially filled with water, which caused it to right itself. The neck began to wobble in a beckoning manner, as if motioning for Levi to follow. His alcohol-laden mind understood the message. As he put his pole down to stand, he lost his balance and fell into the river. Levi was never a good swimmer; the bad leg and liquor didn't help. Quickly tiring, he slipped under the dark water. His old hat was left on the surface and peacefully floated away. He was found down river a week later, snagged and bloated under the docks in Conway.

After Levi's funeral, John and Letsy returned home. Their faces still reflected the sorrow they felt. The service was short; Levi didn't have many friends. He was placed beside Everett and his mother. Now they all rested peacefully together. Word was that Sarah died in childbirth not too long after Levi's death. A terrible darkness had destroyed the whole family.

Chapter Twenty-Five

Winter had blown into the little farming community with a fiendish wind and cold. Many folks were ailing, and more than a few had died from consumption. Letsy spent a lot of her time helping the neighbors nurse their sick. The lumber business, however, was booming, and John was doing well working for Clyde Smith.

Late one afternoon, John was walking home from the job. He was bone weary. He and his crew had been felling some of the great loblolly pines, which were so plentiful in the virgin forest of the area. As he walked, a familiar mist began oozing out of a briar thicket and onto the road. Recognizing the signs, John stopped to listen to the other side. He sensed that he was about to be visited by Blind Jolene once again. They had not spoken in a long time. He was curious as to why she was coming without being asked.

"Well, hello stranger. To what do I owe the honor of such a surprise visit?" John said kindly.

"Ha, yo' be a funny man, John Waters. Yo' knows why I bes here. I be done give yo' way too much time to be talkin' wit' de li'l one. She need be knowin' what be ahead fo' her! John Waters, yo' be forgettin' 'bout yo' gift too. What be wrong wid' yo'?"

The cold winter wind blew against him; he stuck his hands deep in his pockets to keep them warm. John had blocked out his gift, trying his best to put it out of his life.

"Jolene, after going after that treasure so many bad things have happened. I lost all my cousins, members of my family have been sick. I just don't know. I think sometimes that what I have is a gift of the devil, and God is punishing me for using it."

Jolene came closer to John; he could feel her energy everywhere around him. "Mr. John, dis here thinkin' yo' be doin', it be real bad. Yo' be a blessed man. Now, I tells yo' dat takin' da ol' pirate treasure, dat not be too smart. Yo' boys make him bad angry. I hears bad tings be happenin' to folks dat be holdin' pieces o' it."

"I don't have any of it, Jolene. It hurts me to think that the treasure is the reason why so many of my kin have died. You know, if it hadn't been for my gift, we wouldn't have found it."

Jolene moved around John as if she smelled something rotten on him. "Mr. John, Blind Jolene be feelin' der be somethin' evil 'round yo' an' yo' family. Yo' best be findin' out what it be. Yo' gots to find out what it be 'afore somethin' bad be happenin' to yo'. De most impo'tant ting be dat yo' tells dat chile 'bout da gift. The Good Lord might be comin' anytime and takin' yo' away."

"Jolene, you worry too much about my dying. I feel great; nothing is going to happen to me, so stop your worrying."

Jolene held out her arm. Using her powers, she summoned the sand from the road, which was suctioned directly into her hand. She closed her fist but allowed the sand to seep slowly back to the ground. "Yo' destiny done be writ'. Yo' not knowin' when yo' time on dis here earth be done 'til the last minute afore da dark."

She opened her hand. Only a few grains of the sand remained.

"Don't yo' be fogettin' to use yo' gift, Mr. John. I be seein' yo' afore too much longer."

Then she was gone. The mist lingered for a few seconds. Then it slowly drifted back into the briars.

Jolene knew that his time was short, but she was forbidden to tell of a coming death. She would be vanquished from the spirit world, thrown into the nothingness, if she told. She hoped the sand would tell him what she could not.

Shaken by the encounter, John began walking again. He thought about everything Jolene had said. What bothered him most was the thing about something evil around the family. He searched frantically but could find no alternative. He would have to use the gift in his own home now. His promise to Letsy would have to be broken. He couldn't bear the thought of something evil harming her or the children.

When he arrived home, he didn't say anything to Letsy about the encounter with Blind Jolene. He tried to figure out what she meant by the evil around the family. He didn't sleep much after he went to bed—in and out of dreams all night.

One dream in particular kept coming back into focus. He saw himself pinned under a pine tree, and he couldn't move. His legs were broken, and the pain was terrible. He looked up to see Caleb Bland standing over him laughing, as the pirate watched him slowly die. Then he would wake up in a sweat; he'd grab his legs only to realize it was all just a dream.

Next morning at breakfast, Letsy mentioned that he had been very restless all night. She wanted to know if anything was wrong.

"No, just a bad night. I'm curious though, Letsy. Is there anything strange around here? Is something bothering you?"

She turned away, hesitated, and then wiped her hands on her apron. That was enough! Without even using his gift, her husband knew something was wrong.

"Why no, John, it's just been a bad winter. The kids have been sick and my helping the neighbors has just worn me down."

John stood, picked up his lunch pail, and then walked to the door. He turned and looked at Letsy. "Are you sure, Letsy? You know you can talk to me about anything."

"Yes, John, I'm sure." She walked over to him, hugged him, and gave him a kiss. Assuring him, she sent him on his way.

John walked a ways down the road before he opened his mind to the gift. He let the powers flow through him as they filled his mind with visions. He closed his eyes as the past started to release its secrets. The gift began to tell him what had happened. He saw Everett ride up to the house and give Letsy the broach. He could see that she adored it and also that she knew that he would not approve of her keeping it. He could see it now, wrapped in cloth, lying in the bottom of her cedar chest. He cleared all other thoughts from his mind so he could concentrate on what he needed to do. It had to be removed from the house before any more bad things happened. He continued walking. He decided that he'd talk with Letsy when he got home, for he knew that this evil must be dealt with soon.

As long as he didn't touch the stone himself, his powers were safe. He had to be very tactful in how he approached his wife. He didn't want her to think he was angry or upset about her having taken the broach from Everett. It would work out. He would explain to her about the curse, and that once the broach was thrown into the river, the curse would be ended forever. She would understand.

John arrived at the crossroads where he met the rest of the crew. They drove the oxen deep into the piney woods where they began another day of felling trees. His crew was rough, but they were dependable, hard-working men.

Two of the men immediately started in on a big pine. They worked the two man crosscut saw back and forth. The undercut had been cut about one-third of the way through. They had sawed deeply enough from the opposite side so that the blade was fully supported when they stopped for a break. Without warning, the wind picked up. Pine straw blew around, and the wind forced them to pull their collars up against the cold. Their eyes watered, making it difficult to see one another.

John stood by the oxen as he hitched the leather harnesses to the towropes. Suddenly, a strange sensation came over him. The chill of the wind penetrated to the bone, a different, eerie kind of cold. He felt frozen in time, and then a vision appeared to him. He saw his body, dead, trapped under a fallen pine tree, just as he had seen in the dream. Letsy and the children were crying, and Clyde Smith and his wife were trying to comfort them. Many people stood in the yard as a group of men, his closest friends, carried a handsome pine coffin out of the house. They loaded it on to the wagon in the yard. The vision vanished.

He then remembered what Jolene had told him: "Yo' don' know yo' time be up 'til seconds befo', den' yo' instincts bes tellin' yo'." Only then did he remember the sand in her hand. At that moment, John realized his life would end within seconds.

Suddenly Blind Jolene appeared before him.

"Mr. John, it be too late; yo' n'er did tells de chile 'bout de gift. Now she be left to learnin' 'bout it her own self."

She then held up her hand and allowed the rest of the sand to fall. She was gone as quickly as she had appeared.

At that instant, John heard the distinct snap of the big pine as the wind finished the job the men had begun. The trunk, weakened by the saw cuts, could no longer resist the force of the howling wind. Instinctively, John planted his foot in an effort to leap to safety. As he did, his foot lost its traction on the slippery pine straw, and he fell flat on his back. He lay there, helpless, crushed beneath the large pine.

Death came quickly. With his last breath, his soul floated free of the broken shell of his body. His spirit stared at the mutilated corpse. Though the others tried desperately to free him, it was too late.

Again Blind Jolene was standing with her arms crossed right beside him. After a few seconds, she turned to him. "Mr. John, yo' done left yo' family in a heap o' misery. De chile got no way o' knowin' 'bout de gift, an' worse yet, Miss Letsy gots a piece o' dat treasure dat be cursed. My, my, my, da troubles she be goin' hav'. Des nothin' we's kin do here, fo'yo' done shed yo' body. Yo' be just like me now, John Waters."

With a great sorrow in his eyes, John looked at Blind Jolene and asked, "Why didn't you tell me when you had the chance that I was going to die today?"

"John Waters, yo' knows I's cain't tell. Jolene not knowin' it goin' be dis day. I be knowin' fo' some time yo' time be near, but I's not knowin' it be dis near." Som'ting or someone be workin' evil on dis day. It be gitin' even fo' someting an' I thinks we bot' knows who it be. Come on now, we be leavin' dis here place cuz we gots tings we needs be talk 'bout."

Before John could say another word, they were both drawn into the spirit world, the other side, which would now be his home for eternity.

Chapter Twenty-Six

Letsy was in the little kitchen mixing a batch of corn bread. As she stirred, her thoughts drifted to the emerald broach. "How in the world am I going to tell John? Will he understand why I want to keep it?"

She knew it would be impossible to keep the secret from him if he suspected anything. She rationalized: "If he really wants to know, he'll find out. There's just no use. I have to tell him as soon as he walks in the door."

Figuring she might need assistance, she asked the Lord to help her do what was right. She lifted the hot black skillet from the coals. The spoonful of lard had melted, and the skillet sizzled as she poured in the cornmeal mixture. Placing the lid over the skillet, she put it back onto the hot coals. She went to the window as if she had been drawn there, and then she looked outside. Wiping the dust from the glass with her apron, she saw John standing under the big maple tree.

"What in the world is he doing home so early?" she thought. Opening the door, she walked out on the porch but found no one. She figured she was so worried about telling him that she was beginning to imagine things.

She felt a sudden coldness, a weakness, as if part of her heart had been cut away. Something bad had happened; she knew it. She went back inside and found her shawl. Wrapping a scarf around her head, she walked to the place where she thought she had seen John. She stood there for a while, silently.

Remembering the cornbread, she ran back inside and pulled it off the coals. She placed a dishtowel over the top of it to keep it moist, and then she went back outside.

This time she heard a horse and buggy approaching. Not far behind, was a mule and wagon driven by Isaiah Brooks, one of John's closest Negro friends. Somehow she sensed immediately that her husband was dead. Her knees weakened, and she fell to the ground. Looking up through her tears, she could see the face of Clyde Smith whose expression confirmed the worst. The mule and wagon had stopped a little ways down the road.

Clyde got down from the buggy and helped Letsy to her feet. "Letsy, honey, I've got some terrible news."

"It's John, ain't it Clyde? My John is dead; I can see it in your face!"

"It was a bad accident, Letsy. They did their best to save him, but it was just too bad."

Her tears flowed as if her own life were being taken. Clyde held her head on his shoulder to comfort her. She was shaking all over.

"What in God's name am I going to do?" she sobbed.

"Don't worry, Letsy. We'll take care of things."

"I want to see him, Clyde."

"No you don't, honey. He's messed up real bad."

"What do you mean, 'messed up'?"

Trying to find the right words, Clyde hesitated a moment. There was no easy way to tell her. "Letsy…," Clyde began, "a big pine fell on him and crushed him. He's mangled up pretty bad. Let us take him and get him cleaned up before you look on him."

"No, Clyde. I'll see him now. I must. Let me go, Clyde."

Pulling away, she walked toward the wagon. He tried to stop her, but she was determined. As she approached, Isaiah looked down at her.

"Missy, yo' not be needin' to sees yo' man like dis."

"Yes, I do Isaiah! I must see him now."

He jumped down into the bed of the wagon. Carefully, he kept the canvas over John's body while pulling it back from his face.

Letsy turned her head away, then she slowly turned back, to look at John's face. It was as if someone were working magic; Letsy felt she was alone with John. A soft breeze blew all around the wagon, and not another soul was in sight. John's head turned to Letsy.

Opening his eyes, he looked at her and said, "Letsy, I will always be with you and the children. I love you."

She reached out and wiped the blood and dirt off his face.

"And I'll love you forever, John."

Letsy felt such relief that they had been given the chance to say these words to each other before they parted for the last time.

"Miss Letsy? You okay, honey? Miss Letsy, can you hear me? Are you okay?"

Clyde's voice, as if from a great distance, came to her and jolted her back to reality. John was dead. Isaiah covered John's head again, and then climbed back upon the wagon seat.

"Mr. Clyde, I be getting' da mens to hep. We be getting' Mr. John all clean up now and be findin' him a right proper pine box. Ms. Letsy, we be bringin' him back to da house in a bit fo' da settin' up. Is der sometin' special yo's wants to line da box wid, Miss Letsy?" Isaiah asked.

Letsy thought for a moment, "Yes, Isaiah, there is. Just the other day John and I were in the mercantile and he took a fancy to some deep blue satin material; he thought it was so beautiful. He wanted to buy it for me so I could make myself a dress. If they still have it, tell Joe to put it on our ac…"

Before she could finish, Clyde spoke up saying, "Tell Joe to put it on my account, Isaiah."

"Yessa, Mr. Smith, I sees to it."

"One more thing before you go Isaiah," Letsy added.

She disappeared into the cabin returning with a white shirt and black jacket. Holding them to her face, tears ran down her cheek as his scent filled her senses. "Here, please dress him in these."

She looked down and then wiped her face with her apron. She felt a renewed strength, the same strength she had mustered when she confronted John after Lavenia died.

"That'll be fine. I'll be ready. Clyde I need to get the children from school. Could you carry me over there? I don't want them to hear of it from anyone else before I can be with them."

Letsy brought them home to tell them the sad news. It hit Franklin the hardest. He had never had the opportunity to resolve the anger he felt for his father. He now wanted to tell his father that he forgave him for the mistreatment his father had given him. Now he'd have to carry it forever.

Thomas and Hallie pulled themselves together for their mother. They knew she'd need them now more than ever.

Later that day, Isaiah and a helper brought John's body home. They prepared a place inside for the pine box before heading down the sandy lane to the cemetery to dig the grave. Before leaving, Isaiah hesitatingly suggested that the burial should be done first thing in the morning. She understood his meaning; even the thought turned her stomach. Hallie quickly fetched a cold rag and applied it to her forehead, easing the feeling a little.

She was moved by all the folks who came by with gifts of food, people she had not seen in years and family she didn't even know she had. Later that night after the children were asleep, she was left alone with the pine box and the empty shell that now was all that was left of her warm and loving man. It had been a long and stressful day. She stood all alone in the middle of the room staring at the box. Isaiah had done well. She would have to do something for him and his family. She stepped up beside the coffin and ran her trembling hand across the wood. "Oh, John, my heart hurts so. Words can not express the pain I am feeling. I am not sure I can make it without you." She laid her head on the box and sobbed uncontrollably.

Behind her, two spirit forms materialized from the shadows. Letsy had no sense of their presence.

"Jolene, I can't bear to see her suffering, I have to find a way to comfort her."

"Mr. John, I nos yo wants to gos to her, but yo caint. When her time bes comin' den yo kin go and hep her to make da crossin'. Come now, wes must be goin'. The two forms slowly faded back into the shadows.

Letsy was exhausted; the stress and crying had taken its toll. Taking the lantern off the table, she started for her room. She would be alone now, no warm body to snuggle up with in the bed and no early morning conversations. She would take her coffee in the mornings in silence.

She sat on the edge of the bed in the same place John sat the day he struggled with the thoughts of the hidden whisky bottle. Opening her diary, she discovered she had not made an entry since January 20, 1869. "The last entry I made was the day Everett gave me the broach." She thought.

Going over to her cedar chest, she found the little box with the broach inside. Opening it, she took the magnificent emerald out, holding it in her hand. A faint cold pain traveled up her arm. She shuddered.

"I'll put this away. It might just come in handy one day if I need money."

She took John's Bible, the broach and her diary and walked over to the secret hiding place in the floor where John kept his magic bag. Using John's knife, she pried up the piece of floor. Inside was another box that held John's other items, some photographs and letters. She put the diary, broach and Bible in the box and returned it to the secret place beside his magic bag. After covering it with the floorboard, she pulled the rug back over it. "You should be safe until I need you," she whispered.

She lay across her bed and was soon sound asleep.

Little Nellie, being the youngest, continued her daydreaming, not really able to understand what had happened and not yet aware that she would never see her father again. She continued talking to her imaginary friends, quite content in her own little world and totally unaware of the power within.

Letsy and the children walked out onto the porch. To their surprise, the front yard was filled with people. It was burial day, and she felt a certain comfort that so many had taken their time to show concern for her and the children. They fell in behind the wagon and followed it down the road to the small cemetery. Letsy could still smell the fresh earth, which reminded her of spring planting.

Meanwhile, the same two spirits stood back away from the group that had gathered. John and Jolene watched as the preacher said his words and then turned to Letsy to comfort her and the children.

Jolene broke their silence. "Well, Mr. John, what's yo' gwine do now?"

"I don't know, Jolene. This is something I'll have to deal with. I should have listened to you a long time ago. I should have told Nellie. You know that bothers me, but not as much as Letsy having that damned broach. I had decided what to do about it, but I didn't get the chance."

The boys who had worked with John slowly lowered the box down into the dark hole. After the service, Letsy and the children stood by while each shovel of dirt fell back into the grave. Each shovel full that hit the box sent a vibration through Letsy that slightly moved her body. It took all the courage she could muster to stay there, her eyes fixed on the grave. Closing out the voices around her, she retreated deep inside herself. She had numbed herself to the rest of the mourners, as if she were the only person left alive in the whole world.

Chapter Twenty-Seven

Letsy Waters sat in her rocker on the front porch of the little house in which she had lived just about her entire life. The year was now 1922, and she was in her late 80s. She had started growing old the day John died. She rocked back and forth looking out over the yard. Her eyes were weak, and her bones ached from the years of hard work.

She could hear Nellie in the house cleaning the breakfast dishes. Nellie was the only one of her children who had stayed. The others were gone. Nellie had married Luke Bass, the son of a tobacco farmer. His family home was not too far from the Waters homestead. After she had married Luke, Nellie demanded that they live with Letsy because she knew her mother could not handle the place on her own. They had added a new room to the house and a few other conveniences for the kitchen that made the little house more livable for the family.

It was springtime, and Luke had left early to help his brothers plant the year's tobacco crop. That left the two women at home alone with Nellie's granddaughter, Annie. Luke and Nellie had been blessed with three children, two boys who were now serving in the army and a daughter who died giving birth to Annie. The child's father tried to take care of her, but it was just too hard for him. He asked Nellie and Luke if they would take her and raise her. Bad luck seemed to follow him; a few months after leaving Annie with Nellie and Luke, he was killed in an accident on the Waccamaw River.

Annie was busy playing in the yard while Letsy kept an eye on her. As Letsy watched Annie playing, she reminisced about her own children.

What could she have done to make life better for them? But now here she was, an old woman waiting for her own time to come, way too late for any changes.

Franklin ended up drinking himself to death. There was nothing she was able to say or do to help Franklin with his demons. He had relied on the bottle as his escape from the bad memories, much the same as his father had done before the epiphany.

Faced with the never-ending work on the farm, Thomas grew discontented with what seemed to him a dismal future. He decided to leave. No one had heard from him since.

Hallie had married a cruel man who beat her all the time. Finally, after one too many beatings, Hallie had died. They said he beat her so badly you couldn't even recognize her. He would spend the rest of his life in prison, but Letsy took little comfort in that.

She withdrew further with each loss. She no longer enjoyed going to town, and she completely stopped going to church. She was content to sit on the porch and watch the road, as if she were waiting for someone.

Nellie seemed to be blessed, though. When she met Luke, her intuition told her he was a good man. She had a way of sizing folks up, for good or bad. She sensed from whom to stay away as well as whom she could trust. Luke was well thought of by people in the community. He was always helping folks, and he took care of what was left of the Waters family.

A light breeze that gently touched her face seemed somehow familiar, as though it had touched her before. The strands of gray hair that tickled her face made her turn her head toward the old maple tree. Her knotty, wrinkled hands pulled the strands back. Retrieving a pin from her twisted up bun, she secured her hair.

At first, she shivered only slightly, but then the wind intensified. It felt almost like a cold hand resting on her shoulder. She blinked her hazel eyes against the bright morning sun that warmed her face. On such a nice day, why in the world was she feeling such deep coldness around her? Her shawl had fallen down behind her. She pulled it up over her shoulders and continued rocking in the old chair. Suddenly, the empty rocker next to her began to move rhythmically.

"What in the world? The wind must be playing tricks on this old woman," she thought.

She reached over to stop the chair, and as she did, she felt the chill intensify. As her hand reached the armrest, someone or something took hold of it. It numbed her old thin skin. She jerked her hand away, and rubbed it with the other to warm it. Slowly, she looked back to the other rocker. Were her old eyes playing tricks on her? Sitting right there beside her was John! Was she finally losing her mind? She had heard stories about old folks seeing people from their past, but this was just too much. Frightened by the image, she started trembling. The apparition, so lifelike, just grinned at her. She could see his deep green eyes—they were John's eyes—and his presence left her speechless.

Annie still played in the yard, oblivious to the scene unfolding on the porch. Letsy finally found her voice, shaky as it was. She asked Annie if she could see the man in the chair sitting next to her.

"Granny Letsy, there ain't nobody in that chair. You must be playing with me." Annie laughed and continued her play.

"Sweetie, there is! It's my John! He's sitting right here in this rocker."

"Granny, there's nobody on that porch but you. You're just playing with me."

"Oh, no, baby! I wouldn't do that. Oh, just never mind."

Still shaking, she turned back to the rocker and mustered the courage to whisper, "John, is that you?" She kept her voice low so Annie wouldn't hear.

"Yes, Letsy, it is. I didn't mean to upset you. You're the only one who can see me."

"Oh my God, can it really be you? Why are you coming to me like this? You've been gone so long. I'm not sure if you're real or not."

She continued to tremble, and then she started to cry. Her old wrinkled hands clasped each other in a futile attempt to stop the shaking. Her first thoughts were that the angel of death had come for her.

The apparition smiled at Letsy in John's familiar, loving way. "Letsy, I am real but only to you. Please don't be upset. There are things I never got to tell you. I've struggled with them since I passed. It's important that I tell you before your time comes."

The spirit moved closer to Letsy. She looked deep into his handsome eyes.

"You know the powers I used when I helped other folks?"

Still trembling, her weak voice answered him. "Yes, John, I do." Puzzled, she added, "Oh! But I've never told anyone! I've kept it a secret all these years."

He patted her hand. "I know you have. It would have been all right if you had told someone, after all, I am gone."

She reached for her little hanky and wiped the tears from her cheeks.

"Letsy, I don't want you to keep it a secret anymore. I want you to tell Nellie. She needs to know about it. She has the power too."

"Why Nellie?" questioned Letsy.

"You know why, Letsy. Remember when she was talking to Blind Jolene? You remember that, don't you?"

"Yes, I do now, but I've forgotten so much, John. I'm so old now; my memory's gone." Again the tears flowed.

"I know, Letsy. That's why I want you to tell her as much as you can remember. She has the same gift, and she needs to know about it. You've got to tell her everything you can remember. Tell her about the good things I did with it; tell her about the treasure hunt. Tell her that she, too, has this gift and that it will be passed down to one of her children."

Letsy shook her head. "But John, Nellie will think I have lost what little mind I have left."

John glanced out at Annie. "I know, Letsy, but with each new birth, the gift is passed on. Annie has it now. It'll go on for generation after generation, just as it always has. It may not be strong in some, but one day a child will be born whose powers will be as strong as mine. The story must be told when they are old enough to understand the gift.

Pausing a moment, he turned his right hand over to expose a birthmark that resembled a snake "But only a few will be marked by the serpent; they will be the most gifted and will have the knowledge needed to use all the powers. The powers, if not used correctly, can drive them to the dark side as almost happened to me. That's why it's important that the story of the gift be told.

"There's something else. I know you've forgotten about it, the emerald broach that Everett gave you a long time ago. You've got to tell Nellie where it is, and she must throw it in the river. It is cursed; it was part of that treasure we found. If it's not thrown into the water, a river or the ocean, it'll curse our family forever as it has for years now. This you must do, Letsy, and do it soon. Letsy, I must go now, but I'll see you again soon."

With that said, John's spirit vanished as quickly as it had appeared.

Letsy struggled to stand. Her old weak heart was taxed to its limits. Looking for her husband, she slowly turned around and called his name repeatedly.

When she finally accepted that he was gone, she tried to think of where she had placed the broach. Over the years, she had begun habitually to misplace things. She strained to recover the memory of this one thing. After John died, she had taken the emerald broach and placed it in a smaller box with some of John's things. She put them away somewhere, but she couldn't for the life of her remember where.

Picking up her cane, she started into the house; she stopped for a minute to think where she might have hid them. "What in Jesus' name did I do with that box?" she thought. As she struggled to remember, her confusion turned to desperation.

"You know, I think I may have thrown that stuff away. Or maybe I gave it away," she offered quietly to no one.

She flopped back down in the rocker. "Oh Lord, I just don't know. John, you'll have to forgive me; I just can't remember anymore."

She sat, staring out toward the old maple tree.

Wiping her hands on her apron, Nellie came out on the porch. "Mama, who in the world are you talking to out here?"

"Oh, just talking to myself and Annie here."

Annie looked up at Letsy. She rolled her eyes to show that she thought her Granny was crazy.

Nellie sensed that something had made her mother uncomfortable, and so she quickly changed the subject. "Well, I've done the dishes and put everything away. Would you like to help me with some stitching on the quilt?"

Yes, honey, that'd be fine. Could we bring it out on the porch?"

"Sure, Mama. I'll gather it together, and we can work out here."

Letsy reasoned to herself that this would be a good time to talk with Nellie about the gift. She wanted to say her piece before she forgot what John had asked her to do.

When Nellie returned with the quilt, the women went right to work. Although Letsy was old, she could still hold her own when it came to stitching on a quilt. It was one of the few things that gave her the satisfaction of knowing that she could still help Nellie.

Nellie had a way about her that was calming. She loved life, and she didn't let the misfortunes of her siblings cause her unhappiness.

"It is such a gorgeous day, Mama," she said, smiling.

"Yes, honey, it is that."

Letsy stopped stitching. Taking a deep breath, she spoke to Nellie. "Honey, I need to tell you some things about yourself that you may not be aware of."

"Well, what in the world could that be, Mama?" Nellie asked in a puzzled tone.

Letsy began telling her daughter about John and his special gift. She told her it was in the bloodline, all the way back to a time before his family had come to the new world. She told Nellie of her father's problems dealing with it throughout his life. She related the story of the treasure hunt and how Everett came to give her the emerald broach. Many of the details were missing because her old memory was unable to recall everything. Most important, she had forgotten where she had put the broach.

Finding it hard to believe her mother's outrageous stories, Nellie was stunned, to say the least. As her mother rambled on, Nellie listened with a large amount of skepticism. She wondered, though, if the ghostly forms she had always dismissed as the changing slant of the sun's light actually could be apparitions. And what about the sounds, the voices far away, that distant hum, the people talking? At times, she had thought she was losing her mind. Was her father's power, her power, the reason she had made so many good decisions in her life? Could this be why her life had taken such a different turn from her siblings' lives?

"Really now," she thought. "Is this nothing more than just my mother's feeble old mind playing tricks on her?"

Letsy finally admitted that, sadly, she could no longer remember what she had done with the broach. Nellie told her not to worry about it, that they would find it. Later that day, Letsy insisted that they begin the search for the broach. They looked everywhere, even out in the old barn and shed, but they found nothing. Nellie's heart wasn't really in the search. She just didn't totally believe the story. Ironically, if she had only been taught to use the gift, she could have found the emerald broach in minutes.

A few days later, Letsy sat again in her rocker on the porch. Annie and Nellie were inside getting ready for supper. Suddenly, the wind blew as it had the day John appeared.

A voice whispered in her ear, "Remember the secret place."

Filled with excitement, she struggled to stand up. She grabbed her cane and opened the screen door. Quickly, she crossed the room to the hallway.

Annie and Nellie stopped what they were doing and watched Letsy disappear into her room. Nellie could tell that her mother was on some sort of mission. She followed her silently and then watched from the open door. As she observed the strange events taking place, she came to the conclusion that Letsy's old mind was gone.

Looking down at the floor, Letsy circled the room and talked under her breath. She would occasionally bang her cane against the wood floor.

Backing away from the door, Nellie closed her eyes with grief. She knew the time had come, that her mama had to be watched now more closely. Worse yet, she didn't want to leave Annie alone with her. She returned to the kitchen and resumed her cooking.

In the meantime, Letsy continued her search for the hiding place; she forgot that Luke had put down a new floor over the old one. Growing frustrated, she gave up her search and returned to her rocker on the front porch. By the time she had sat down, she had completely forgotten why she had gone inside.

Feeling John's presence, she turned and looked over to the other rocker; there he was, rocking back and forth. "You did your best, Letsy. I guess I waited too long. Now it's time for us to go."

"What do you mean, John? Where are we going?"

A beautiful light appeared to Letsy, wrapping its warm, glowing rays all around her. It was such a beautiful sight and indescribably comforting. From its source, people motioned for her to come with them. She stood up and started toward them. She looked back for John, only to see her mortal body slumped over the chair. She now understood; her time had come. John had come to get her as she always knew he would.

After Letsy was laid to rest, Nellie spent a lot of time trying to understand what her mother had told her. She struggled with the possibility that there might be truth to what her mother had said. Parts of the story fit so well. Other parts offered explanations for some of the strange occurrences in her own life. She sensed that she might one day have to face something that she'd rather avoid. Ultimately, her decision was to put that time off for as long as she had the option.

She and Luke soon sold the old place and moved to his family farm nearer to his brothers. They both seemed happier having more family around. Annie would now have friends to play and attend school with.

The old house fell into ruin. A wisteria vine that grew on the corner of the porch eventually covered the homestead completely. Undergrowth grew up around until the old house was almost hidden from view. The nearby fields became part of a large tobacco farm. The old house and barn stood like an island in the great ocean of tobacco, just another forgotten memory. Still, in a hidden and forgotten location, lay the broach, the connection to the curse that had devastated the Waters family for generations. Now, seemingly lost forever, it was free to continue its lethal haunting.

PART TWO

Chapter Twenty-Eight

The River's Edge Café smelled of fried food, sweaty workers, and attorneys doused with cheap cologne. The noise included the steady hum of muffled conversation, with an occasional out-burst of laughter and plates clanging against one another. The Café was across the street from the County Courthouse, which was always crowded when court was in session.

Without speaking, Rainey Alexander and her mother sipped their coffee. Both women stared through the dirty window as people came and went from the Café. Occasionally, Rainey would recognize someone, acknowledge their greeting, and then return to her silent vigil. Both were recovering from the sentencing of Tom "Storm" Spencer earlier that day before Judge Thornton. Ten years. Most likely he'd be out in three.

"What a waste!" Rainey thought. "Hopefully he'd get some type of anger counseling while in prison." Her intuition was that if something wasn't done to help her brother soon, the next time he might be facing a murder charge.

Tom was Rainey's twin brother. She was born first, after a long hard labor for Annie, their mother. Tom came soon after, delivered with no problems. They were as different as night and day: Rainey, with green eyes and dark auburn hair; Tom, blond with stormy blue eyes. Rainey had followed her mother's side, and Tom, his father's. Part of Tom's inheritance was his father's dark disposition. Early on he had been pegged with the appropriate nickname "Storm."

Tom Spencer had been known to go a little crazy when he drank too much, but this time he had gone over the line. During a fight, Tom had cut up a local good old boy really bad. The police found him crouching over his victim. He was still holding his yellow-handled, razor-sharp Case pocketknife, which was covered in blood. It took five officers to finally get him under control for Tom was half out of his mind. He spent the first night in a straight jacket under suicide watch in the county jail. He had been on the edge most of his life; it didn't take much to push him into a mindless rage. Rainey herself had given up on her brother after he tried to choke her during an argument. She loved him, but he was not the same brother she'd known as a child.

Rainey sensed the other patrons trying to get a closer look at her and her mother. Everyone knew Rainey was in town for the sentencing. The place had not changed one bit; people still thrived on gossip and on other people's misery.

The waitress plopping their food down in front of them snapped both women back to life. Monday's special: fried fish, slaw, and French fries. The waitress reeked of cooking odors, cheap perfume, and lots of hair spray. The strong smells almost took Rainey's breath away. Tearing the ticket out of her little book, the waitress laid it on the table. Rainey quickly grabbed it before her mother could.

"Lunch is on me, Mama," she said smiling.

The waitress remained beside the table. Puzzled, Rainey looked up.

The waitress grinned really big. Then she asked, "Rainey, you don't remember me, do ya?"

She did look familiar, but Rainey couldn't for the life of her place the face. Could it have been the poorly applied makeup or, perhaps, the bleached hair with dark roots that deceived her memory?

"Who is this woman? Do I know her?" she asked herself.

"It's me, Brenda Sue."

"Oh, my goodness, Brenda. I am so sorry. I've had so much on my mind. I just didn't recognize you."

Rainey took her hand and held it for a moment. "Brenda, this is my mother."

"How are you, Mrs. Spencer? I know all about Tom. I know this has been real hard for you. But you know, he's better off in a place where he can get some help."

This advice had spilled out of Brenda Sue's red painted lips before Annie Spencer could say a word.

Rainey saw tears well up in her mother's eyes. "Thanks, Brenda, but could you…? Please?"

"Oh, sure. I'll leave you two alone. I know you're not in any mood to talk about it. If I can get you anything, just flag me down."

As she turned to leave the table, the waitress looked back at Rainey and silently mouthed, "I'm so sorry."

Rainey held her mother's hand across the table. She spoke low so the others couldn't hear.

"I know this is killing you mother, but there's not a thing we can do now. Tom has chosen this path."

Annie wiped the tears from her eyes with her napkin. "Rainey, I can't tell you how heart-broken I am about this. My whole life has been this way. I still don't understand why your daddy had to die in that car wreck. You and Tom were so young. I did my best raising you kids, but somewhere I failed with Tom. It's so hard for a mother to take the place of a father."

Rainey moved the food around on the plate with her fork as she considered Annie's statement. "You did your best. The odds were just against you when it came to Tom. Now eat your lunch before it gets cold."

Feeling that the mood needed to change, she smiled at her mother across the table. "Do you remember the story you used to tell me about your Great-Grandfather John? I loved that story and so much wanted it to be true. It would have been so cool to have the kind of gifts he had. And that treasure hunt! Just think how exciting it would have been. I know it was just a story, but I've thought many times how it might be if we could have powers like that."

Glancing up for a moment, Annie turned her head as if she was looking for something far away. "Honey, I know you always thought it to be a fairy tale, but your great-grandmother Nellie, she swore it to be the truth."

Rainey recalled what she could of her great-grandmother. She was only six when Nellie died, but she did remember a few things about her. The one thing for sure was that she was probably the oldest person she had ever known. Rainey would lean on the arm of Nellie's rocker. She'd stare at her face and count the lines in her wrinkled skin. The smell of snuff permeated her clothing. The small Maxwell House Coffee jar, half-filled with spittle, caused Rainey to back away with fear when the lid was removed. Eventually, Nellie would grow weary of her hanging on to the rocker and run her off.

"Nellie was a sweet old lady, but, I just found it hard being around her. She was always so caught up in those books and in that half pint she kept in her apron. I'd sneak around and catch her taking a little nip on it now and then, when she thought no one was looking. I now wished that I had made the effort to get to know her better."

Rainey laughed. "Mom, do you remember how she would sit in the den and look out the window? She swore that there were people in the big magnolia tree in the front yard. And at night, she'd get up and swish a straw broom under her bed. Remember, she said there was somebody under it."

Annie sighed deeply. "Yes, I remember. Those were difficult times, her growing old. I hated it when I had to put her in the nursing home. She was the only mother I knew because my real mother died when I was born. Grandma Nellie told me the doctors had told her not to have any more children, but she ended up pregnant again and bled to death during my delivery."

Again, Annie sighed. "My father died soon afterward in a drowning accident on the river. All I ever remember is Nellie was my mother and Luke my father and great grandmother Letsy helped out too."

Rainey found herself gazing at her mother. She followed the movement of her lips, but she heard nothing she was saying. She had heard the story too many times.

As Annie continued, she mentioned Letsy again. "Grandma Nellie told me how Letsy would sit on the porch and talk to herself, as if she was having a conversation with someone. She told the story about the evil spell cast on the treasure that John and his cousins had uncovered. That's the story of the treasure hunt, the one I first told you about when you were a little girl."

"I know, Mama. I will never forget that story." Rainey found parts of her family history dull, especially compared to the exploits of the gifted John. He was far more interesting than any of the others.

"You know, it's funny. While I was doing my research on the family, I had the chance to speak with some of the old folks that were still around. Some of them knew of other stories passed down about John Waters' ability to do mystical things. Those stories make me think there could be some truth in it all." Annie shrugged her shoulders.

Rainey's mood perked up considerably. "So, you mean to say that the story could possibly be true?"

"Well, sure, I guess so. But I've never really thought about it in that way."

Rainey's mouth dropped open.

"Mama, look at our lives, look at all the heartache our family has experienced. I'd have to say it's altogether possible that some kind of curse has been on us. Wouldn't you agree?"

Annie whispered across the table to Rainey, "I guess we could have a curse on us. But even if we did, how would we find someone who could break such a spell? Maybe there's a local witch or root doctor looking for work? I can't say as I know of any right off the top of my head; how about you?" Annie chuckled at the comment, drank down some ice tea, and watched her daughter's expression fade.

Rainey rolled her eyes. "Now, Mama, according to the story, some part of that treasure would still have to be in our family. If you don't have anything and your brothers are dead, you're the only one left that remembers Letsy and the story. Or is it possible that there is something hidden somewhere, in a place that is in some way connected to us?"

Annie shook her head. "But Rainey, honey, there is no one else; so just forget all this nonsense."

"Oh, come on now, Mama, work with me here. Don't close your mind to the possibility of something that could be real. Think about it, please?"

Annie shrugged. "Okay. The only place that comes to mind would be that old house out at Adrian. That's where John and Letsy lived, and my family too, but I only lived there briefly, as a child. The last time I was there, the old place was still standing but it had taken to leaning considerably. It's most likely unsafe to go in."

Rainey's eyes scanned the café, but her mind was in high gear on this new information. Refocusing her attention back at her mother, she declared, "Let's go out there. Let's go right after we eat."

In disbelief, Annie hesitated for a few seconds and then adamantly replied, "No, not just no, but absolutely no. I am not going out there."

Rainey folded her arms in disgust. "Mama, I don't think you know what to believe. I think a part of you wants to find out and then a part of you just wants to bury your head in the sand. Forget Tom, Daddy, and everything that has ever happened to this family. I agree. I'd like to run away, too, write Tom off, and never come back here. But I can't. I want to know why. What about all the family research you've done? Isn't there anything in it that might tell us something?"

Rainey had her mother's attention now. She could see Annie wasn't comfortable with her own daughter's accusations, but Annie knew Rainey was right. She had always tried to run from her past. There were many things in her personal history that Annie wasn't exactly proud of. She did her best to keep them under wraps.

After several minutes of soul searching, Annie brought herself back to the present. "There are some documents I've found that might lend some truth to the story."

"Are you suggesting that now you think the story could be true, that your great-grandfather actually found a buried treasure that had a curse on it?"

"Now mind you, I'm not absolutely certain of any of this, but I believe it might be so. Now that I think back, not one of my ancestors had a normal life after that treasure was supposed to have been found. All of them had some sort of tragic ending to their lives; even John died in a terrible accident."

Annie leaned a little closer to Rainey and whispered, "I've even found out where they came from."

"And what does that have to do with the story?" Rainey asked.

Annie perked up; obviously proud of all the knowledge she had gained in her research of their family. "You, my child, have Scottish blood running in your veins. Not just any Scottish blood, blood from an ancient clan believed to have mystical powers."

Annie could see that her daughter's creative mind was shifting into high gear. Regretting a little that she had let the conversation go this far, she added, "Rainey, even if there was such a broach, nobody today would know where it was. Anybody could have it by now; for all we know, it could be a thousand miles from here."

Rainey pushed her plate away. As she downed her sweet iced tea, she shifted that creative mind into overdrive.

Sensing that Rainey was formulating some sort of plan, Annie glanced around the restaurant. Many of the other patrons were looking their way; she wiped her hands with her napkin, pushed her partially eaten plate of food aside, and gathered up her purse. "I'm ready to leave. I've had enough of people staring at us. I'll be outside at the car."

The heat of the day was at its peak. Annie fanned herself with an old power bill she had found in her purse. "Where is that girl. I'm melting out here! "Annie thought to herself.

Finally, Rainey left the Café. Annie watched as her daughter moved across the parking lot; her body shimmered in the heat that rose from the asphalt. Annie took pride in her beautiful daughter and seized the opportunity for a little prayer that nothing bad would ever happen to her.

The two women climbed into the car. Rainey grabbed the wheel as usual, instantly her fingers recoiled in agony from heat. She started the engine, which allowed the air conditioner to spew its initial blasts of hot air into the interior. It had its work cut out for it, as both the temperature and humidity had to be in the nineties.

"Man, oh man. I'd forgotten about the heat and humidity down here. The mountains have really spoiled me, and yet there's something about this heat that I love. I guess it brings back fond memories of my childhood."

Memories as sweet as a cold Pepsi on a hot summer day. Back when she and Tom were inseparable. Before neither one noticed the opposite sex, when they were one, the "Spencer twins." Just kids, hanging out; getting into trouble. They spent their summers either swimming in the river or holed up in Tom's tree house. With their mother working, they were left to take care of themselves; in other words, they both grew up pretty fast.

―――――

She lifted her hair off her neck with one hand, draping the other over the hot steering wheel. She slowly maneuvered through the streets of Conway back to her mother's house.

Annie knew Rainey was still thinking about their conversation back at the Café. "Rainey, you know I've spent a lot of time at the courthouse doing research. Some of what I've found might indicate there could be something to this curse thing. I came across records that related to the men who went with John to look for that treasure. Every one of them died a tragic death after they allegedly found the loot. Even John himself, he ended up dying when a tree fell on him. I know none of these things actually prove anything by themselves, but if you consider all of them together...."

Rainey didn't respond. She was in deep thought. Continuing to twist her hair around with her fingers, she stared at the road ahead of her. After several minutes without a word, she pulled over onto the shoulder of the road. Placing the car in park, she turned and faced her mother.

"Mama, as long as I can remember I've been having this recurring nightmare that scares me to death. Lately here, I've been having it two or three times a week. It's about to get the best of me. I'm afraid to close my eyes for fear I'll have it again."

"Tell me about it. Maybe I can help."

Rainey took a deep breath. Resting her head on the steering wheel, she started. "Well, it begins with a man's voice, and what is so weird is that he has an English accent. I don't know anyone with an English accent. He seems to be far away; it's foggy and I am trying to follow the voice in the fog. Then I see something hanging from a tree. When I get close enough, I can see it's a man's body. The body looks as though it's been hanging there a long, long time. Can you believe it, a rotting corpse, hanging from a tree, and it's talking to me? I think that it's asking me to help it, but I can never figure out how it wants me to help. Oh God, it's so gross looking. I don't even want to think about it. It's been occurring more and more often; it's really bothering me. You know how I am about dreams. There are dreams and then there are message dreams, and this one has a message. When I wake up, I have this overpowering desire to help this man; I feel guilty that I can't."

Rainey was visibly upset; Annie felt it best not to comment further right then. Having just seen her brother carted off to prison, Rainey had enough stress. Their shared inability to help Tom in his darkness had left both women feeling quite helpless. It was possible that the situation had some bearing on these dreams.

"Okay, let's just go home, and you can take a nap. We'll talk more about your dream when you're rested." Annie then added in her best, Scarlett O'Hara accent: "And since you'll be leaving tomorrow, I'll make your favorites for supper: fried chicken, mashed potatoes, and butter beans."

Rainey managed to smile reassuringly. "Sounds good. I haven't had butter beans in ages."

Chapter Twenty-Nine

"Rainey, my beautiful one, do you hear me? Rainey, Rainey Alexander, help me. Please help me." The eerie, constant voice comes from far away. "You must help me. Come, help me." She picks her way through vines; the fog is so thick she can move it with her hands. She can barely distinguish the dark images moving ahead of her. The voice continues to summon her.

Suddenly she feels a strange sensation, as if she were flying across the ground toward the body hanging from a tree. As she approaches, the corpse spins around. The eyes are blood red; flesh hangs from the rotting face and hands. With a wave of his dangling arm, the sinister form beckons her to come closer.

Who is this? A feeling of familiarity rushes over her; he is someone from long ago. His clothing suggests the eighteenth century: a waistcoat, a ruffled blouse, and high leather boots. Why is he calling her name?

As she nears, he speaks to her. "Rainey, I need you. Something very precious was stolen from me, and only you can find it. I have waited for you for many years. You have the gift; just like John Waters, another of your line. He helped them take it from me; you have the power to help me get it back. There is an emerald broach that was in the treasure stolen from me; it belonged to Annabelle, my Annabelle. You see, I promised her I would keep it for her forever, but your ancestor John waters stole it from me. I beg you to help me get it back!"

The body spins around again. The glare of the red eyes burns into her soul. Two distinct emanations come from the apparition: one is sympathetic, in dire need of help; the other is evil personified. The evil, which seems the stronger, causes Rainey to scream as loud as she can.

"Rainey, honey, wake up! It's okay. I'm right here."

Rainey sat straight up on the couch. Standing over her, Annie tried to comfort her.

"Mama! Mama!" She cried. Grabbing hold of her mother, Rainey tried to catch her breath before she blurted out, "It's the broach, the one from the treasure hunt. That's what the man in my dream is looking for! The broach, he wants me to find that broach!"

Speaking fast and breathlessly, she squeezed her mother's hands and continued. "Mama, you've got to tell me where the old house is. I'm going to see if I can find it!"

"Rainey, it's the middle of the summer. That old house is probably full of copperheads, spiders, and who knows what else. You don't want to be going off into those fields this time of year. Besides, they're probably still full of tobacco; you'll get filthy."

Annie Spencer found Rainey's enthusiasm disquieting. "Who in the world is this man that you keep dreaming about?"

Rainey, still drenched in sweat, looked at her mother excitedly and said, "Mama, I believe he could be that pirate from the story, the one John took the treasure from. He wants that broach back!"

Annie started to cry. "God, this has got to stop. Do you realize what you're saying? If others were to hear this nonsense, they'd think we're both crazy, just like your brother."

"Mama, no one will find out about this unless one of us tells. I'm not going to say a word. Now, if I'm right and it is the pirate, we could both be in real danger. Think about what's happened to our ancestors."

Annie pleaded, "You can't go out to that old house alone, and I'm too old to go with you."

"Mama, I don't know if there's anything to this or not, but if I don't at least try, we'll never know. We'll always wonder if there really was a curse on the family. And Mama, I've got a lot of questions I want answered. There's a lot I remember from my childhood that seems strange, things I've never understood. I've dreamed of this man since I was a little girl. I know now he's telling me something. He's calling me from somewhere, Mama, and I have to find out if there is anything to it."

Annie plopped down on the couch. Shaking her head, she said, "What in the world have I started?"

Rainey paced back and forth as she ranted about the man in the dream. Sensing that her mother knew more, she urged Annie to tell her anything else she could remember.

"Mama, what else have you learned? You've got to tell me everything; I have to know it all."

By now Annie was very upset, her face tensed with worry. "I think I might have to take one of my pills. This is getting the best of my nerves."

She kept a bottle of Xanax in her medicine cabinet for times of emergency, and this was sure beginning to seem like one of those times. Rainey wasn't going to give up; she could be darned persistent.

After a few minutes Annie gave in. "Well, I don't know if this will explain your nightmare, but I will tell you why I believe there may be something to this curse."

Annie paused to gather her thoughts. Then she began. "When I was little, maybe nine or ten, Grandma Nellie had a breakdown of some sort. Grandpa Luke had to put her in the hospital in Columbia for a while. I don't know what happened or why they took her away so fast. One night I eavesdropped on Grandpa Luke and the preacher; they were out in the kitchen having coffee. Now Grandpa Luke was saying something about Nellie talking with a voodoo woman who often came to her at night. He said there were other spirits that she could see and could talk with. Now I'm here to tell you, my Grandpa Luke was a good man, and he took good care of us. But he was a Bible thumper, and there was no way he was going to allow his wife to act in such a way. He said it was the work of the devil; so he had her committed. He came from a prominent tobacco farming family, and he didn't want rumors circulating about him or his family. When she came home, she never again mentioned such things in front of him, but she would tell me stories about her family. Now we joke about her seeing people in the old magnolia tree, but maybe, Rainey, she really did see them. I wish she were still alive. I'll bet she could tell you all you need to know."

Annie continued, "After she returned home, she didn't have much to do with Grandpa Luke. She started drinking, and she never set foot in another church. One day I was out playing in the yard. She came out the back door and sat down on the steps. Pulling her little pint out of her apron, she took a sip and returned it to the pocket. She called me over to sit with her and talk. I must have been around nine or ten; this was after we had moved away from the old place at Adrian. She wanted to talk about her mother, Letsy. She always did this when she was drinking. I guess she just really missed her."

Annie paused for a second. "Now, I remember Letsy as just a sweet old lady, but according to Grandma Nellie, Letsy told her about John's supernatural gift and how he could talk with dead folks. For the most part, I always thought that it was just the alcohol talking.

The story I remember best… and only because I saw it transpire before my very eyes, was the day…"

Annie sighed deeply, then continued. "I remember the day just as clear as a bell. Grandma Nellie and Letsy started acting mighty strange." Annie paused again, "Have I told you this story? You know how I've started to repeat myself here lately."

"I'll stop you if you have. Please go on." Rainey said with deep interest.

"I was out playing in the front yard of the old place at Adrian. Letsy was on the porch in her rocker. As I played I noticed she was looking intently at the chair beside her and appeared to be talking to it. After a few minutes, she asked me if I could see her husband, John, sitting next to her. There wasn't anyone in that chair so, of course, I thought she was just playing with me. I told her that I didn't see anyone. I went about my play but noticed she continued talking to the empty rocker. Then, out of the blue, she started to cry. In a few minutes Grandma Nellie came out and asked Letsy who she was talking to. Letsy told her no one and then looked down at me. I guess she feared I might say something to the contrary. Grandma Nellie went back in and brought out a quilt and started to work on it. I acted like I wasn't paying any attention, but I was listening. Letsy told Grandma Nellie the story about some kind of gift that was in our family. Finally, I heard Grandma Nellie say she'd look in the old barn to see if she could find it. Letsy was insistent about going out to the barn with her; it was obvious that she was anxious about something. When they came out of the barn, Grandma Nellie went inside. Letsy began to pace back and forth on the porch. She was wringing her hands and mumbling to herself. I couldn't, for the life of me, figure out what they were looking for."

"Well, what then?" Rainey pleaded.

Pausing for a moment, Annie took a deep breath and continued. "The next day, they just about tore the house up. I kept asking what they were doing, and Grandma Nellie kept answering 'cleaning.' After several hours, she stopped and told Letsy not to worry about it anymore, that it was gone. Whatever it was, Letsy was really disappointed that Grandma Nellie wasn't able to find it. For days after that, Letsy would sit on the porch for hours in silence. I just figured she was pondering something deeply. I knew, though, it had to do with whatever they had been looking for. "A few days later, Grandma Nellie found Letsy in her rocker. She had passed on.

"That's just one of the stories Grandma Nellie told me about Letsy. The best was the story about the treasure hunt, yes, by far the best. She had a way with words; she would draw you in and then she would laugh and say, 'You know it's just a story, so don't say anything to Grandpa Luke, okay?'"

Clutching a pillow tightly, Rainey fell back against the couch. Her mind flashed back to the treasure hunt. "I think they were looking for the broach. It's the one that belongs to the pirate, and the one I keep dreaming about. It has to be. I'll bet he cursed the broach and whoever possessed it, too."

Rainey always followed her intuitions. Something in her gut now told her she was on the right track.

"Now Rainey, I know for a fact that all those men who rode with John on the treasure hunt had tragic deaths. The courthouse records pretty well establish that fact. Let me see… what did I do with all the records I copied at the Courthouse?"

Annie disappeared into her bedroom. In a few minutes, she returned with a book.

"If you're determined to go on this wild goose chase, you should know who your people were and where they came from. This might help you."

Annie passed the book to Rainey as if it were a sacred document. Rainey could feel energy flowing from the book the instant she touched it. There was a quick flash, a vision of someone, a man. Shaking her head, she deliberately cleared her thoughts before she opened the book.

Waters Family Research—Our Scottish Lineage. As she slowly turned the pages, she came to a section of old photographs. The people in these pictures were stoic.

"Why was it that the people back then didn't smile when they had a picture made?" She asked her mother.

Annie laughed. "Well, I've heard that the folks had to wait so long for the process that they became impatient with each other, and the photo reflected it."

The names of each person were written under the picture. As Rainey ran her fingers over their images, the names rang out in her mind, as if she had known them all her life. In fact, she had never even heard of most of them.

Annie pointed to one of the pictures that showed an older woman, a girl, and four boys. All four of the boys were dressed in confederate uniforms. "Now, this bunch here was Bertha Waters and her children. It was taken right before the boys went off to war." Pointing out the two youngest ones, she said, "These two were killed in the war. The other two are Everett and Levi. They're the ones that went with John on that treasure hunt."

Mesmerized by the old photographs, Rainey studied them closely. "Did Bertha not have a husband?" she asked.

"Oh, yes, it's my understanding that he was kicked in the head by a mule and died from his injury. He was John's uncle."

"What a terrible way to die," Rainey said. She felt she knew them all. "Now, Everett, I'll bet he was a mean scoundrel, and Levi, from the way he looks, he had to be a fun-loving joker."

Annie confirmed her opinions of Everett and Levi. "You're right about Everett; arrest records prove that he was quite the trouble maker."

Looking further down the page, Rainey came to a photograph of a man and woman. The names under the picture read, "John and Letsy Waters." "Oh, so this is John Waters? He does have a mysterious look about him, so handsome. And Letsy, she is such a beautiful woman. Now I understand why I'm so gorgeous; it's those good genes," she added, laughing and winking.

Staring at the picture for a few minutes, she found John's face to be hypnotic. Unable to take her eyes off of him, she could almost hear him speaking—but surely it was her imagination at work.

Closing her eyes, Rainey ran her hand over the picture. Another quick flash. The man was trying to communicate with her. She had never had visions like this before. Fear welled up in her, but she pushed it aside and tried to open her mind to any possibility.

Annie had no idea what Rainey was experiencing. "You keep this awhile and read it. I think you'll find a lot of interesting people in it."

Rainey snapped back to conscience thought. "Thank you, Mama. I know I will."

She spent most of the night reading and looking at the old pictures. She tried to commit their faces to memory. What had they been like? She found herself wishing she could go back in time to meet them. She read everything written about the families of John and Letsy and of Bertha. She was saddened to read about their tragic fates. She had expected to experience more of those strange visions as she read, but there were none. Had John, or whoever it was, given up?

Chapter Thirty

The next morning she was up early. Annie found her out in the tool shed plundering around.

"Good morning. Are you going to do some gardening?"

"Good morning, Mama," said Rainey as she backed out of the shed with a hoe and ax in hand. "No, I just think I might need these if I'm going to the old house."

"So, you really mean to do this?"

"Yes, Ma'am, I do," she said determinedly.

"You know I can't go with you. You're on your own with this mad adventure."

"I know, Mama. Not to worry. You don't mind if I stay here with you a few more days do you?"

Annie smiled. "No, if it means I can have you around a little longer, then please stay. But do watch for snakes. I'll bet that place is infested with them."

"How about your husband, I know he has to miss you?"

"No, Addison's in Washington for two weeks on some sort of military training."

Annie crossed her arms over her chest, adding, "Oh, I didn't know that. You never tell me anything about him; it seems everything is always such a secret."

"Good men are hard to come by, so I keep him under lock and key—for my use only."

"You can't fool me, Rainey Alexander. I know he's some kind of secret undercover type person."

"I have no idea of what you are talking about, Mother dear. He's just in the Army."

Securing the tools to her shoulder, she and her mother started back to the house for coffee and a little breakfast. During breakfast, Annie told her how to get to the old place. She guessed the current landowner wouldn't mind if she looked around, but as far as she knew, nothing was left in the house.

The dusty road was well traveled. It was tobacco-cropping time. Rainey had passed several pickup trucks pulling tobacco sleds loaded with the bright green leaves. No doubt they were headed for the barns. The dust from the road almost blinded her each time she passed a truck. As it settled, she prepared to pass the next truck up ahead. The lower leaves, or lugs, of the plants were being cropped now and had to be taken to the barns for curing. This was the routine in tobacco country this time of year.

At least the path through the tobacco to the old house might be easier now. Progress had changed the way of working tobacco: no more field hands or mules, only the machines that had taken their places.

Between the passing trucks and clouds of dust, she could see the railroad crossing her mother had told her to look for. The car thumped up and down over the tracks as she looked to her left for the three tobacco barns in a row. She saw them, and just beyond them, the old house.

It sat back in the field about fifty yards, an island in a bright green sea of tobacco plants. The idea of a clear path was immediately eliminated.

She steered the car onto a pullout and then parked. Apparently, she'd have to wade through some tall weeds and the forty to fifty yards of tobacco before she got to the house. She was really glad she had the foresight to wear long pants and boots. The possibility of going through all that in shorts and sneakers was totally out of the question.

Rainey had a severe aversion to snakes and spiders. She didn't understand why. As a child she had played daily in the fields and ditches behind the house as well as along the Waccamaw River with absolutely no fear of anything. And yet, here she was, a grown woman who was terrified by both snakes and spiders. Nothing that she could recall from her past explained this change. Suffice it to say, she avoided both at all costs.

At first glance, at the edge of the tobacco field, she thought how beautiful the huge green tobacco leaves were. They measured about a foot or more in length and at least a foot wide. Their deep color and soft leathery texture made them desirable. An old friend who had passed away recently came to mind. He swore that Adam and Eve wore tobacco leaves after the Lord kicked them out of Eden. Who knows, he could have been right!

Gingerly stepping into the field about three rows, she scrutinized every plant for the possibility of a snake or spider that might be lying in wait. She followed the row until she found herself right in front of the old house, about twenty or thirty yards away. Vines covered it completely, and the growth around its perimeter had not been bush-hogged in many years.

Saying a little prayer, she took a deep breath and stepped out of the neatly cultivated tobacco rows into the tangled mass of weeds. As she threaded her way toward the house, she had the unmistakable feeling of tiny feet on her lower leg. Screaming, she assumed immediately that a spider had begun its climb upward under her jeans to a spot where it could sink its fangs deeply into her flesh. Rainey stopped. She tried to determine exactly where it was on her leg. Shaking uncontrollably, she reached down and placed her hand directly over the creature to hold it in place; she hoped she had mashed and killed it with the same motion. She felt confident that by grabbing it in that manner, through her jeans, she wouldn't have to actually touch it with her hand. Thank God she had worn jeans! She twisted her hand around her leg tightly to lock the creature in. Still shaking, it was difficult to tell if she had stopped its progress. She managed to hold still long enough to feel if she had, indeed, stopped its climb. Her fingers were beginning to turn white; nonetheless, she formulated a plan to get the giant spider, or whatever it was, off of her. She would continue to hold it in place. At the same time, she'd unbuckle her belt and unbutton her jeans. She could then slowly slide the jeans down until the pants were just above the spot where the creature was trapped. She should then be able to relax her grip and shake the thing off as the pant leg fell further down. Quickly she unfastened her belt and undid the button. Then she pulled the zipper down.

Shaking her hips like a hula dancer, she worked the rather tight fitting jeans off her hips and down her thighs. Suddenly, she realized that she was outside in the open where someone might be watching. Here she was with her jeans almost down to her knees. Frantically, she pulled her jeans back up with her one free hand, but in doing so, she lost her balance and fell to the ground.

"Oh great!" she said. "How many more of the damn things are down here waiting to get on me."

Quickly struggling to her feet, she raised her head slowly above the weeds and looked all around. Seeing no one, she mumbled, "Thank God! Now to get this thing OFF me!"

Once again the jeans slid off her hips as she worked them back down her legs to where her hand was still positioned. By this time, her fingers had turned ghostly white from the lack of circulation.

At last, the pant leg was directly above the spot where the creature was trapped; she carefully inched it down while easing her death grip on the intruder. As the cloth went further down, she was shocked as she got her first sight of the intruder: a small pine seedling covered with short needles. Rainey stood upright shaking her head in disbelief. "I can't believe I just did what I did for a baby pine tree!"

Without further attacks, she approached the first step up to the porch. She carefully tested its strength; it felt a little weak but seemed capable of holding her weight just fine. A bit more confident, she started to the next and then the next until she had made it onto the porch. It creaked under her weight, but she stood for a moment to look around. Dirt daubers were busy building mud nests on the front wall. She looked back over the field to the horizon. In the distance, dark clouds were forming. A thunderstorm was on its way.

"I need to be moving along here, or I'm going to get caught in a storm," she thought to herself.

Gazing around the porch, she could visualize Letsy in her rocker and Annie playing in the yard. How time had changed everything! The old house was slowly being consumed by nature.

She wished it was the dead of winter as she looked over the cobwebs neatly placed in every little nook and cranny. "Lord, I wish I wasn't so afraid of spiders. This place is infested with them, she mumbled.

As she slowly stepped toward the front door, the porch again creaked and groaned under her weight. She turned the doorknob and pushed the door at the same time. It opened easily, letting sunlight illuminate the dark corners of the main room.

By now the wind was picking up, and she could hear thunder in the distance. "I've got to get moving," she thought. "What if this floor won't bear my weight, and I fall through? There'll be hundreds of spiders down there!"

The room was empty except for a layer of old hay on the floor. Apparently, someone had used the house for hay storage. Light filtered in through the grids of the windows, the glass panes having all been shattered. Thin wispy pieces of cotton drapes hung over the windows. Moving in and out with the breeze, they had been shredded from their constant contact with the jagged glass. The fireplace stood at one end of the big room. She envisioned the former occupants standing in front of it in the early winter mornings.

"I bet this place was really comfortable," she thought as she slowly turned to scan her surroundings. She could see where the kitchen had been. Everything except a few of the cabinets had been torn out to make room for hay. Another clap of thunder rolled over the shaky house; she needed to get busy.

Talking out loud made her feel as if she were not alone. It bolstered her courage. "Well, I guess I'll start by looking in the cabinets."

The cabinets revealed nothing except mouse droppings and more spiders. It was a good thing she could see into them clearly because it would have been virtually impossible for her to feel around blindly inside them. "Nothing here. Maybe the fireplace has a loose brick or two; it could be hidden behind one of them."

Walking over to the fireplace, she looked closely at the bricks. "Why didn't I bring a pair of gloves?" A shiver ran up her back; she was afraid to move even one brick. Spiders. Luckily none of the bricks were loose.

"I have got to get over this spider thing," she vowed.

The sun's rays through the windows suddenly disappeared as if a dark cover had been thrown over them. The wind blew through the broken windows and the cracks and crevices of the old house. The thunder sounded very near.

"Oh, great, I guess I'm stuck here until this storm passes."

Rain began beating down on the tin roof hard. It sounded as if the old house might fall in on top of her.

Reluctantly continuing her search of the fireplace, she was totally unaware of the black snake lying in the corner of the room just a few feet away. Unintentionally, Rainey moved a little too close to the shiny black reptile, which moved very quickly toward an escape hole in the wall. Catching the movement out of the corner of her eye, Rainey jumped back and landed on the weakened floor with a dull thud. A dusty cloud erupted into the air. "Oh! Oh my God, you scared the daylights out of me."

Trembling visibly, she fought hard to regain control. "I'd best take my hoe and ax with me to the other rooms," she muttered as she composed herself. That poor snake had no idea of the anguish he had just caused her.

The rain continued. Thunder crashed, and a bolt of lightning lit up the room as if it had hit right outside the door. Rainey instinctively ducked.

Taking her tools in hand, she entered the hallway. There was evidence that rooms had been added on to the house a few times. On one side of the hall were two small rooms, each with one window. On the other side was one larger room. She figured the larger one must have belonged to the parents, Letsy and John. The two smaller rooms were probably for the children.

All of the rooms had been used for hay storage, just as the main room had. She decided to search the smaller ones first then move into the main bedroom. As she walked through the door of the first room, she passed directly through a spider web that wrapped itself invisibly across her face. Spasmodically, her arms flailed as she tried to wipe the threads away. Her heart was pounding so hard she could feel it, and she was breathing as if she had just run a mile.

"Get off of me! Oh, God, I hate spiders," she screamed.

Again, struggling to compose herself, she looked around the room. She could see there was no place to hide anything in the first bedroom, not even a closet. She moved back into the hallway, but not until she very carefully examined the doorway for more spider webs.

With storm clouds still filling the summer sky, the hallway was almost as dark as night. As she stepped toward the next room, the feeling of someone standing next to her caused her to stop dead in her tracks. Her hair moved ever so slightly. "Was that the wind or someone's breath?" she asked herself. "It was very warm and had a lifelike smell." Beads of sweat popped out on her upper lip, and she had the strongest urge to run from the old house. Rationalizing, she figured that she had come this far, so she couldn't stop now.

Then she heard a faint whisper of a man's voice, "Follow me." Startled, she dropped the ax and hoe. She reached down to pick up the tools, and at the same time she glanced toward the end of the hallway. In the faint light, a ghostly apparition appeared to slip into the master bedroom. Was it daring her to follow? A chill shook her, and her heart pounded in her chest.

"Who's there?" she whispered. "I've got a hoe and ax with me." Holding the ax up in front of her, she slowly slid along the wall. As she got to the opening of the larger bedroom, she stopped.

"Oh, please don't let there be another spider web," she thought. Taking a deep breath, she stepped quickly into the room. The floor felt unstable. Moving deeper into the room, she scrutinized all the walls and corners, but there was no one there.

What was it that I saw? I'm sure it was the figure of a person, but I couldn't make out facial features, she thought.

Suddenly, before she could turn around, the floor gave way under her feet. One leg disappeared into a dark hole all the way up to her ankle.

"Spiders! Spiders! Spiders! There's got to be spiders in here," she screamed as her foot touched what felt like another floor. Quickly regaining her balance, she pulled her foot out. The panic subsided and rational thought returned.

"What in the world am I doing? I'm going to get hurt in here if I'm not careful."

Although she couldn't see clearly, she could tell there was some sort of small storage area below the floor. Some kind of hidden floor had stopped her fall. Dropping down on her knees, she grabbed at the wood around the collapsed flooring. She tore away jagged pieces of wood so she could see a little better. Then she spied it, what appeared to be the perfect little storage compartment.

Now was the time for bravery. With admitted phobias of both snakes and spiders, this woman would have to put her own little hand into a dark hole, a hole that could contain one or both of her most feared enemies.

"Okay, I can do this. I know I can. There's nothing in there that will hurt me this time," she said defiantly. All the while, she questioned why she had not brought gloves.

Mustering all her courage, she carefully inserted her hand into the hole. Even though she was shivering and numb, her fingers felt what seemed to be a soft bag. Grabbing it, she jerked it out and dropped it immediately on the floor beside her. After all, there was no reason to hold it any longer than was necessary, she rationalized. The bag was covered in dust and secured tightly with a leather cord.

"Well, well, well. Could this be it?"

Slowly she untied the cord. Then lifting the bag by the bottom, she eased its contents out onto the floor.

"Hum, what have we here, what in the world is all this stuff?"

The bag contained an old dried up chicken foot, some leather pouches containing different colored powders, some herbs, and a few other items, Rainey could not identify. But to her disappointment, she found no broach.

As she toyed with the idea of putting her hand back into the hole, the sun broke through the window. "Oh, thank the good Lord. The sun's back." Its light gave her the opportunity to see a little more without having to again reach into the hole. She noticed what appeared to be a box.

Accepting the logic that since she had gotten the bag out with no problems, she reached in once more to pull the object out.

This time, however, a sharp chill ran up her arm that caused her pain. Immediately, she assumed something had bitten her, and she repeated the earlier routine of the flailing arms and shrieking. After a few seconds of panic, she regained her composure. A quick inspection revealed no obvious signs of reptilian or arachnoid bites. Relaxing a little, her attention went back to the box.

Slowly she opened the lid. She couldn't believe her eyes; it was full of letters, a diary, a small Bible so brittle she was almost afraid to touch it, a single photograph of John, a few pieces of jewelry, a small doll, and something wrapped in a soft piece of cloth. She carefully unfolded the cloth. To her delight there it was, the emerald broach, the one in the dream, it had to be! She admired it for a long time, as others before her had. It was the most beautiful piece of jewelry she had ever seen. The depth of the color at the center of it was unnaturally beautiful. It glowed, even in the dim light, as if within it there was light. She took the broach into her hand and held it closer. As her fingers made contact with it, she felt an energy so powerful it scared her. A piercing chill ran through her arm that almost caused her to drop the emerald.

North, on his island home, Caleb Bland rejoiced. "Ah yes, she has found it. I never would have imagined it would still be so close to the family. Yes, this is good. You have done well, my dear. I must see it again. For a fleeting moment, he gazed through Rainey's eyes at his beloved emerald broach. She had a sensation as if someone were trespassing in her mind. "Who's there?" She blurted out.

There was no answer, but the feeling of someone or something remained.

Hesitantly, she returned her attention to the broach. The green stone was so beautiful. Some kind of design was scribed into the gold. If she held the emerald up to the light, it glowed radiantly. Tiny jewels encircled the broach.

"I've never seen anything this gorgeous before in my life," she thought.

As she stared at it, she again sensed the presence of the apparition she had seen earlier. When she finally put the broach back into the box, the presence strangely faded. Gathering up the bag and box, she made her way back to the main room of the house.

Outside, the cool rain falling on the scorching soil created steam that rose into the air everywhere. As she made her way down the steps from the house, she remembered the hoe and ax she had left inside. Returning, she again saw the apparition for one split second.

"What am I seeing? Is it a ghost or just shadows?" she asked herself.

Placing the tools under one arm and the box under the other, she began her way to the car. By the time she waded through the rain soaked weeds and tobacco, her clothes were soaking wet and sticky with mud.

"My next stop is to get home and take a shower," she thought. "I smell like a field hand."

Finding courage to wade through weeds and mud, she had worked up quite a sweat. She reviewed her exploits: walking through a spider web, encountering a black snake, blindly running her hand into a dark hole. And there was, she could not forget, her battle with the pine seedling, too. But she was proud of herself; she had journeyed through her fear without being attacked by either a snake or spider. She couldn't help but laugh at herself.

As she drove through Conway, she kept glancing at the box. She couldn't wait to get back to her mother's house. Eventually, she passed through the intersection where her father had been killed. Sad memories rushed through her mind. She missed him. Then her thoughts turned to the dream, the dream that had haunted her just about all her life. "I've been dreaming about this pirate all my life, and now the dream intensifies. Why now?"

She recalled all the unusual events in her life, things she could not explain. She clearly remembered the ghostly visitor who had come to her while she was still a child. She had managed to put that fatal morning out of her memory. Losing her father had been very traumatic for both her and her brother. But now, she remembered it as if it were yesterday.

"Was that visitor real or just my childish mind imagining things? Is it possible that the pirate was a real spirit trying to communicate with me? I remember that he seemed real, he really did. He even told me that our lives would change very soon."

Rainey was beginning to believe that the first time she saw him was significant for some reason; there was some connection that she, as yet, did not understand. It was long ago, and she was very young.

Chapter Thirty-One

The first dream, or encounter, came when Rainey was four years old.

It was in the early morning, five or six o'clock, I would guess. I had made my way to Mama and Daddy's room. Clinging to my blanket, I climbed onto their bed. My bouncing around didn't seem to disturb them; they were both sleeping deeply. This was a day I would never forget, the day my daddy would die in a car crash. At that moment, though, our lives seemed perfect.

Daddy was still asleep, odd, because he never slept past five a.m. He was always up and out of the house early. Now that I think about it, I had tried to wake them but it seemed as though they were both drugged. Something kept them from waking up.

I sat between them for some time. I talked to myself and played with my blanket, I occasionally pushed Mama. The sun peaked through the thin curtains and cast its brilliant rays into the room, and I could see the dust particles hanging in the light. The smell of summer floated in on the light breeze that moved the curtains back and forth.

I kept doing things to try to wake them, but they continued sleeping deeply. Something caught my eye at the foot of the bed. Something or someone was slowly taking shape and seemed to grow from the floor up. I stared in disbelief as it materialized before me.

It was a man, or like a man, and had long black hair that hung down around his dried, tanned face. He sported a thin mustache and goatee, but his facial hair was neatly trimmed. He was covered in dirt; his clothing was faded and torn. It seemed as if he had just dug himself out of the grave. His eyes were blood red. He wore a broad leather belt that covered a knife tucked beneath it, and an empty scabbard dangled against his leg. Those scary red eyes glared at me for what seemed to be the longest time before he spoke, with a rough English accent.

"I will not rest until it is returned," he said in a wicked whisper. "Your family is cursed until my beautiful broach is brought back to its resting place. One day, when you are older, I will call on you to help me. You will search until it is found and returned. Your ancestor John Waters took it; he used his powers to find it. Now he is lost in the spirit world. I am left with no means to retrieve it except you, my dear. By the time John Waters discovered that the emerald was in the possession of his wife, it was too late. My curse sent him to his death before he could cast it into the waters and break the curse forever. One day, it will be your fate to right the wrong that was done."

The specter paused for a moment then drew closer to me. I cowered with fear; I shook uncontrollably.

"Do not fear me, little one; I mean you no harm. Now is not the time. You are too young and have much to learn. You will know the right time and place, for in a few years, you will understand the gift of your people's past."

Pointing to my hand, the specter continued. "You bear the mark of the serpent. You have been blessed with a precious gift and one day after you are enlightened, you will learn how to use it. When the time is right, I will awaken your memory, and you will find my broach. For now, listen to my instructions."

I sat and listened and said not a word. Scared out of my wits, I was not able to scream or run.

"Not far from here is an island. You will find a marsh on the west, an inlet to the north and south, and the great Atlantic on the eastern border. On this island is an oak which has lived for many, many years. Here I will wait for you when you bring the broach. When you are older and the time is right, you will know. Do not be afraid. I will always protect you, but only you, from my curse. Until it is returned, your family will see much sorrow. Until you are enlightened, you will not see me in your waking hours, but I will always be in your dreams." Then he was gone.

I stared at the empty space where he had appeared. I felt as though I were in a trance. After a few minutes, I moved. Quickly I jerked my blanket up over my head and hid. About that time, Mama and Daddy began to stir.

That was the very first time he ever appeared to me.

He was right, too; tragedy would come to us. Late in the afternoon that same day, a patrolman came to our house to tell Mama that Daddy had been killed in a car accident.

A horn blowing shook Rainey back to reality. The light had changed to green as she sat lost in her memories.

"Okay, I'm going, I'm sorry," Rainey mouthed as she raised her hand to apologize. "I can't believe this. He was real! This pirate came to me when I was only four years old. I need to find a map of Horry County. I've got an island to find." She turned around to drive back into Conway, for she was now on a mission.

"I bet the library will have county maps, even some old ones. I can make copies. I know I can find this island."

Somehow she remembered everything he had told her that summer morning. "So, you've stayed with me in my dreams, just as you promised. You knew I'd help you find your broach," she said out loud.

The streets of Conway had hardly changed over the past fifteen years. The mighty oak trees still held a place of prominence in town, forcing many streets to go around them. The memories of her younger days came rushing back. She and Tom were as different as night and day. She had been the wild child, and Tom had been a smart student. He played football and was popular with the girls. Everyone agreed that he was destined for great things. He had a bit of wild side, too, but their mother always let him slide. Rainey, on the other hand, had a hard time concentrating in school; her creative mind was always occupied but not necessarily with the lesson of the day. After graduation from high school, Tom went off to college while she stayed in town, working a number of dead end jobs and dating guys with only one thought in their little pea-sized brains.

After Tom finished college, he changed; he had become a different man, and the changes were for the worse. He had developed a mean streak that had never been apparent before. The good looking, blue-eyed boy who never met a stranger wore his new nick name, "Storm," like a badge of honor. Local folks referred to him more often as "Storm Spencer" than as "Tom."

She and Tom had had harsh words on occasion, and their bond as twins was strained as never before. While the verbal disagreements were unsettling, the soon to come physical attack was the final warning. She knew that she had to get away from him before something really bad happened. She made an off hand comment to him about his life style, and the next thing she knew, he had her by the throat. If a neighbor hadn't pulled him off, he might have killed her. Tom was like a man possessed by a demon; his eyes unnatural. This wasn't the first time he had become violent.

She was reluctant to leave their mother but knew she had to find a new life.

The library hadn't changed a bit. To her, it was still the most interesting place in town. As she walked up the front steps, a man exited and that smell of old books filled her senses. "Wow," she thought, "the smell. Some things haven't changed after all these years."

As she entered, she felt the contrast from the stifling summer air outside; the cool air conditioned comfort felt wonderful. An older woman sitting at the desk gave her a quick glance before returning to her work. Looking up again, the woman asked if she could help.

"Yes. I need to locate maps of Horry County, old and new." Rainey whispered in her best library voice.

The woman focused on Rainey for a minute and then removed her bifocals. She could feel it coming.

"Do I know you, honey?"

Before Rainey could say a word, the woman recognized her. "You're Annie Spencer's girl; I knew you were a Spencer. Let's see… its Rainey isn't it? Yes, that's your name. I've been here a long time, but I don't forget faces… sometimes the names, but not the faces. I'm so sorry to hear about Tom's misfortunes, he used to be such a kind boy. What can I help you with, dear?"

"Like I said, I need to find the map room. I need to make a few copies of county maps." For the life of her, she could not remember the librarian's name. She glanced around for some type of name plate, feeling like a fool. She was intimidated by the woman in the same way she had felt as a young teenager checking a book out. There was something about a librarian that made her feel small and insignificant. Maybe it was the loud sound of the date stamp on the card along with the look they gave you… knowing that if you were late bringing it back, you would be cast into the pits of the late charge minions.

The librarian pointed to the map room. Finding the county map section, Rainey laid out the most current map of the county. She knew about where the island would be. With her finger, she followed along the coast to Little River. Locating the only island in that vicinity, she tried to figure a way to get there.

She then looked at older maps until she found the first one ever made of the area. It was fascinating; so little had changed. After making copies of both the old and new maps, she paid for them and returned to the car. The day was wearing on, and so she thought it best to go home. She couldn't wait to tell her mother about her day and the discoveries she had made.

As Rainey pulled into the driveway, she could see Annie at the door waiting. The look on her face left little doubt that she had been worried.

"I've been worried sick. Did you get caught in that thunderstorm?"

"I did and it was some storm! I was in the old house, and so at least I had shelter. It was something else, Mama. It rained so hard I thought the roof was going to give way."

Annie felt the excitement in her daughter's voice. "Well, Rainey, tell me, tell me what you found!"

"Mama, I have to show you this bag I found and the odd things in it. If John was into magic, the items in this bag could have been some of what he used. But that is nothing compared to what I found in this old box."

Rainey held the box in her arms as if it were a baby. "Let's go inside. I'll show you what's in it."

Annie cleared a place on the coffee table as they both sat down on the couch. Her curiosity was intense; she could hardly wait for Rainey to get the box open.

"Mama, what I've found will shock you. I know now that all the things you told me are true."

Opening the box, she picked up the cloth that held the broach. Again the painful chill ran up her arm. Slowly she opened the cloth and laid the broach down in front of her mother.

Annie was speechless. She instinctively reached out to touch it, but Rainey stopped her.

"Mama, don't! It's possessed by something evil. When I touch it, there's this cold chill and a pain that runs through me."

"Oh, how awful! But oh, my Lord, Rainey, it's so beautiful. What would something like this be worth?"

"I have no idea, but we can't concern ourselves with its worth or our own desires. It has to be returned to its owner, and I know where to find him."

Annie, taken aback with Rainey's statement, asked, "What do you mean you know where to find him? He can't still be alive?"

"No Mama, he's been dead for a long, long time." Rainey had a faraway look in her eyes. "Mama, do you remember the day Daddy died? I told you that day I had a bad dream about an evil man coming into the bedroom and talking to me."

Annie shook her head. "Well, yes, I guess I do. I remember you telling me something about a dream. As a matter of fact, now I remember you were in tears, it scared you so bad."

"Mama, today after I left the old house, I was driving through Conway. My mind was wandering when I passed through the intersection where Daddy was killed. Suddenly, I remembered this dream from long ago, and it was as real as this broach sitting here. I remembered every little detail about the man and every word he spoke. He told me about the curse and about returning the broach to him when the time was right."

Stopping for a moment, Rainey turned to her mother, "And Mama, he told me something else, too, that I was blessed with some kind of gift."

Turning her hand over, she revealed the serpent-shaped birthmark. "Mama, this mark means something. He told me that."

Looking at the mark on Rainey's hand, Annie offered, "That's just a little birth mark."

"No, Mama. He told me I was blessed with the mark of the serpent. He said it was the mark of the gift!"

Shaking her head, Annie spoke, "Honey, this is nonsense. You don't have any kind of special gift; you've never experienced any unusual things in your life, nothing that others haven't."

"You're wrong. I know I have, Mama. Do you remember how tough it was for me in school? Remember how much I was teased by the other kids about my imaginary friends?"

Annie was not ready to accept that her daughter might be a recipient of any supernatural gift. "Rainey, lots of children have imaginary friends."

Rainey began to feel frustrated. She realized how difficult it would be to convince her mother she might possess any special powers.

"Don't you remember how the other kids made fun of me? I always told them I was hearing voices and strange sounds. I always thought they, too, heard them. Now this explains it. I wasn't crazy. It was something mystical, and it was really happening to me." Rainey's eyes welled up as she patted herself on the chest. Tears spilled down her cheeks.

Annie took Rainey in her arms. "It's Okay. I'll take your word on this, and we'll see what happens." As she hugged her daughter, Annie looked down at the broach. "But honey, I don't want to see this beautiful piece of jewelry lost forever. Maybe there's a way we can keep it?"

Rainey wiped her eyes with the back of her hand. "That's the way it's got to be, Mama. He wants it back."

Regaining her composure, Rainey pulled the rest of the contents out of the box.

"There're a lot of letters here. There's a doll and, oh yes, this little Bible."

Rainey opened the Bible. Apparently, the pages had gotten wet at some point. A note was written on the first page: For my husband, may the Spirit of Lord walk with you, Love Letsy.

"Mama, look, it's a note that Letsy wrote to John in this Bible. This must have been his. I wonder if he had it with him when he set out to find the treasure."

"If John was a religious man, he most likely did," replied Annie.

"Look here, there's a page marked. It's in the book of Psalms."

The pages were so dry and brittle she had to be careful not to tear them.

"It's the Ninety-first Psalm."

Rainey read the underlined part. "He will cover you with His feathers and under His wings you will find refuge; His faithfulness will be your shield and rampart."

"That's beautiful. I must remember that," Rainey said.

Putting the Bible aside, they continued looking through the letters in the box. Some were sent from John to Letsy during the war. Others were from people neither Annie nor Rainey had ever heard of. Another small book Rainey discovered was Letsy's diary.

"This is Letsy's diary, Mama! I feel a bit like I am intruding into her private life."

Annie laughed. "I don't think she'd mind, especially after all these years."

"Some of these writings go back to the Civil War. Here, listen to this one:

"'May 5,1864. John has left me with child after his last leave home. I don't know what in the world I will do with another mouth to feed.'"

Annie thought for a moment. "That baby must have been Nellie. I'm so excited that you've found these; they mean so much to me. Read on."

Rainey turned a few more of the pages, "Listen to this, Mama:

"'May 25, 1865. The war ended last month, and John has returned to me a changed man. He is full of anger, and his drinking is unbearable. He has taken work on a riverboat that travels frequently to Georgetown. He is always gone. His absence, though, is really a relief, for when he is home, he beats me for no reason and scares the children to death. Sometimes I think I am living with a mad man. But I still love him, and I pray he will change.'"

Annie and Rainey looked at each other as they both thought, could this be true?

"You know, Rainey, that was a bad war, brother fighting brother. I'm sure a lot of men returned home not quite the same. Maybe Letsy was exaggerating a little, too."

Rainey continued. "This sounds interesting:

"'August 20, 1868. John is away working on the river. I met a nice man today named Will Rhodes. I fed him supper. Later, after the children were asleep, we went out on the stoop and talked for a long time. He was in the war, too. I found him very attractive and am ashamed to say that we shared an intimate moment. I pray John does not find out for he will kill me, I know. I have been so terribly lonely. Will gave me a gift; it's a treasure map drawn on a piece of leather. I don't believe in such things, but I put it away in my chest. It will remind me of him. I will feed him in the morning and send him on his way.'

"'August 21,1868. Will wasn't in the shed this morning. He must have left during the night. It was best that he did. I let things go too far, and I shall worry on it for the rest of my life.'"

"Mama, Letsy had a one night-stand!" Rainey couldn't help but laugh. "And they didn't think people did such things back then, did they?"

Annie took the book from her. "If you're going to make fun of it, you can't read anymore," she said shaking her finger at her daughter.

"I promise I'll behave. You read some more."

Annie flipped through the pages. Occasionally, she found where pages had been torn out, and some had been left blank with nothing more than a date written in.

"Oh, listen to this. It's about Lavenia, her oldest child.

"'October 1, 1868. I am so heart-broken. Lavenia has passed on; she was so sick the doctor was unable to help her. John is not here, and I don't know when he will be. We must bury her today; we cannot wait any longer for his return. Damn Him!"

The next few pages were blank.

"I guess she was grieving too much to put anything down. The next entry is a week later.

"'October 6, 1868. John has finally returned. I found the courage and told him to leave. I will not live in fear of him any longer. He is now at the cemetery saying good bye to Lavenia. He was very upset, but I will not continue to live this way.'"

"Well, I guess she must have laid the law down. You know a woman can only take so much abuse before she begins to fight back," Annie said, shaking her head in disgust.

Rainey took the diary from her mother. "I want to see if there's anything about the treasure hunt or the broach."

She continued to look through the diary, to search for anything that might help her understand exactly what had taken place back then. She wanted something that might tie in with her dreams, something about the broach. Anything.

Meanwhile, Annie continued looking through the box. She pulled out letters and scanned them. She found what seemed to be a dried up piece of leather.

"I wonder what this is."

Rainey took it from her and examined it closely. The drawings and writing had almost faded completely.

"It looks like some sort of map. Oh my God! Mother! I'll bet this is the map the man gave Letsy."

Laying it on the coffee table where she could get a better look, Rainey continued. "Yes, look here's the coast line and an inlet. It's got 'Little River Community' written on this spot. And here's an island with some type of mark. I can barely make it out, but I believe it's an X."

Rainey ran her hands through her hair. "Mama, I think this is the island that man told me about, when he appeared to me. This is where I have to go. This is Waities Island, and I know exactly where it is."

Pulling out the copies she had made at the library, she compared them to the map drawn on the piece of leather.

"Yes, this is the place!" Rainey shrieked. "With this old hand drawn map and the updated county map, I should be able to go right to the spot."

Annie, too, was excited, but the fear of something happening to her only daughter was strong. Rainey was all she had left, and she knew she couldn't bear it if something were to happen to her. Annie couldn't help but feel that Rainey was in danger.

Rainey continued reading the diary. She hoped to find some entry that might help her understand what she was up against.

"'January 20, 1869. Everett stopped by this morning. He gave me a broach that was in the treasure John helped him find. I tried to turn it down, but he insisted. It is so beautiful; I have never seen anything like it in my life. I know John would not take it because he could lose his powers, and so I have hidden it in my chest. I know I will have to tell him about it, but for now I'll keep it hidden. I'll tell him when the time is right.'"

Jumping up from the couch, Rainey screamed, "I found it, Mama! She talks about John's powers in this part." She handed the book to Annie so her mother could read it.

Leaning back on the couch, Rainey raised her arms over her head. Phew! The pungent smell of body odor reminded her that she needed a shower badly. "I've got to take a shower; I'm still filthy from digging around in that old house."

The warm water was refreshing as it ran down her body. Squeezing shampoo into her palm, she lathered it into her dark hair and slowly massaged her scalp. Soap was running down her face, so she couldn't open her eyes. Feeling a bit of panic, she had the strangest sensation that she was being watched. She desperately reached for the towel that was hanging over the shower door.

"Who's there?" she called, but there was no answer. She seemed to be alone.

"I know someone is in here with me; I can feel the presence," she thought to herself.

Quickly rinsing her hair, she soaped up the wash cloth and started rubbing her body. Feeling the stubble on her legs, she reached for the razor. As she leaned over, she again had the sensation of being watched. She looked out through the glass door, but she still couldn't see. Even if anyone had been there, the steam would prevent her from seeing.

"God, is my imagination running amuck?" she thought to herself.

She finished her shower and dried off. After putting on a pair of clean jeans and a clean shirt, she returned to the den where her mother was still busy reading the old letters.

Sitting down beside her mother, she didn't say a word. Annie was completely absorbed in the letters. She was glad she had found the box and the bag for it meant a lot to her mother.

"You know, Mama, I was so wild when I was younger. I'm really surprised I didn't drown in the river or get killed in a car wreck like Daddy. That crowd I ran around with back then was just a bunch of no-counts; we didn't have a care in the world. I bet I smoked enough pot to fill this room."

She couldn't help but laugh at herself. "Do you remember the first time I got stoned?"

Annie looked at Rainey with disgust. "I sure do. You didn't think I was on to you, but I knew you'd been into something."

"I was just being a typical rebellious butt-head teenager. Then it was over. After high school, we all went our different ways. It was time for me to grow up. They went to college and I went to work."

"You could have gone to college, too. We would have made some kind of arrangements."

"I know, Mama, but Tom needed it more than I did, and I didn't want you to have to make even more sacrifices."

Annie's voice filled with anger. "I worked myself to the bone to put him through school, and look where he is now? So much talent down the drain. It sickens me to think that he's sleeping tonight in a prison cell."

"Well, let's not get into all that again. There's not a thing we can do to change the past. What's done is done. Let's talk about something we have some control over."

Annie picked up all the letters and placed them back in the box. "Enough of this for tonight. I'll read the rest of them tomorrow." Annie went on to bed leaving Rainey on the couch to watch television.

Rainey stretched out on the couch and buried her head in the soft pillows. Her mind was still working on what she was going to do the following morning.

"I'll rent a sea kayak and paddle over to that island. Yeah, that's what I'll do. " With that figured out, she clicked on the TV and escaped into the world of sitcoms. As usual, the "great relaxer" worked its magic, and Rainey was soon fast asleep.

"Rainey, my lovely Rainey, do you hear me?" She heard a voice in her dreams.

"Yes, I hear you. Who are you? What is your name?" Deeply asleep, she could hear his voice as clearly as if she were wide awake. This was a dream, but he was there.

"I am most satisfied with your findings, and I cannot wait to reclaim my beautiful broach."

Rainey could see herself walking on a beach. Off in the distance stood an oak. A full moon illuminated the myrtle bushes and palmetto trees. The undergrowth around the oak was dense and thick.

She called out, "Are you in there, near the tree?"

"That is where I will be. You will know the place. Your instincts will not deceive you. The moon will be full, and you will be able to find your way. It must be tomorrow night. I will be waiting. I will reveal myself when you arrive."

Rainey woke with a start, the conversation from the dream crystal clear in her mind. Sitting up on the couch, she realized her trip to the island was his doing. Somehow, he was orchestrating the entire adventure.

She reached over for the box, opened it, and took out the broach. She held it close, scrutinizing its every detail. It felt as if she were holding an ice cube charged with electricity. That cold and mysterious pain surged again up her hand and arm.

"This has to be done. I'll leave tomorrow afternoon so I can at least find the tree before dark."

Out the front window, she could see the moon hanging in the night sky. "Yes, the moon will be full tomorrow night. I'll be there, and then I'll find out exactly who you are."

Chapter Thirty-Two

The next morning, Rainey searched the phone book for a sea kayak rental shop. She located one in the area and punched in the number.

The male voice on the other end sounded young and spirited. "Ocean Kayaks, may I help you?"

As she poured herself another cup of coffee, she cleared her throat. "Yes, I'd like to rent a sea kayak for two days." After his assurance that there would be no problem, she pulled a credit card from her purse.

"Price is not a problem. No, I've never used one but I'm pretty good with a canoe. Great, then I'll pick it up in a couple of hours. Alexander is the name, Rainey Alexander." She was pleased to have located a shop close to the spot from where she had chosen to leave.

Annie had been listening to the conversation. "So, you really are going to the island today?"

"Yes, Mother, I am," she said seriously.

"I'll be worried sick about you paddling around in that marsh. What if you get stuck out there?"

"If I'm not home by tomorrow afternoon, you call the rescue squad. Anyhow it's the middle of summer; there'll be lots of other people out in boats."

"What! You mean to tell me you're going to stay over night?" Annie interrupted.

"That's right, all night long, and I'll be just fine. I know how to take care of myself."

Rainey's mother realized that further objections were futile; she could hear the determination in her daughter's voice. Rainey had always been hardheaded.

"Okay, what'll you need? I'll help you get it together," Annie said reluctantly.

Rainey smiled. Giving her mother a hug, she reassured her that she would be fine.

"I'll need some water, snacks, bug spray, a blanket, a towel, flashlight, matches and, oh, if you don't mind, can I take your little pistol?"

Annie didn't like the sound of that. Rainey sensed her mother's apprehension in her face.

"Oh, all right, I guess so. You'll need something if you're going to be out there alone."

She stuffed everything into a backpack, including a few sandwiches that Annie had made. She placed it all in her car. When she returned to the house, she found her mother holding the broach.

"No, Mama, I told you not to touch it!"

Frozen stiff, Annie stared at the broach. Removing it from her hand, Rainey sensed that her mother, too, had felt the chilling pain that came from just holding it.

"My lord, I didn't believe you. It scared the daylights out of me! I just figured you didn't want me to get attached to it. Now I know what you mean."

Rainey wrapped it back in the cloth and then placed it in a zip lock bag. As she placed the bag into her fanny pack, she sternly told her mother, "Forget you ever saw it, Mama. Before long it'll no longer be a part of our lives. Hopefully, our family will then be free from this evil curse."

Seeing the dirty bag containing the mysterious items lying on the coffee table, she wondered if she should take it along. Something urged her to take it. She stuffed it into her backpack; she reasoned that a little more weight shouldn't hurt.

Hugging her mother goodbye, she headed for the car. "I'll see you tomorrow so don't worry."

The rental service had her kayak ready to go. One of the employees gave her instructions on its use, but she found her mind drifting to the island. She felt it pulling her.

"Do you understand, ma'am?"

"What! Oh, oh yes, the rudder. Yes, I understand how that works."

"Okay, then you're set to go. Is there someone who can help you get it off the top of the car?"

"Oh, sure," she lied. Surely she could handle it by herself; it didn't appear to be that heavy.

The spot she had in mind for launching her adventure was a small access park in the marsh across from the island. She'd found it while perusing the copy of the county map. It was as close as she could get.

Following Highway 17 north, she took the Cherry Grove exit. She turned at the road that led up into Little River Neck. She was amazed at the development that had taken place in the many years she had been gone: pricey, gated communities, not at all as she had remembered.

She came to a dead end. "I must have missed the sign for the park," she thought to herself.

Turning around, she drove slowly and looked to her left down each of the crossroads toward the ocean. Finally, she found the sign, which was almost completely hidden by overgrown weeds.

The road, which was about a half mile long, ended right at the marsh. Although the park was very small, it did have a walkway that led to a dock on the water. She could launch her boat from there. After parking her car in what she thought was a safe location, she started untying the kayak.

The voice of an old man startled her. You be needin' some hep gittin' that boat off yo' car, Missy?"

When she turned around, she spied a man sitting on a bench under a tree. It appeared that he might have been taking a rest from work. Rainey was never one to turn down a helping hand, especially when it came to lifting heavy objects.

She thought for a moment and then said to him, "I'd love a helping hand."

The old man had a gray beard and, the best she could tell, no teeth. His skin was golden brown and his eyes were hazel, almost yellowish green. He groaned as he stood up from his place on the bench. "Yo' must be gwine float da marsh."

"Why yes, I am." She wondered if her car would be safe parked here overnight. "Can I leave my car here over night? Do you think it will be safe?"

"Yes'um you can, but it might not be here in da morning."

"I was afraid of that." She muttered.

"Yo' gwine be back tomorrow, yo' be stayin' out in da marsh all night?"

Stumbling for a minute for the right words, "Yes, I'm staying out. I'm studying the tides, and I need to be out at least twenty-four hours."

"So yo' must be some kinda science woman?"

"Yes, you could say that I am." She was getting proficient at telling little lies. She felt a little bad about lying to an old man, but she didn't want anyone to know where she was going or why.

He helped her get the boat off the roof and carry it down to the little dock. She secured the backpack in the forward storage compartment and a small cooler in the rear.

Without saying a word, the old man watched her for several minutes. "I tells yo' what. Yo' see dat der house up der in da woods?"

Her eyes searched the woods and finally found a little shack sitting quite a way back from the road. It was almost entirely concealed by trees covered with vines and moss.

"Yo' kin parks yo' car up in der. Dat's where I lives. I kin keep an eye on it fo' yo'."

Rainey eyed the old man and then said, "You sure you don't mind?"

"No, I's most often always around. Dis here little park really bes mine."

"But the sign says, 'City Park'." Rainey said.

"Dat's right, da city be owning it. But I's take care of it. Peoples always trashin' it up and all. So I's keeps it picked up and take care of da flowers. Da city don't tend to it so good."

He turned around and waved his arms all around the area. Proudly he stated that "Dis here land use to be mine, it was in da family for mo' den a hun'ert years, 'til the city takes it fo' unpaid taxes. Da only thing I's got's left is dat old shack up yonder."

Rainey felt sorry for the old man, losing his land over taxes. She then wondered if he could be trusted. She had a strong feeling he could. "You really do have a nice view of the marsh and the island," Rainey offered.

"Yes'um it is. I loves it here. Now yo' be careful out der on de water and especial' if'in yo' gwine on dat isle." The old man pointed his finger to a spit of land on the other side of the marsh.

Rainey smiled, thanking him for the help. She pulled her car into his driveway and locked the door. Glancing around, she felt a strange familiarity with this place.

She bid farewell to the old man and slid into the kayak. Slowly she started paddling. She struggled with the rudder at first, but finally she began to get the knack of how the thing worked.

Chapter Thirty-Three

Paddling through the winding creeks toward the open sound, she was awed by the beauty of the place. The tall marsh grass shielded her view of the rest of the inlet. Cutting through the water, schools of baby fish flew through the air to escape the oncoming kayak. Each time she rounded a bend, wading birds would fly ahead and then settle back down, only to repeat the action as she approached them again and again. To her surprise, right in front of the boat, two dolphins broke the water to catch a breath. They followed her for some time before they disappeared into the open sound at the place where the creek joined it. Pausing for a moment to take a drink, she gazed across the sound toward Cherry Grove Point.

"Good Lord, look at the houses and high rise condos. I remember when there were no more than two or three small beach cottages out there. Before long, there won't be any natural shoreline at all," she thought.

Picking up the paddle, she started rowing again. It seemed fairly easy, as if the boat was being pulled along by the tide.

"I can't believe I got lucky enough to have the tide with me. At least," she reasoned, "I shouldn't be completely worn out when I get there." It was late afternoon, and the sun was really bearing down on her. She realized that she needed to get off the water, or she'd soon be looking like a lobster.

Stepping up her stroke, she could see the shallows of the island. She pushed hard on the paddle. The boat lunged forward and beached itself in the wet sand. She placed her hands on the gunwales and pushed down on the boat to climb out of the cockpit. Unaccustomed to a kayak, she lost her balance and fell toward the right; the boat dumped her unceremoniously into the shallow water.

"Oh no, I didn't want to get wet. I didn't bring a change of clothes," she muttered.

She rinsed her arms and then splashed water on her legs to wash away the wet sand. Only then did she look around at her surroundings to assess her situation.

"Oh, what the hell, I may as well cool off." Sinking back down into the warm salty water refreshed her, at least temporarily. She'd still have to live for the rest of the trip with that sticky salt all over her body. There would be no shower tonight.

Luck was with her to a degree. Since the kayak hadn't turned completely over, the backpack was still dry. She pulled the towel out and dried off. She also congratulated herself for wearing a bathing suit under her hiking shorts and T-shirt. Laying the pack and cooler to one side, she grabbed the boat and pulled it further up on the beach, well above the high tide line.

"Now to find a place to hide this boat," she thought.

She decided to drag the boat far enough up between the dunes so the tide couldn't get it. Furthermore, no one would be able to see it from the water. After dragging it into position, she went back down to the shore of the inlet and gathered enough dead marsh grass to conceal the kayak further. Finishing this task, she brushed her hands off. In a panic, she suddenly thought of the fanny pack. She breathed a sigh of relief when she found that it was still closed and fastened around her waist. To be on the safe side, she opened it to confirm that the broach was still safely tucked inside. Fortunately, the pack was somewhat waterproof, and so the contents were still dry.

She put on her pack and picked up the cooler. She looked around to get an idea of the direction in which to go. She found a trail leading off toward the dense wooded area of the island. She decided this particular way was as good as any. The sand made walking a struggle, and she quickly found herself tiring under the strain of the pack and cooler. Stopping to take a break, she looked toward the dark forest that lay ahead of her. She felt very alone and for the first time questioned her decision to return the broach.

"I know people would think me crazy if I told them what I was doing out here, but it is real. I know I have to do this, or I'll never know for sure," she reasoned.

Approaching the tree line, she could see the path begin to diminish. As it narrowed, it led directly into a small passage through the thick underbrush, most likely a deer path. "I'm not sure I can do this", she thought. "How do I know this place isn't crawling with snakes and spiders?"

Inspecting the small opening that led into the thick growth of Myrtle trees and cabbage palms, she recalled her brave passage through the tall tobacco on her way to the old house. Having made that journey without incident buoyed her courage for the one ahead. Into the thicket she plunged.

Immediately, the limbs of the brush snagged and caught the pack. After fighting to untangle herself several times, she removed it. Rather than leaving it, she dragged it for a few feet before realizing that she had passed through the worst of the undergrowth and was now under the canopy of the forest. She checked the pack and herself for any eight-legged hitchhikers but, to her relief, didn't find any.

It was beautiful; palms trees with their spikes encircled the trunks and penetrated the lower bushes. Spanish moss, like gray tangled hair, hung from the oaks. The sunshine filtered through the canopy and cast rays of light on the forest floor. It was quiet. The only sound was the rhythmic, intoxicating pounding of waves on the beach. Within the shelter of the small forest, the ocean sounds seemed far away. She wanted to spread her blanket, lie down, and take it all in. A nap, of course, was out of the question, given the likelihood of spiders or snakes.

Snapping back to reality, she knew she couldn't let the beauty and tranquility of the place make her complacent. Her mission, her first priority, was to find the old oak. Then she would wait to see what this specter might have in store.

Pulling on her backpack and taking up the cooler, she waded through the lower growth of cabbage palm. She tried to stay on the deer paths where the walking was much easier. Her direction was toward the tallest trees she could see. After covering a considerable distance, she came to a clearing where apparently someone had been digging holes.

"I bet the locals have heard legends about the treasure buried here. They must come over to look for it," she thought.

The clearing was completely enclosed by the forest. Taking in the area, her eyes fell upon a massive, old live oak. The tree's giant limbs spread out like octopus tentacles in every direction. Some were so heavy they grew along the ground. They were large enough to be used as walkways into the interior of the magnificent tree. Lichens and mosses of all descriptions grew over the bark. Gingerly stepping along one of the larger limbs, Rainey drew closer to the twisted and gnarled oak. No doubt this was the tree. With a trunk easily eight feet across, it had to be at least three hundred years old, probably more.

One limb had actually broken off the trunk, leaving a large hole. The limb lay on the ground, where it was slowly rotting away. Searching for somewhere to wait, she found a somewhat flat, smooth place on the fallen limb. Here she spread her blanket out and sat down.

"This should be a perfect place to wait for whatever is going to happen," she decided.

As the daylight started to dim, the deep shadows of the forest began playing tricks on her. The sights and sounds of the coming night became a little spooky. To reinforce her courage, she busied herself by rounding up some dead wood to build a fire. At least a fire would give her the comfort of seeing her immediate surroundings.

Clearing a place for the fire, she carefully stacked the wood. She then lit the dry oak leaves she had placed beneath the dry branches. Off in the distance, the ocean waves pounded the beach. Soon the eerie sounds of night creatures filled the air.

Staring into the fire, she began to wonder if this journey was a mistake. She even felt a little foolish believing this pirate spirit actually existed. Glancing away from the fire for an instant, she saw a bright white light shining through the dense forest. Suddenly, several lights shone through the forest.

"Oh no, someone's coming. What am I going to do? Where is that gun?" Digging in her pack, she found the little revolver and held it close as she crouched behind the large limb.

She waited. Staring directly at the lights, she trembled with anticipation. The lights flickered. Whoever it was appeared to be walking directly toward her. The intensity of the light suggested someone was getting real close. Suddenly, she realized that the lights were not coming toward her; they were rising into the sky.

"Oh, how stupid! Those aren't flash lights; it's the moon coming up through the trees."

The big bright ball slowly cleared the tree line and completely revealed itself in the clear night air. The denseness of the forest had been very effective in disguising the moon's size and its brilliance as it rose.

As the moon climbed higher and higher, the trees, silhouetted against the night sky, grew black and lifeless. The sand had begun to take on a glow from its light. The sounds of the night creatures, which had become almost deafening, suddenly stopped. She couldn't understand the silence.

She began to shiver. It felt as though fingers were sliding across her back.

"What was that? I hope that's not a bug on me, she muttered.

With her arm, she brushed as far as she could across her back. Failing to touch anything, she convinced herself it was nothing and returned to watch her fire.

Suddenly, something as cold as death itself grabbed her shoulder. Jerking around quickly, she saw nothing but the darkness behind her.

Trembling, she called out, "Who's there?" No response. Then quietly to herself she said, "Did I just imagine that or did someone touch my shoulder? Oh, for God's sakes, it's just my vivid imagination!" Nothing but silence came from the darkness. To calm herself, she turned her attention back to the glowing coals.

"This place is giving me the creeps," she thought.

Chapter Thirty-Four

She threw a piece of wood into the fire. As sparks swirled and flames rose into the night sky, she caught sight of a man, or the form of a man, standing just outside the limits of the light. Her breathing quickened, and her heart was pounding out of her chest. She was so numb from fear that she couldn't feel her arms or legs. It was all she could do to sit there motionless while her instincts told her to get up and run.

This manly form floated across the ground. It came closer to the fire until she could see it clearly. It had the look of the devil himself, but no, it was the man she had seen so many times in her dreams. The darkness behind him came alive with ghastly apparitions, which seemed to look to him for instructions. They became more agitated as their numbers increased until it looked as if they were on the verge of rioting. Without looking back at them, the man, the form, waved his arm slightly, and they were gone. He alone stood in the light of the flickering fire.

He spoke, "Greetings, my dear. Welcome to my home." Lifting his arms with a sweeping motion, he turned, as if to introduce her to the island itself.

Rainey fought back the fear. Her instincts by now were yelling inside her, commanding her to run faster than she had ever run in her life. She managed to capture her voice at the brink of a scream.

She forced her voice to ask, "You… you… you must be the pi… pi… rate from my dre… dreams?" Her instinct was to scream.

"Yes, my darling Rainey, I am," he replied with a sinister laugh. "Oh! My manners. I know your name my dear, but as yet, you do not know mine, do you? You only recognize my dreadful face. Forgive me. I do wish I looked more respectable." A captivating smile spread across his lips as he glared at her with his blood red eyes. "Let me work on my appearance a bit here."

Right in front of her eyes, his facial features changed, and he turned himself into as handsome a gentleman as she had ever seen.

Bending slightly at the waist, he crossed one arm in front of his body and extended the other arm toward the ground in a sweeping motion. "Captain Caleb Bland, at your service."

Rainey could sense he was wicked; but there was also something about him, perhaps his appearance now, that captivated her. He was handsome by any standards, and an unmistakable charm emanated from within him. Nevertheless, there was no mistaking the fact that he had to be in concert with the devil.

He crossed his arms over his chest and turned toward the old oak. "So, what do you think of my home?" he asked, again spreading his arms as if to present the tree as a country estate. "Of course, this is not what I was used to when I was a mortal man, but it has served its purpose well."

Taking considerable time to muster her courage, she somewhat cautiously offered, "The tree is beautiful, and it is certainly very unique." She was not sure exactly what he was, and she strongly felt she had reason to fear him. Something deep inside, perhaps from her soul, continued sending her warnings.

"You know, my dear, I suffered terribly that day long ago."

Coming closer, he reached up, pulling back his collar to expose the marks from the bloody rope burns around his neck. The collar of his shirt was bright red with blood, as if the stain had just been made.

The fright in Rainey welled up again. Standing up, she attempted to step back over the limb. Her foot became entangled in the blanket; she fell back and landed sprawling on the soft sand.

"Yes, that very limb is the one from which they hanged me. I did not even have a proper gallows," he said, pointing to the limb over which she had just fallen.

Rainey stood up, never taking her eyes off him.

Squint-eyed, he continued with his story: "A terrible storm blew through sometime back and ripped it from the main trunk. It was already weakened, of course, and diseased. The truth is, the tree has been waiting for you also, Rainey. It possesses a soul just like a mortal, but it has outgrown its life span."

He pointed to the large dark hole where the limb once grew and added, "That is where you will place the broach. You do have it, don't you? I would be most disappointed if you had come all this way without it."

"Yes, I have your broach." The fear within warned her of the impending danger he posed. Her fear kept telling her to run, run right now! Something else, however, told her flight would be useless; this curse was not going away no matter how far she ran. The curse had haunted her family for over a hundred years; to think that running a few hundred yards would have an effect was ludicrous. It was all up to her, and running was not an option. As long as this curse remained, his only reason for being was to haunt her and her family.

"I have it; don't worry," she said bravely.

"Rainey, my dear, you do intend to give it back, do you not?" He came close to her. Every particle of intuition was now telling her that she was in the presence of a demon. Shrinking away from his glaring eyes, she moved to the opposite side of the fire.

"It is time! Take the broach and place it in the hole in the tree where the dead limb once grew."

She felt as if she were being pulled apart. Something was saying "no, don't do it, and don't give it to him." Something else was pleading "yes, give it to him, and get it over with." God, what should she do? She sensed that he was using some kind of power to force her toward the dark hole, to make her put the emerald there.

Again he instructed her, "Rainey, place it in the hole! Do it now!"

Approaching the tree, she unzipped the fanny pack and pulled out the broach. She freed it from the soft cloth and looked at it for what she thought would be the last time. It began to glow bright green. As the intensity of the glow increased, she felt the sensation of extreme cold climbing up her arm that began to throb with pain. Her eyes darted toward Caleb. He encouraged her to continue. He pointed to the hole.

"Rainey my child, you are helping me. I will be forever in your debt for bringing my broach home." The ghostly forms that had appeared earlier returned. They flew around him from every direction, again looking to him for instructions.

Climbing up on the fallen limb, she followed it to the trunk. Anticipating further instructions from Caleb, she turned once more in his direction. He was ghastly and dark and sinister.

She thought, "Am I doing the right thing or am I going to regret this for the rest of my life?"

"That's it, my child. Now put your hand deep inside the hole until you feel the bottom. Leave my broach there, and it will all be over."

As she stretched her arm up toward the dark hole, something grabbed her.

At the same instant, Caleb, who was grinning in a manner that could be mistaken as sheepish, asked, "Are you ready to join me, Rainey?"

"What do you mean, 'join you'?"

Caleb roared with laughter, and the handsome face changed into the half-rotted visage of her dreams. "You see, my dear, my Annabelle is not here with me, and she can never be. She went where many of you mortals go, to the place you call Heaven, where, as you might imagine, I can never go. What I need is a lady companion as beautiful as my Annabelle to wear the broach for me, here in my Hell. Rainey, I have chosen you. You are even more beautiful than she, and it is you who will be my companion here for eternity." His insidious laughter filled the night.

A chill ran through her again, this one as cold as death itself.

Whatever it was that gripped her arm used its unbelievable force to throw her to the ground.

"What the hell was that?" she screamed. Picking herself up off the ground, she realized she had dropped the broach.

"Oh God, the broach. I dropped the damned broach!" Quickly falling to her knees, she started feeling through the sand and leaves.

She glanced up at Caleb who was obviously in a very animated conversation with someone. She could see his lips moving but couldn't hear his voice. Whatever was going on with him appeared to have his full attention. At that moment, she was no longer important to him.

"Here it is! Thank God, I found it." She held on tightly and turned back toward Caleb. Looking out into the darkness, he was spitting mad.

She thought again about running away, but she knew running would be hopeless. He'd follow her.

Caleb kept circling with his back to the fire. Looking outward, he was searching for something.

Wiping the sweat from her brow, she caught the movement of another apparition as it entered the light of the fire. She couldn't be sure, but this spirit, a man, looked familiar. At that instant, she recognized him; it was John Waters, the John Waters.

He spoke directly to her. "Rainey," he said, "do as I tell you. Do not ask any questions."

While she could hear him clearly, he was not actually speaking. It was as if he were inside her head. Confused, she started to question his order, but before she could utter a word, he raised his hand for her to be silent. Her voice failed her.

"Open that old cloth bag. Inside is a leather pouch with some yellow sulfur dust. Pour the sulfur out on the ground. Make a circle that you can stand in. Hold tight to the broach! Do not let it leave your hand. You will be safe in the circle. Do not try to interfere with whatever happens outside that circle. Stay calm; I have the situation in hand. Caleb and I are old adversaries, and we are about to renew an old, old relationship. Now when I tell you to do something, just do it. Don't ask questions. Is that clear?"

His voice was clear, but he wasn't speaking aloud. She realized that he was inside her head.

The reality of this situation finally dawned on her. She was witnessing a spiritual battle of epic proportions. At this moment, Caleb Bland was one very angry demon. She sensed, however, that John had the upper hand, which she found comforting.

Quickly finding the bag, she untied the leather string. She found the little bag of sulfur and managed to pour it, though in a somewhat uneven circle that more resembled a triangle. She stepped inside the uneven ring, fearing the imperfection of her hastily drawn circle. "What if it doesn't work?" she thought.

Caleb Bland was outraged. "So, John Waters, you have returned to the scene of your crime. You should have known that I wanted you to return, so I could destroy you also."

Then John Waters made his case. "I know now that I should have never taken the treasure, but I didn't know better at the time. Be certain of one thing though, Caleb: you will not take Rainey into your hell for any reason. She is innocent; she had nothing to do with what I did. We would not be here right now if she had not tried to return the broach to you as you asked. I knew you would try to deceive her. The deaths of the others over the years as well as my own should have been punishment enough on the family."

Rainey was totally into this conversation when she realized that both sides of this discussion were taking place in her mind. In her wildest dreams, she couldn't have imagined she'd be a party to such a confrontation. She could understand, but not hear, every word, including her own name tossed about between the two spirits. She felt the urge to speak, but remembered John had told her to stay quiet. Whatever the outcome of this argument, she knew there was nothing she could say or do that would change it.

Out of the corner of her eye, she again caught some movement in the direction of the old oak tree. It appeared to be moving. In fact, it was moving as though it were a living animal.

"You will not stop me, John Waters. I will have back what is mine and even more. This is your punishment for what you did those many years ago. Your bloodline will never have peace, never! Your descendents will forever be cursed. Your darling Rainey will come with me and forever be mine!"

John turned to Rainey who still stood inside the sulfur ring as he had instructed. Somehow he used his gift to send his message to her. John's power blocked Caleb from hearing his message. The demon would not be forewarned.

"Rainey, follow my instructions. Do exactly as I say, and do it now. You must throw the broach in the water. Run as fast as you can to the beach, and throw the broach as far as you can. It must remain there for all time. The water will cleanse the broach of the spell. Once this is done, the curse will be ended. You will be finished with this evil specter; he will never slip into your dreams again. No matter what you hear behind you or see in front of you, remember they are only spirits; I will not allow any of them to harm you. Now, go!"

As if by magic, the sulfur ring flared up into giant flames.

"Run Rainey! Run now as fast as you can," willed John.

Springing into action, she ran as she had never run before. Behind her, she heard the horrible screeching of Caleb Bland in the night. She was so frightened and running so fast, she couldn't feel the sand beneath her feet. It was as if they were not even touching the ground at all. As she tore through the forest, a cloud covered the moon, and what little light she had was now gone. She stumbled into the blackness and listened for the sounds of the surf. She fought the undergrowth with every step. It felt as though Caleb's ghouls were grabbing at her, trying to hold her back from the beach.

Suddenly, the moon reappeared, and Rainey could see her way again. By now she had strayed from the faint path, and it took her several minutes to find it again. She continued toward the beach as John had instructed. Meanwhile, the phantom spirits had followed and were flying around her like a swarm of bees. Their horrible piercing cries caused her agonizing pain. She thought her eardrums would surely burst. Mustering all her will, she blocked out the screams as John had instructed. Soon she heard the loud crashing of the surf. The beach, at last! She frantically searched for an opening through the dense brush. Forcing her way through the foliage, she burst out onto the open beach. She fell, flat on her face, onto the soft white sand.

Evil followed. The swarm of specters, attempting to stop her, crowded in closer and closer.

"No way!" she thought. "No way!"

Scrambling to her feet, she sprinted across the open beach. Her heart pounding, she neared the water at last.

Like a beacon, the moon guiding her to the water's edge. The grotesque faces of the demons came at her from every angle. Their wailing filled up the night sky.

She finally reached the water's edge. Splashing out into the surf up to her waist, she stopped. Cradling the broach in her hand, she paused for a second to admire it for the last time. The green stone glistened in the light of the moon. She drew back her arm and then threw it as far as she could into the dark water. The stone, flickering in the light of the moon as it flew from her hand, finally dropped into the water. If John was right, the emerald would never be found again, and the curse would be ended. To Rainey's horror, as the broach splashed into the sea, a brilliant bolt of lightning lit up the night sky. It struck the exact spot where the broach had hit the water.

The stone disappeared forever beneath the surface of the water. The terrifying sounds of the shrieking specters were gone, and the struggle between Caleb and John was ended.

The only sounds left in the night were the crash of the ocean and the rush of a warm breeze coming in off the water. Rainey stood there awhile, calming herself by the sea. It was peaceful, a peace she had never felt before.

In just a few minutes, she was shaken back to reality by a large breaker smashing into her. She shuddered with the thought of what she had just been through, and she prayed silently as she waded ashore. On the beach, she turned once more to see where the broach now rested.

She watched wave after wave crash onto the beach. They glittered with florescent sparks and, mixing with each previous wave, they slowly retreated back to sea.

Rainey spoke to herself. "I did what John told me, but have I done the right thing? Of course, I have. What other choice was there? I just pray that this evil veil will be lifted from my family." She pondered her situation. Should she wait until morning to go back to the tree? Or should she forget about it and get back to the mainland? No, perhaps not, she could get lost in the marsh this time of night.

The total silence was reassuring, especially after the hell she had just experienced. Her curiosity was great, and she knew she had to return to the site under the ancient live oak. She couldn't help but feel that John might want her to return there for some reason. Then again, maybe it was Caleb Bland who wanted her back. She decided that waiting on the beach for daylight would be the best course of action.

It had been an exhausting night. She was hungry and thirsty, but more than anything, she wanted to go home. However, something inside told her that she had to go back to see what remained.

As the sun began faintly to light the eastern sky, she was on her way toward the forest. It was still fairly dark, but by the time she walked up the beach and found her way through the undergrowth, there would be enough light.

She pushed her way through the bushes and found a deer path that lay in the right direction. After walking what she believed to be more than far enough to reach the tree, she began to think she was lost. She thought this was the place, but there was no tree. Searching the ground frantically for some sign that this was the right location, she saw the remains of a fire, barely smoldering. Then she spotted the blanket and her other belongings. Slowly turning around in a complete circle, she was shocked to find there was no tree. Yet this, she had no doubt, was the place. The fire, her blanket—there was no mistake. She could see her own footprints in the sand. Strangely, there were no others. There was no tree, but there was a rotted stump, surely the remains of a tree that had been gone for years. Even though that tree had been gone for a long time, this was the right place.

Piecing things together, she began to understand exactly what had taken place the night before. She realized the tree was not real at all but just an illusion. Caleb had used it as a landmark, so she could find him. She recalled how it moved, as if it were animated. It was actually in the process of disappearing before her eyes! The unbelievable truth was beginning to dawn on her. That tree no longer existed; it was all part of an illusion created by Bland just to lure her and his precious broach to within his reach. He never intended to let her go.

"Thank you, John," she whispered with a long sigh.

Collecting the root bag along with the rest of her things, she made her way back to the kayak. She quickly drank down a whole bottle of water and then devoured a peanut butter and jelly sandwich in record time. She now had the strength to paddle back across the sound and up the creek to the park.

Stroking the water with the paddle, she found herself deep in thought about John.

"I wish we'd had the opportunity to talk longer. I wanted him to tell me all about his special gift. I have so many questions I want answered. He might have been able to tell me if I, too, possessed the gift. Maybe it just wasn't meant to be, or maybe I'll see him again one day. "

She stopped paddling long enough to look at her birthmark. Yes, it did look like a snake.

Chapter Thirty-Five

To her surprise, the old man was waiting on the dock. "I's be thinkin' it was 'bout time fo yo' to be comin' off dat water."

Rainey grinned. "Yeah, it was quite a night."

"Well, did yo' learn a lot 'bout the tides or what ever yo' be learnin'?"

"I did." She then realized she didn't even know his name. "You know I don't even know your name."

"Oh, Lord chile, I's sorry, they calls me Jobe Vereen."

Reaching for his hand to help her out of the boat, she felt a strange sensation as they touched. "I'm Rainey Alexander. I'm glad to see you again, Mr. Vereen."

"I knows who yo' be," he whispered secretively.

"I'm sorry. What did you just say, Mr. Vereen?"

"Oh, I just sayin' I's glad to see yo' is back."

Rainey was a bit confused; there was no doubt in her mind that he had muttered something else.

"Les us git dis here boat back up top o' yo' car. I knows yo' must be give out."

After loading the boat, Rainey looked out toward the island. It was then that she noticed a fire burning near the edge of the water. Still smoldering, it appeared to have been burning most of the night. Two chairs weaved from grape vines were positioned next to it. She figured he spent a great deal of time sitting around a fire.

When Jobe bent down to pick up her pack and cooler, she noticed a bag hanging from his neck. It was a neat little leather bag tied up tight that hung from a long piece of leather. She was curious but decided not to ask. She had enough for one night, and her bed was calling her.

After rechecking the ropes on her car, she turned back to thank him for his help. He was gone. There was no sign of him. Even the house looked different, all grown over with vines and weeds. She glanced back to the fire, but it, too, was gone. Obviously, no one had spent any time there for a long while.

She was startled, to say the least, but after the occurrences of the last few hours, nothing was out of the realm of possibility. Could Jobe Vereen have been a spirit, too? Seeing John and Caleb clashing on the island, being chased by a bevy of specters, finding a tree that moved as if it had a life of its own and then vanishing.... Why shouldn't she believe that Jobe also was a spirit? Maybe he had been sent, by someone, just to help her out. After last night, she reasoned, anything was possible.

She then began laughing hysterically. She laughed so hard tears flowed down her cheeks. It took several minutes, but she finally composed herself.

"That Caleb Bland wasn't so powerful after all. Did he really think I would actually put my hand down into that hole, all the way to the bottom? Obviously, he didn't know exactly with whom he was dealing. Just try to picture this: Rainey Alexander, who has this morbid fear of snakes and spiders. Some scary specter tells her to reach into a dark hole in an old tree in the middle of the night? Not a chance!" The absurdity of the thought went a long way in relieving the tension she had been under for the past few hours.

On the drive back to her mother's house, she thought about John and Jobe. Clearly, spirits were able to appear to her, and she could both see them and communicate with them. There had to be a way to find out just how these things occurred. She needed to explore this so-called gift. Was it really something within her family that could be passed on? Or had it already been passed on? So many questions. Somehow, she had to contact John. She just had to.

The old home place came to mind. There was something about that ghostly image of a man she had seen there. She decided to go there, right now. At the next intersection, she turned in the direction of the old house. She was going back out there to find him.

Pulling up into the same spot she had parked a few days earlier, she sat for a moment to gather her thoughts.

"Now exactly what am I doing here? Is there really something calling me to this place, or am I just imagining this?"

Slamming the car door behind her, she walked toward the house. She was taking the same path as before, but she wasn't thinking about spiders and snakes now. She found herself on the porch but couldn't remember how she got there. Trembling a little, she walked slowly into the front room. For some reason, this time she didn't fear the little creatures watching from their webs or snakes crawling on the floor.

Standing in the middle of the room, she opened her mind and silently called to John.

"John, are you here? Please help me. I want to know about the gift."

She sensed a movement from behind and started to turn even before hearing a voice. She saw a tall man standing in the hallway. It was John.

The instant her eyes fell on him she understood that she, too, possessed the gift. Tears filled her eyes and then cascaded down both cheeks. She felt overwhelmed, both terrified and grateful. An aura surrounded him; she felt herself being drawn to it. Alarmed yet attracted by this aura, she attempted to hold herself back, to keep her distance from him. He smiled reassuringly and motioned her to come forward.

"Come, Rainey, we have much to discuss," he said with a passion that erased all her fears and hesitation.

She approached him and allowed herself to be as one with him. "Tell me everything, great-grandfather; I want to embrace, not fear, this power." She felt relief; she had so many questions. "Tell me everything I need to know."

He spoke calmly. "I can only tell you that you possess the gift. It is not a given that you will be able to use it as I have. The powers of the gift are many, and each of those powers must be developed within you yourself. Communicating with spirits is a challenging accomplishment, but it is fraught with dangers. You must learn to use these powers only in the right way. If you are not careful, the dark side can take control and slowly destroy you. All of these powers can be lost."

John walked over to the fireplace. He stared down at the hearth where many hot fires had once burned. Rainey sensed he was reminiscing about his life with Letsy and the children in this house. She began to tremble when she realized that she was reading his thoughts.

He remained silent for a few minutes, and then he spoke to her sternly. "Rainey, this gift you possess must never be used for wrongful deeds. You have already seen what can happen if it is. Your first lesson will be to concentrate on listening to the other side. Along the way, you will encounter a few of my spirit friends, and they will help you to learn. They have many ways to communicate with you, and you must train yourself to hear them. But be warned: when the veil is opened, evil can slip through. Distinguishing between good and evil will be your first challenge. Everything the gift enables you to do depends on your ability to free your mind and concentrate. Now, close your eyes and quiet your soul. Clear your mind and listen."

Closing her eyes, she did as he said. She could hear the steady rhythm of her heart beating. After a few minutes, she began hearing the murmuring of many voices, voices of souls speaking out to her, calling her name. She found it quite terrifying for these were the same noises she had heard as a little girl. Over these voices, she sensed John's will, telling her, "This was your first lesson, learning to listen to the other side. When you master this we will move on."

Opening her eyes she found him gone. The little house was empty, but she knew that he would always be there for her. She had found the power that had been there all along. From that day forward, she knew life would never be the same.

The End

About the Author

Sally Glass was born in Conway, South Carolina. She grew up in Conway and Myrtle Beach, attending the local schools and was active in sports. She is a self-taught artist with no formal training but with a very creative side that, prior to the writing of Caleb's Curse, was directed toward painting and sketching. Sally resided in the Horry County area until the late 90s when she moved to North Carolina. She and her husband George now reside in the Blue Ridge Mountains where she continues to work on her writing.

The inspiration for this novel was a tale told to her as a child by her mother. The story inspired her to explore one more creative adventure, that of writing. Utilizing her knowledge and love of the area around the Waccamaw River to turn what was a brief adventure story into her first novel. This story is her first attempt to allow others to sample the imagination and creativity she has always possessed.